A Tease and a
TRAIL RUN

A Tease and a
TRAIL RUN

By Maddie Evans

A Brighthead Running Club Romance

Philangelus Press
Boston, MA

A Tease and a Trail Run, Copyright © 2019, Maddie Evans.

Print ISBN: 978-1-942133-33-9
ASIN: B07V95HQV6
Library of Congress Control Number: 2019946160

Cover art by Charlotte Volnek
Edits by Heather Turner, Versor Editing
Brighthead Logo by Rayha Studios

Dedication

To Madeline, for all her support and thoughtfulness during a very difficult time. Thank you for getting me back on my feet. I am honored to share your name.

Chapter One

Charlotte stepped out of Uncle Gregory's Audi into the kind of family home she was resigned never to have.

Aunt Eleanor rushed into the garage. "Oh, you look amazing! How was your trip?"

The only amazing thing was how Charlotte was still standing, and she leaned hard into Aunt Eleanor's hug. "Fine. Delayed an hour, but I was more worried about Uncle Gregory waiting for me. It's been so hot lately."

Uncle Gregory lifted her suitcase from the trunk. "Not a problem. You know that. Let's just get you inside so you can relax."

"I've been sitting too long," Charlotte protested as she followed Aunt Eleanor into the kitchen.

A border collie clattered up to her on the white tile floor. "Pepper!" Charlotte exclaimed. "Who's a good girl? Is it you?"

Wagging, Pepper jumped, then backed away. Uncle Greg said, "Down," but Aunt Eleanor handed Charlotte a treat. When Charlotte held it on her palm, Pepper bolted it right down.

Charlotte's heart twinged. No, this kind of family life would never be hers. Not after the last six weeks. No happy couple. No suburban home on five acres. No family dog waiting in the kitchen. Just Charlotte, but Charlotte alone could be enough. She'd have to be.

"There you go," Aunt Eleanor cooed to the dog. "Charlotte's going to be spending a lot of time with you while we go meet Anna's baby, so you'll need to be on your very best behavior."

Aunt Eleanor got a tall crystal glass from the cabinet and filled it with ice water from the fridge. They'd renovated since Charlotte's last visit: the living room with its grand piano was gated off, presumably because of the dog. All the appliances were hidden behind cabinet doors, and a new back deck looked out on her aunt and uncle's vibrant property.

The next stop was a second-floor bedroom at the front of the house.

"Anna's room?" said Charlotte. "You're not giving me my old one?"

Aunt Eleanor drew back. "You could have that room, but we made this the primary guest room after Anna got married. It has a private bathroom."

Charlotte blinked as she looked around. "It's fine. I just wasn't expecting this."

Everything was unexpected lately. Every single thing she'd envisioned for this summer just...wasn't. Even details like which bedroom she'd wake up in.

But that's what happens when you discover your whole life is a lie. It would be better just not to assume anything, about anyone, ever again.

Eleanor smiled, mollified. "This room has so much more personality, plus the sea view."

Her aunt opened the window, admitting a breeze from the ocean. Charlotte went to stand beside her. "I forgot you can see the lighthouse from Anna's window."

"You'll have to visit it this summer. The Brighthead Historical Society has tours , but I forget which days."

History always felt more secure than the future. "I'd like that."

The shoreline wasn't visible from the window, but

Charlotte could view waves further out where the sky stretched down to the ocean. This eastward-facing room would have amazing sunrises...and would feature them amazingly early as well. She glanced at the drapes: room-darkening. Good. Although an early bird, Charlotte didn't quite want to catch worms at five a.m.

Aunt Eleanor sat on the bed. "I was talking to your mother again about the wedding. I'm so sorry."

Charlotte forced a smile as she turned away from the waves and the motion, the salt and the uncertainty. "You don't have to be sorry. It's better I found out now rather than after we were married. It's a lot easier to cancel reservations than to separate finances during a divorce. And at least we never filed taxes together."

"You're quoting your mother?" Charlotte straightened, but Aunt Eleanor added, "I can hear Margaret's voice in what you're saying. You were right to call it off, but that doesn't make it easy."

How would Aunt Eleanor know? Uncle Gregory had never cheated on her. Charlotte turned back to the window, blinking hard. No, don't think about it. Don't think about the wedding four weeks from now that wouldn't take place. Don't think about Hunter and his side dish who was prettier or nicer or less controlling than she was. Don't think about every single lifetime plan torpedoed by a single folder full of photos and cell phone records. Instead Charlotte clenched a hand in the thick fabric of the light-blocking drapes. "Well, at least it worked out that you needed a house sitter for when Anna had the baby. Staying in Brighthead for a summer will be like when we were kids."

No, it wouldn't. Years ago it had been her and Anna running wild on the property all summer, usually with the gardener's son and sometimes with other kids Anna knew. Endless days of sunshine and rocky beaches, waves, ice cream, and the occasional horseback ride. Everyone had grown up and moved on. Everyone but Charlotte, and here she was again.

Aunt Eleanor could call it "house-sitting," but it was just a crash landing, no survivors.

Speaking of crash landing...Charlotte opened her carry-on bag and withdrew a gift-wrapped package. She'd changed her mind twenty times about whether to actually give this gift, but now that it came down to the moment, she didn't want it for herself anymore. Just get rid of it, and maybe she'd also get rid of her failed dreams.

Charlotte faked enthusiasm. "Can you bring this to Anna? I'm sorry if it's a pain, but it's too valuable to send it through the mail."

Aunt Eleanor brightened. "Did you crochet something for the baby?"

"You'll see," she teased. But then Charlotte flinched as Aunt Eleanor took the package out of the room.

No, really, this was for the best. Charlotte wasn't getting married, whereas Anna's life was moving forward in the best way possible.

Pepper wandered in while Charlotte unpacked her suitcase and carry-on. When Aunt Eleanor had first pitched the house-sitting idea, it hadn't been entirely obvious that she was giving Charlotte a way out of Philadelphia. Aunt Eleanor was an excellent diplomat. She had to be, with a sister like Charlotte's mother.

The Fletcher/Mattingly wedding should have taken place on July 19th, followed by a week-long honeymoon, followed by the start of a new life in downtown Philly. Hunter would work in the surgical practice at the hospital, and his new bride would work as a professional textile conservator. Charlotte's fellowship with the Kist-Brannigan Museum of Fine Arts had ended this May, with the understanding that she'd write and publish a paper during the summer. Armed with a successful fellowship, a publication, and her Master's, it would have been natural to locate either contract work or a full-time position at one of the museums. There was enough history in Philadelphia.

Then, the Day of Discovery. Hunter was cheating. Well, now he wasn't cheating. Now he could just have the other woman. If they wanted to get hitched right away, he could even use the same venues and vendors. They could go be happy, and Charlotte could just get flung to the side like a crumpled fast-food wrapper: useful while necessary, but easily rid of once you were done with it.

She never could have competed. She shouldn't even have tried, except that Hunter claimed he loved her. She should have known shapeless brunettes weren't cornering the market on young surgeons.

Charlotte had packed her things tight in the suitcase that should have gone to Hawaii. (Maine was exactly like Hawaii, right? Oceans, rocks... And Hunter having an affair was exactly like being monogamous.) Jeans, shorts, T-shirts, blouses, a light jacket, an airy cotton dress, sandals, sneakers, heels, a swim suit, pajamas. All of these vanished into drawers that smelled of fresh wood. Was Charlotte the renovated room's first long-term guest?

Out of the carry-on came her books, her computer, her research materials. Even at the tip of civilization, they still had internet service, so she could finish her publication. Then came her yarn, her crochet thread, her hooks, her beads, her patterns. She hadn't been sure the crochet hooks would make it through security, but in the end no one had questioned her.

She'd have long days in solitude, perfect for crocheting a hostess gift for Aunt Eleanor. Maybe an afghan. Maybe a gorgeous slippery shawl in a gradient of colors...except she didn't want to crochet another shawl. She'd just handed her last shawl off to her aunt in baby shower wrapping paper.

Unpacked, Charlotte sat on the bed with its artfully arranged oversized pillows. Calling this "Anna's room" was a misnomer. There wasn't any of Anna about it any longer. Her posters and paintings had come down, and up were landscapes and a modern piece spread across five canvases. Even with an art degree, Charlotte couldn't identify what it was supposed to be.

A queen could stay here, if queens ever set foot in Brighthead, Maine, what with the star quilt, the thick cream-colored carpet, and the gleaming oak furniture. The quilt, though... Charlotte's heart shrank from the thought of leaving it where the dog could sit. Maybe Aunt Eleanor had put it in this room because it gave off a rustic feel, but she'd pack it away once her Aunt and Uncle left for Michigan.

She'd packed away lots of things too late to stop them from getting ruined. Her heart. Her certitude.

Charlotte put her hands over her eyes, and Pepper raised her head. "You don't actually have to be on your best behavior," she told the border collie. "I don't expect that of anyone anymore."

Chapter Two

Brandon patted the monitor as though it were a guilty puppy. "Any day now."

On the other side of his desk, the Lighthouse Athletic Club member shook her head. "I didn't mean to cause so much trouble. I only thought that because my gym membership was up for renewal, I should pay for another one."

Brandon looked her in the eyes and intoned, "Brutal."

Finally the computer showed the next screen of the membership renewal. Brandon ran the credit card, and the computer started grinding away at the next part. "If you want to go run five miles on the treadmill, I'll just have your card waiting when you're done."

"I'd much rather procrastinate." Brandon recognized this member from the body pump classes on weekday mornings. He knew her favorite colors but hadn't known her name until five minutes ago. She added, "You'd think taking money would be the first thing the owners would figure out."

Brandon gave a nasty side-eye to the outdated computer with its low-end software package. "Taking money, yes, but the corporate overlords aren't so much into paying it out." He handed back her card. "You're all set. I threw in an extra two months."

She smiled. "You didn't have to do that."

"I wasn't sure how long the transaction would take,"

Brandon protested.

His boss approached after the member left. "I need to talk to you about the Lighthouse Run."

"Sure." Brandon swiveled his chair to look at Michael, the branch manager. "There's nothing to talk about. The historical society cancelled it."

"It's been uncancelled. Corporate announced this morning that we're taking over the Lighthouse Run because we have the same name."

Brandon recoiled. "That's bizarre."

"They think it'll be great advertising." Michael half sat on the counter. "They're already dumping the work off onto our branch, since we're closest."

Brandon motioned "go on" with his hand. "And that means...?"

"Alex from the head office wants you to design the logo."

Brandon recoiled. "What?"

"I told him no." Michael glowered. "It's awesome for you that you've got a graphic design business as a side hustle, but when you're working here, you're not a graphic designer. You're not getting paid to do graphic design, and we certainly haven't given you the equipment for graphic design." Michael glared at the computer that couldn't run a credit card without choking. "He wants to reward you in *exposure,* and he dangled the idea that they'll hire PacerStudios to handle advertising and rewrite the website if they like the logo."

Brandon's head spun. How much could he charge for that kind of work? Asking for his standard rates would doubtless make them laugh in his face. More likely they'd fire him just for suggesting it. And redoing their website? Would they hire his business, or just expect him to slip it in between everything else in his job description? And how much would they battle him over the stupidest things?

Talk about the nightmare client. Disagree with them on the details and he could lose the day job that actually paid the bills. Agree with them and he could turn out a lousy website...and then lose his job for that reason.

Michael folded his arms. "If they're willing to hire you for the big package, then one little logo isn't going to make a difference to the bottom line, so they should just go ahead and contract your business."

Too many companies expected graphic designers to work for free or, more insultingly, for that nebulous thing they called "exposure." Who benefitted? Well, the company benefitted from a great design, but how many people glanced at a logo and thought, "I have to hire that artist"?

Brandon rubbed his chin. "So where do things stand?"

"Right now they stand at me answering the phone all afternoon because I didn't want him to spring this on you." Michael's visage darkened. "He loves the logo you did for the Kelty Duncan Memorial 5K. That's not a joke, either. I handed him a race shirt so he could see our logo on the back, but he barely even noticed."

If that were true, ironically, the gym would be one client Brandon gained from exposure. Free work that led to more free work. What an awesome system.

Granted, he hadn't designed Kelty's logo for the money or the exposure. But Alex from corporate didn't know that. It was none of their business. Literally.

The phone rang, and Michael reached over Brandon to pick it up. "Lighthouse Athletics. Yes, barre class is at nine on Tuesdays and Thursdays. Absolutely. Thanks!" He turned back to Brandon. "Have a rate sheet in hand for when he talks to you. They want a free logo, and you're convenient."

Brandon grinned. "Here you said they liked my design."

"They like *free* a lot more. You do good work, and there's no reason they shouldn't pay for it." Michael slid off the counter. "They're idiots if they don't promote you into the marketing department. But given their track record...be prepared to stand your ground."

Chilled, Brandon said, "How likely am I to remain employed if I refuse?"

Michael shook his head. "Firing someone because he won't do highly skilled work that's far outside his job description? That's got to violate some kind of law."

As if he could get a lawyer to fight something this nebulous. Brandon turned back to his screen. "Well, thanks for the warning."

It stank that you could be loyal to your job, but your job wouldn't be loyal to you.

Brandon rounded the edge of the Sparrows parking lot along with four other runners making up the "slow" contingent of the Brighthead Running Club. Although the day had cooled off a bit, the air hadn't gotten less humid, so you could probably wring out his clothes. Everyone else looked the same, and their pace reflected it.

Not a big deal. He enjoyed slow runs.

Sparrows was perfect for nights like tonight, and not just because of the air conditioning. At the back was the function room where twenty to thirty runners could hang out for a couple of hours, while off to the side were huge bathrooms where runners could change out of their sweaty gear. Brandon took advantage of a clothing change before heading to the back.

He hadn't yet reached a table when Eleanor called, "Brandon, look who's here!"

Sitting at Eleanor's side was a willowy young woman with sky-clear eyes. He exclaimed, "Charlie? Welcome back!"

As she stood, he rushed over but stopped short of a hug. No matter how much he'd toweled off before changing, she doubtless wanted nothing to do with actual physical contact.

"You look great! When did you get in?"

"About three hours ago. Aunt Eleanor and Uncle Gregory took me out to dinner, and here we are."

Charlie slipped back onto the bench at the corner booth, so Brandon took a chair opposite her. Also in the booth was Aileen Duncan, librarian at the Brighthead library and relatively new member. He asked, "How long is the house-sitting gig?"

"Anna's having the baby toward the end of the month," Eleanor said, "and afterward, we'll stay a couple of weeks until the christening. But you know how babies come when they want."

Brandon nodded. "My sister went a week overdue. I swear I heard her doing jumping jacks trying to convince Aria it was time to leave." When Eleanor laughed, he said, "So, boy or girl? Or are they still keeping it a secret?"

"It's not even a secret." Eleanor sounded miffed. "They asked the midwife not to tell them."

Charlie winked at Brandon. "They want it to be a surprise."

Eleanor shot back, "It can be just as much a surprise in the ultrasound room as the delivery room."

"And if the ultrasound is wrong," Brandon added, "they can be surprised twice."

Charlie grinned. "I remember now, you always had to get in the last word."

"More like I predict what can go wrong. Speaking of which," he added, "do you have my phone number? If you need anything or have any questions, *I'm* not going to Michigan."

Charlie nodded. "You're on a list they magneted to the refrigerator. There's the electrician, the doctor, the veterinarian, you, the police, the fire department, the navy, and the CIA."

In the corner, Aileen laughed. "You should add the library, in case you run out of reading material."

Charlie laid a hand over her heart. "That would be a true emergency, but I believe Aunt Eleanor has emergency novels stashed on the property."

Eleanor sighed as though very much abused. "I apologize for being considerate."

"Call me before you phone the coast guard," Brandon said. "But call the fire department before you call me."

"I'm relatively good at triaging." Charlie leaned her chin on her clasped hands. "So what's been going on with you? I haven't seen you in like ten years."

Had it been a whole decade? Charlie had spent every summer with her aunt and uncle for ages. Then one year toward the end of high school she just didn't show up, and summers had felt emptier. "I've started a graphic design business, but the rest of the time I'm working a desk job over at Lighthouse Athletic Club."

She'd straightened at mention of the business. "What kinds of things do you design?"

"Logos, websites, ads, whatever people need." Doreen came to take orders, and Brandon asked for a lemonade. Eleanor said she was fine with her herbal tea, but Charlie asked for a refill on her iced tea.

Aileen said, "Brandon designed the logo for the race we organized over Memorial Day. He did an amazing job. Hang on."

While Aileen hunted up the logo on her phone, Brandon asked Charlie, "And you? What have you been up to?"

"I just finished up a fellowship with the Kist-Brannigan Museum of Fine Arts, so I'm free for the summer." Charlie tugged at a lock of hair, uncomfortable. "I'll do the writeup of my work while I'm at Aunt Eleanor's. Should keep me busy."

"You have to do more than that," Brandon urged. "It's tourist season, and you've got all that property to wander around. Plus the dog," he added.

"Plus the dog." Charlie looked mischievous. "I do need to

get the publication done in July."

"What kind of fellowship was it?"

"Antique textile preservation and restoration."

That was a job?

Aileen started. "How amazing! What kind of training does textile preservation require?"

"Bachelor's in Art History," Charlie said, "and I finished up my Master's of Science in Historic Preservation last September. I was fortunate to land the fellowship with Kist-Brannigan, but after this I'm on my own."

Aileen said, "There's a textile museum in Bar Harbor. Actually, I think every historical society around here could use someone if you decide to freelance."

The whole conversation had flown away from Brandon, so he let them chatter away. Then Aileen showed Charlie the 5K logo he'd designed, and she said, "Oh, that's neat."

A billion hours of design merited, "That's neat." Well, if Kelty were still alive to see her own logo, she'd have been similarly understated. But if she hadn't died, they wouldn't have held a race in her memory, so...

Brandon, on the other hand, adored that logo. It was the last thing he could give Kelty, so he'd put more time in on that than a lot of his paying gigs.

Eleanor tried to sound tempting. "It would be wonderful if you got a job around here, Charlotte."

"We'll see," Charlie said, in a way that Brandon translated as, "Under no circumstances."

Mention of the historical society jiggled something in his brain. "Oh! Remember how the Lighthouse Run got cancelled? It's back on. The club may want to do something for that."

Eleanor perked up. "The historical society changed their mind?"

"No, more like someone stepped in thinking they could make money."

Aileen said, "What's a lighthouse run?"

Charlie murmured, "I'm glad I'm not the only one who doesn't know."

Eleanor said, "It's a charity run in August to benefit the lighthouse preservation fund. You start on the beach while the tide is out. You run the causeway to the lighthouse, circle the island, and then run back to the beach. It's a little over two miles. You finish before the tide comes back in."

Brandon added helpfully, "Or else you drown."

Charlie raised a glass. "Here's to motivation!"

Aileen said, "I'll sit this one out, thanks. At my speed, you'll be dredging the bay for my body."

He turned to Charlie. "What about you?"

"I won't still be here by then," she said. "Anyhow, I don't run."

As Brandon crossed the room to talk to club president Julie Capriotti, it struck him how disappointed he felt. Disappointed by both halves of Charlie's statement.

Chapter Three

On her second full day in Brighthead, Charlotte navigated back to Aunt Eleanor's house with a car full of groceries and a GPS cheerfully admonishing her about lefts and rights in five hundred feet.

This was the world's scariest place to drive. No one ever heard of a straight line or a right angle, and you could travel a main artery for miles in any direction without even one street sign to confirm you were still on the same road. Meanwhile overhead was a complete lack of street lights. When the sun went down (admittedly at about nine o'clock) it would be you and your headlights, plus the GPS voice playing the role of your best friend. At least as long as you still had service.

Why did streets change names at random? Why could she take South Street south and suddenly it was North Street? Why, when there was a detour, did she get two detour direction signs never followed by a third, no matter how many turns the detour required?

"In five hundred feet, take a right onto Sky Ridge Drive," said her phone, and Charlotte sighed. Nearly there. The road wound along the hilltop for quite a distance, but only a half-dozen houses stood facing the sea. She'd get inside, unpack her food, and exercise the dog.

Aunt Eleanor's house came into view, with its beautiful landscaping and three horses in the front yard.

Problem: Aunt Eleanor and Uncle Gregory didn't own any horses.

The horses stood grazing, their tails flicking. She eased into the driveway, cautious as Pepper bounded up to the tires. Then, with the car in the garage, Charlotte went back out to make sure this was real.

All three horses were quite definitely on the Boucher property. No one had told Charlotte about a neighbor who grazed his livestock on the perfectly manicured lawn. Or horses that paid for their meal in fertilizer.

Pepper's tail went like crazy, but then she pivoted and circled the horses again, pushing them nearer one another.

Of all the things that made no sense in Charlotte's life, this one made sense the least. She went back inside to unload groceries, but Pepper stayed with the livestock.

While hurrying to get all the food into the fridge, she kept an eye on the beautiful horses, each taller than herself, and none of them wearing tackle or tack or whatever it was horses should wear to leash them when not in use. They didn't have tags, and she wouldn't have gotten close even if they had.

Instead, she walked to the fridge for that long list of phone numbers. Not the fire department. Was this a job for the police? Did police even come for random blessings from the equine fairy? What if someone came along the road and thought she'd stolen their horses? What if the horses *were* stolen and she got accused of taking them?

It was Brandon's number she called.

"Charlie! What's up?"

"There's kind of a problem." She walked back to the bay window. "There are three horses in the front yard, and I'm not sure what to do with them."

Silence.

"Does this happen a lot?" she prompted. Maybe Mainers found stray horses on a regular basis, and she'd just phoned Brandon with the equivalent of asking maintenance how to handle the grey squirrels climbing the apartment building's maple trees.

"No, actually. I'm just as confused as you are. I'm going out on a limb and guessing Eleanor didn't order three horses for delivery this morning?"

Charlotte's shoulders tensed. "I didn't sign for them."

"I'm pretty sure horse breeders don't just deliver free samples. I'll pop over and see what I can do. Ten minutes. Don't let them leave."

She said, "I want them to leave."

"Someone's got to be looking for them, so you want them safe until we find out whose they are. My dad probably knows."

Oh, of course. Mr. Pelletier was Aunt Eleanor's gardener.

Charlotte went back outside, where Pepper focused on those horses with her pointed ears raised and those beautiful eyes so arresting. It was unnerving in every way, this near-wolf and three half-ton animals all waiting for the lone human to do something.

Instead she sat on the rock wall. Mr. Pelletier would surely come by and recognize the horses even though they all looked the same to her. Well other than the colors. She wasn't going to get on the phone with the police and start describing them. *I believe he's an Arabian gelding thoroughbred, seventeen hands at the shoulder, with a white blaze and socks on three feet.* Best leave that to the experts.

Aunt Eleanor had taught elementary school for twenty-five years, which was why Charlotte got sent out to her during the long summer breaks. Brandon was the gardener's kid (and the housekeeper's kid too, come to think of it) who used to bike over to hang out. Aunt Eleanor would open up the piano and give lessons, but when the playing was over, the kids would wander the property and make lean-tos out of sticks, dig holes, and create cairns of stone. Some afternoons they'd descend Sky Ridge Drive to the rocky beach and play in the water.

A beat-up Ford Focus pulled into the driveway, and out

stepped Brandon with his thoughtful eyes and chocolate hair. "Good news! Dad may know whose these are."

"Can't you just text him a photo?"

"I could, but it's a nice day, and we still have to get them back." He jumped up on the rock wall, hands on his hips, and gazed at the horses. Against the blue of the sky, he looked so tall. And strong. Wearing shorts and a T-shirt, it was obvious he worked out often. "Good job, Pepper!"

Pepper's tail went into high gear, but then she popped back into her previous position: sitting alert, head high, staring straight at the horses.

Charlotte said, "Why good job?"

"She must have seen them wandering. She knows they're not supposed to be on the road, so she herded them somewhere safe."

Charlotte blinked. "Pepper herded three horses?"

Brandon looked down at her. "Border collies are the world's best sheep dogs. It's why you need to take them running every day, or at least something else to do."

Charlotte shook her head. "She can't have herded them. There's an invisible fence."

Brandon laughed, and Charlotte burned with irritation. Was he laughing because he thought she was just some ignorant flatlander who had no idea about anything? When he didn't know what to do with the horses either?

Brandon gestured at the edge of the property. "Eleanor called that fence the most useless money they'd ever thrown away. You should have heard Eleanor ranting the first week after she got the dog. She was furious at Gregory because an hour after the thing got installed, Pepper had already figured out how to get around the invisible fence."

"Wait, what?" Charlotte stood. "No one told me that."

"Pepper goes onto that hill by the white birches, runs down as fast as she can, and she jumps." Brandon shielded his eyes with one hand while pointing with the other. "The fence gets really loud for a minute...and then it stops, so she's free to wander the countryside."

"Good grief, what am I supposed to do with a dog that escapes?" Charlotte wrapped her arms around her waist. "I can't stay beside her the whole summer."

"She knows she's supposed to stay on her territory. Bet me the loose horses looked too much like an emergency." Brandon paused. "If you think about it, she had to brave the fence multiple times to herd them in, so that's dedication."

One of the horses separated from the others in search of better grass. Pepper popped up, circled around it, and brought it back to the other two.

"Impressive," Charlotte said. "That instinct to herd, I mean."

"And the instinct to be herded." Brandon shook his head. "Any of those horses could put a hoof right through her."

A pickup truck reading "Pelletier Landscaping and Gardening" pulled into the driveway. Mr. Pelletier was already on the phone as he got out, and he approached them talking easily to some anonymous person on the other end. "Well, that's one mystery solved. They'll be here when you want them."

"Soon?" Charlotte said under her breath. "You want them soon, right?"

Brandon grinned. With the sun in his eyes, he looked mischievous.

"They're tearing up the lawn," Charlotte explained.

"We can fix the lawn," Brandon said. "Dad? You can fix the lawn, right?"

Mr. Pelletier returned the phone to his pocket. "No problem. By the time Eleanor and Gregory are back, I'll have it grown over."

No one seemed to think this was as big a deal as Charlotte did. Good thing she hadn't called the police. They'd have made a show of handcuffing the horses and loading them into the back of the police cruiser, all the while saying "ma'am" and radioing dispatch with call numbers that translated to, "Total waste of our time."

Brandon said, "You're going to need Pepper good and tired in the mornings if you leave her in the yard. Eleanor used to take her for early runs, and Greg would take her biking. Maybe bring her to the beach and throw Frisbees for half an hour."

Mr. Pelletier said, "She's a working dog. On the south part of the property where there's that pond, she'll herd the geese too."

Charlotte shuddered. "I hate geese."

"Everyone hates geese," Brandon assured her. "Remind me to look up when goose-hunting season is."

She laughed. "You think I could cook one?"

"What would Ma Ingalls do?"

Mr. Pelletier left to mow someone's lawn, but Brandon stayed. "I don't work until two o'clock today."

"Second shift?"

"More like the gym closes at ten, so that's when they need me until." He stretched. "I can stay until the horses go home."

Charlotte stretched out her legs on the rock wall, leaning back so the sun soaked into her. This much she remembered of her childhood summers—warm rocks combined with an ocean breeze that kept it cool even when the temperature climbed.

Brandon said, "I could come by in the mornings and take Pepper for a run."

"You don't have to." Charlotte's response came automatically. "I'll figure out something."

Brandon sounded teasing. "*You* could take her for a run."

"You said something about Frisbees. I'll look into that."

A man walked up Sky Ridge Drive, and momentarily Brandon was shaking hands with a solid guy in his sixties. "Jake Farnsworth," he said by way of introduction. The man whistled to the horses, who picked up their heads. Two walked over to him. Pepper circled the third until it stopped grazing and followed. The man fastened halters to all three. "They got open the fence to the upper pasture after I went to the farmer's market, so I didn't even realize they were gone. Sorry they bothered you and your wife."

Charlotte's eyes widened. Not just the wife thing, but the thick Maine accent. The "uppah pastcha" and all those flat R sounds. Brandon's accent wasn't as pronounced. Just adorable.

Brandon shrugged. "Oh, we're not married. I'm just helping out."

"Pity," Farnsworth said. He didn't even offer to pay for the damage to the lawn.

Brandon took one of the leads. "I'll help you walk them back." Then, "Charlie, you want to come too?"

"Sure." She detached Pepper's useless invisible fence collar and attached her leash, then said, "Gate," and Pepper trotted down the driveway.

Chapter Four

Brandon held the lead for one horse as they followed behind the other two. "At least life in Brighthead isn't boring you to tears."

Charlie sounded bemused. "I was looking forward to boredom."

Brandon steeled himself. "I hope you don't mind if I ask, but something's confusing me."

Charlie said, "Something like, 'Why is she here?'"

"Exactly!" Maybe he hadn't needed to steel himself at all. "I remembered last night that Eleanor said you were getting married this summer. She specifically said it was going to happen around when Anna's baby was born."

That was a sanitized version of events. Back before Eleanor's IT band injury, she'd vented during one entire run about how her sister (Charlie's mother) was going to take personal offense at Anna's pregnancy because it conflicted with Charlie's wedding. Charlie had asked Anna to serve as maid of honor, and obviously that couldn't happen with her due date a week from the wedding. "Even if the baby comes early or late," Eleanor had said. "Margaret's going to be so upset."

Come to think of it, "confused" was Brandon's status quo about this whole situation, because he'd been confused back then too. "Why would Charlie be offended by Anna's pregnancy?"

"Not Charlotte! She's a doll. Since neither of them has a sister, Anna's named her an honorary aunt, and Charlotte is delighted to have a niece or nephew. It's Charlotte's mother who's going to take this as a personal affront."

Brandon had said, "When Anna and her husband conceived, somehow I doubt it was your sister they were thinking about," and Eleanor hadn't even laughed.

Holding Pepper's leash as she walked, Charlie's demeanor backed up Eleanor's story. "Yeah, Anna would have been traveling to Philly with a newborn. I told her not even to think of putting herself through that. Can you imagine?" Charlie smiled. "Becoming an aunt was the best wedding present I could possibly get."

Eleanor said later that Charlie's mother did lose her mind, and that there had been screaming. Instead of pursuing that, Brandon said, "Did you change the date because of Anna?"

"I'm not getting married, nothing to do with Anna."

Brandon said, "Oh, I'm sorry to hear that. Calling off a wedding—that sounds huge."

"Of course it's huge!" Charlie sounded prickly, and Pepper looked around at her. "Hunter was cheating."

Brandon exclaimed, "What a jerk! What was wrong with him?"

"Only everything." She huffed. "I confronted him to find out if it was true, and he got all drippy-sorry with me. He hadn't done it, but if he had, he was so sorry I was upset, and now everything would be different." Her voice hardened. "Of course it would be different—and you'd better believe I made it different. We put the dress in storage, cancelled any vendor with a cancellation policy, paid off any vendors who didn't have one, and then I blocked Hunter every way I could."

She stopped when her voice broke. She couldn't keep the anger going. Anger functioned as a cage, but her real feelings had burst out just like Pepper vaulting the invisible fence.

Brandon managed a soft, "I'm so sorry."

"Cheating is the worst. It is absolutely the worst. I'm sorry. I shouldn't be bothering you." Pepper brushed up against Charlie's legs. "I wore out my welcome with all my friends talking about this, but it doesn't go away. When Aunt Eleanor asked if I could house-sit, I knew she wanted to give me a place to crash where I wouldn't bother everyone by moping and ranting. I'm pathetic enough that I took it."

Brandon put a hand on her shoulder. "Hey. Not at all pathetic. You can rant at me."

"Thanks." She wiped her cheeks with the back of her arm. "I don't know what to do now. I'd structured my life around the wedding. My fellowship ended last month, and my lease was up at the end of the fellowship. I need a job, but I'd figured I'd mount a job search after, when things were calmer."

"That stinks."

"I've got a publication to write for the end of the fellowship, but beyond that, it's all wide open. Everything I thought would happen is just...shattered."

Pepper whined at her, and Charlie bent to pet her. "I'm sorry, girl. This isn't your fault. You can't herd a guy into a marriage he doesn't want."

Brandon said, "It's worse than that, isn't it? If this guy tried to work it out with you, he *did* want you married to him. He wanted a wife at home and an easy score on the side."

"Not just any easy score." Charlie hugged Pepper to her chest. "She was another doctor. I could never trust him again. How would I know if a surgery went extra long or if instead he had an extracurricular activity that afternoon? And all his friends who knew, but covered for him?"

"Wow, what slimeballs." The horse tugged at Brandon because they'd gotten behind the other two. "Charlie, I don't want to be rude—"

"Oh! Sorry, the horse." She got up. "Anyhow, that's my sob story. Not good enough to keep a guy happy even before the wedding, not bad enough to be dumped outright, not smart enough to suspect him, not stupid enough to go through with the marriage."

Brandon said, "How did you catch him?"

"It wasn't even me who caught him!" Charlie exclaimed. "My mother hired a private detective."

"She did what?"

"I know, right?" Charlie shook her head. "I asked what she suspected she'd find, and she won't tell me. Gut feeling or something."

Ice-cold even in the sunlight, Brandon said, "Are you *sure* Hunter was cheating?"

"He admitted it over text." She shuddered. "I sent him photos of things they found. He got mad at me. I didn't trust him, he said, and this was all my fault because I would actually pay someone to spy on him."

Brandon laughed out loud. "Wait, he wanted you to believe finding evidence of what he did was worse than him doing it?"

"It actually made it easier that my mother was the one who hadn't trusted him. I might have bought it. Oh, and I'm not perfect either, you know." She rolled her eyes, but her mouth was trembling. "There I was, *playing the victim,* and somehow his decision to cheat on me was all my fault."

"You know that's not true, right?"

His words came out stunned, not strong like he wanted. He wanted to reassure Charlie, and instead it felt hard to breathe. She looked so devastated, and he had a hand full of bridle and couldn't just hug her there in the road. How could a guy who purportedly loved her, who she loved, look at this same pain and deny all responsibility? How could that other man shift the blame back onto Charlie because it was her fault she'd caught him rather than his fault that he'd done the thing she caught him doing?

"I'm sorry." She turned to him, her eyebrows in an inverted V, and forced a smile that was painful to see. "You didn't deserve to hear all that. But that's the story. I'm here because I'm not getting married, but I still get to keep my best wedding present. I get to have a niece."

From his peripheral vision, Brandon sensed a customer coming up to the Lighthouse Athletics desk, and he turned with a smile.

...then had to freeze that smile in place because it wasn't a customer. It was Alexander something-or-other from the corporate office.

"Brandon Pelletier!" exclaimed Alex, as though they'd been best friends since high school. "How's it going?"

"It" was now going less well than "it" had been two minutes earlier, before Alex entered the gym. "Great! The members have been loving those new treadmills with the VR screens. One member said she'd taken the incline off zero-point-zero for the first time in ten years because the hill video was so pretty."

"Glad to hear it." Alex set his elbows on the counter, looking for all the world as though he were not glad to hear it. "I want to talk to you about the Lighthouse Run. It's on again this year, and we're in charge. It was a natural match, you know."

"Lighthouse, lighthouse. Got it," Brandon said. "Michael told me you wanted my graphic design work for your logo. But the run already has a logo."

Alex shook his head. "That's a modified version of the historical society logo, and they won't let us use it. Really there's no reason for us to use it anyhow, since we want to brand this as *our* run. I want people to look at the Lighthouse Run logo and immediately think about Lighthouse Athletic Club."

Brandon smiled, feeling like a 1920s socialite playing a politeness game at a cocktail party. "Then the thing to do is alter the color of our corporate logo and change the text to read 'Lighthouse Run'. Marketing can do that in fifteen minutes. In fact," and he picked up his phone, "I already did."

He handed his phone to Alex, who studied the screen, brows contracted.

This wasn't what Alex wanted at all, and it would take a real push to make him accept it. Alex had in mind the nebulous dream of a *Logo*, something with *branding* and *visual appeal.* The Lighthouse Athletic Club logo was, in Brandon's opinion, replete with the noninspiration you get from low bidders who usually work on national accounts but this time ended up with a local business. *"What's their name? Lighthouse Athletic Club? Slap a lighthouse and a barbell on it and call it good."*

This logo wasn't quite that bad. Quite.

Alex handed back the phone. "We were thinking of something a bit more stand-out."

Brandon said, "Are you thinking of hiring my business as a freelancer, or having me do the work on the clock? Because we have a problem if you want me to do it as an employee. I'm not being paid as a marketing consultant or a graphic designer."

Alex said, "But you'd get great exposure."

"I don't see it that way. The more likely result," Brandon said, "is that you guys get exposed as being cheap, and I get exposed as someone who can be coerced into design work for free."

Alex chucked. "We're paying you to be at the desk."

"I have no problem doing the work I signed up for. But this is not only outside my job description—it's also work my clients contract me to do."

Alex stepped back, thinking.

Brandon leaned back in his chair. "I don't mind modifying the existing logo while on the clock. That's your artwork, and

I'm you're employee. In fact, I'll email those files to you now. Creating new art is another issue. If you want that, let's negotiate between businesses."

He had the email ready to go, a brisk "Here are the original logo files" in the subject line.

To his credit, Alex didn't immediately threaten Brandon's job. Brandon had been uncertain how far and how fast Alex would push things.

Alex finally said, "I'm not sure why you're resisting over something so small."

Brandon hit send on the email. "I'm not sure why you're resisting over something so small either."

Chapter Five

Friday morning, Charlotte was throwing a Frisbee for Pepper when her phone sounded. While Pepper chased down the Frisbee, she answered the video call. Aunt Eleanor appeared on the screen. "Charlotte! Good morning!"

"Hey! How are you? How's Anna?"

"Terrific! She's practically glowing, and she sends you all her love and kisses."

Of course she does. In all her life, Charlotte had never once "sent kisses" to someone, and she imagined Anna hadn't either. "Did you give her my gift?" Charlotte prompted.

"I'll do that at the baby shower tomorrow," said Aunt Eleanor, and Charlotte fought a grimace. That one should have been given in private, but it would be too hard to explain.

Pepper came back. "Hang on. I have to throw a Frisbee."

"Is Pepper there?" Aunt Eleanor exclaimed. "Pepper? Hey, girl!"

Charlotte spent the next five minutes sitting on the grass, holding the phone so the dog could have a video chat with her aunt and uncle. Yes, this was entirely normal behavior and not at all weird. Most likely this was the reason Aunt Eleanor had video-chatted her in the first place: Pepper couldn't text.

"Pepper, put Charlotte back on the phone," singsonged her aunt, and Charlotte dutifully turned the camera around. "Has everything been okay?"

"Everything's fine," Charlotte said, angling the camera so no hoofprints showed. "I went grocery shopping yesterday, and Brandon stopped by. That means he's house-sitting your house-sitter."

"He's a nice boy." Aunt Eleanor paused, then said, "Your mother flew out here for the baby shower."

Another significant pause followed. Charlotte said, "She said she might, since she didn't have to prep for the wedding anymore."

"I'll be seeing her at the house later today. She wants to help us set up, but I keep telling her we have it all under control."

Mom would walk into a situation "all under control" and get it more under control. That's just what she did. Charlotte ruffled Pepper's head. "It's a shame she can't just relax and enjoy the visit."

"That would be nice. Anyway, I'm going to head over to the house soon. Let me know if you need anything or if you have any questions."

As they ended the call, a creaky pickup truck parked on the driveway. Pepper bounded up to the newcomer, and out stepped Farnsworth, the old man who'd come yesterday to retrieve his horses.

Gosh, had the horses gotten out again? But then Farnsworth reached back into the truck and pulled out a square egg crate.

"I owed you a thank-you for keeping the horses safe." He handed Charlotte the egg crate, laden with multicolored eggs. Blue eggs, speckled eggs, some copper-colored, and not a single white one except for where they were coated with gunk. "Fresh this morning." He grinned at her. "You've never had farm-fresh eggs before, have you?"

She nodded, unsure what to say because "These look gross" wasn't the right response. She came up with, "Thank you. It wasn't a problem."

The lawn was still torn up, but apparently dirty eggs fixed that.

"These are much better than store-bought. Trust me." He reached into his pocket and pulled out a rawhide toy for Pepper, who leaped in place. "Come get it, girl! Up!" he said, bending over. Pepper jumped onto his back, and the only reason Charlotte didn't scream was that she still had the eggs—and the farmer was laughing. Pepper jumped down, wagging, and he gave her the toy.

"Dried sow's ear," he explained, which didn't increase Charlotte's comfort level.

He handed her a business card, which she maneuvered somehow while holding the eggs. "We're down the road apiece if you need anything." He pointed to the card. "Also, we've got a stall at the farmer's market on Wednesdays, if you want vegetables. That's why the horses were out so long before we realized."

Charlotte carried the eggs inside. Twenty-four eggs? What was she supposed to do with two dozen eggs?

Actually, considering it hadn't been her who'd taken care of the horses (and Pepper wasn't sharing her sow's ear, that much was certain) Charlotte texted Brandon. "Mr. Farnsworth was just by and gave us these as a thank-you." She snapped a photo of the eggs.

A little later, Brandon replied, "Those will be delicious. Enjoy!"

She texted back, "No, silly. You need to come get them."

From him: "He didn't drive them to my house. Obviously they're for you."

From her: "So help me, come get your eggs."

Ten minutes later, he appeared at the door. "Okay, so we need to have a discussion about awesome things. These," he said, pointing to the square crate, "are twenty-four savage packages of amazingness. They're farm-fresh organic eggs from free-range chickens, and I bet they're still warm."

"I'm aware of all that." She folded her arms. "I've shopped at Whole Foods. The point is, your family did most of the work with his horses, and even if you hadn't, I'm not going to be able to eat all the reward until after they go bad. Which, if they're little treasures, would be a crime against humanity and chickendom alike."

Brandon said, "Quiche? Omelets?"

"I'll keep six. Take the rest home and give them to your dad."

Brandon made a hurt face. "Do you think I live in my parents' basement?"

Charlotte stammered, "Well, no—"

He tilted up his head. "I'll have you know I live in my *sister's* basement. I can give her a bunch of eggs if you want." He brightened. "You probably never met my sister, did you?"

"I've never met a lot of people." She frowned. "Your sister wasn't that girl with the ponytail...?"

"No, that was Kelty." Brandon's eyes flickered away from Charlotte, seeming momentarily gutted.

Oh, right, Kelty! It was stupid how many things Charlotte had forgotten. He probably thought she was an idiot.

Brandon recovered. "My sister's six years older than me, so by the time you were spending summers here, she was working at the ice cream stand. I thought maybe you saw her there. She and her husband have a house in town, and there's this little illegal rental unit that nudges them closer to the mortgage payment every month, plus it houses a handy babysitter. Speaking of which, I need to get back."

"Then take the eggs."

"I'll take some, but only if you come with me."

Shortly they'd cut off the edge of the cardboard egg carton and gotten into his car with the rest on her lap. "Stay on the lawn this time," she told the dog. Pepper was still gnawing like crazy on that sow's ear, which had achieved a state of "disgusting" that Charlotte didn't even want to think about. At least Pepper was enjoying it.

The houses "in town" were tightly packed. Even Pepper couldn't herd three horses onto these lawns. Most of the frontage was driveway, widened to park an extra car, and no one had garages. Brandon left his car at the far end and entered through a door lower than ground level.

The basement apartment consisted of the finished half of a basement. Gosh, this place was tiny. Even in college, none of Charlotte's friends had lived in something this cramped. The flooring was the concrete slab of the foundation, covered with a carpet on one side and newish vinyl in the kitchen area.

"I'm back," Brandon called to exactly no one.

From above, Charlotte heard, "I'll cancel the manhunt!"

She laughed, and Brandon walked under the ceiling grate connecting his apartment to the upstairs. "Didn't want you to think I'd abandoned my post."

From upstairs, the female voice replied, "I was preparing to let her be raised by wolves."

The chief decorations were three of the "Vision of the Future" posters NASA had released back in 2016. Brandon had Mars, Enceladus, and Titan, but he also had a corkboard organizer hanging over his desk.

"Grand tour," he said, pointing around. "Bathroom. Kitchen, living room," (those two were kind of the same) "and bedroom. It's right near downtown, and I have a spot to park my car. Plus free access to the upstairs and all the time in the world to lavish attention on my niece."

Charlotte pointed to the grille in the ceiling. "And Big Sister always watching?"

"A lot of older houses have these." He patted the woodstove directly beneath the grate. "This sweetheart produces a lot of heat. You want the heat upstairs, so you open the heat register and let the air flow up. Also there's the pipe through the upstairs. It's a good system."

He put four eggs into his fridge. "Let's go meet the most

cunning person in the world."

He opened a door Charlotte had thought to be a pantry but was actually a staircase. This deposited them in a kitchen with a cracked linoleum floor and a humming refrigerator. He set the eggs on the counter. "Olivia, I brought you some gold." Then a girl toddled into the kitchen. "Aria!"

He scooped her up and set her on his hip. "Aria, this is Charlie. Can you wave hi?"

Aria gave Charlotte a studious look, not at all certain she wanted to bestow a "hi" upon this strange woman. Charlotte grinned. "Hi, Aria!"

Brandon tickled the girl, and she giggled. "Isn't she cunning?"

The girl's mother came into the kitchen. "Sorry, I was taking care of something." She looked at the eggs. "Where'd you get all these?"

"Jake Farnsworth's horses got into Charlie's yard. He gave her eggs, and she gave them to us."

Olivia's mouth twitched. "You should have eaten them."

"I did keep a few," Charlotte said. "Brandon forced me."

She snapped at Brandon, "Freeloader. You should have forced her to keep all of them." She set them in the fridge without washing them. "I need to head out to work, but—"

"Go!" Brandon waved her away. "Aria, are you ready for our playdate?"

Olivia put her phone in her pocket and grabbed her purse. "I believe it's called 'childcare.'" Aria leaned out, and Olivia hugged her. "See you tonight, babygirl!"

Olivia left, and Brandon said to Charlotte, "She works mornings and I'm working evenings, so I cover when I can." Then, to the girl in his arms, "Want to go see the lighthouse?"

It didn't take long to buckle a car seat into the back of the Focus, and then right after, they were driving toward the ocean.

Chapter Six

Brandon couldn't get Charlie out of the house fast enough. She'd stood in his apartment for two entire seconds before he realized how uncomfortable she was.

She had money. That much was obvious. She'd come from money and quite probably relied on her parents' money to keep up a reasonable lifestyle. He'd die before probing her finances, but given that her family had employed his for at least twenty years, you could conclude her family had more money. His mother had cleaned for her aunt. His sister's house could fit inside her aunt's house, and there would still be room for his parents' house. Her aunt and uncle had left Charlie a car to drive around Brighthead that fifteen years from now Brandon couldn't afford to buy used.

He'd never *thought* about it though. Charlie was just Charlie, the girl whose kite he'd climbed a tree to save.

With his niecelet strapped into the back of the Ford, he drove Charlie to neutral territory. Time for the scenic overlook at the Brighthead Lighthouse.

Although this wasn't neutral territory either, was it? His car didn't have air conditioning other than the traditional kind: open the windows and drive fast. Most of the time in Maine, you didn't need it.

Self-conscious, he parked at the pier and unstrapped Aria, then shrugged on the carrier backpack. A check of his phone showed the tide all the way out. "We're going for a walk, kiddo." Brandon had Aria climb into the carrier so he could pick his way down the rocks.

Charlie's nose wrinkled. "Didn't we used to take a boat to the lighthouse?"

Brandon said, "Probably."

"Is it erosion?"

"It's the causeway," Brandon said. "Remember I mentioned the lighthouse run? We've got about two hours until the tide comes back, and when it does, it'll swamp the path. But right now we can walk it."

Charlie pointed at the seaweed clumped on either side. "Wait, when you said the race is a race against the tide, you really meant it?"

"We're going to walk it now, so not really a race." Brandon laughed. "If you want to do one of those, there's a marathon downstate where you run between the shore and an island, and then you've got to make it back without drowning. It's muddy and they do have spotters out in boats. I'm not that brave."

"Or dumb?" Charlie asked.

"I'm probably exactly that dumb. It's my fortitude that's in question." Brandon grinned. "We'll get a couple of hours where the water's just on either side of the walkway, and then after that, it's covered."

She looked over the sides. "And you can run on this? Like, without breaking your foot?"

Brandon chuckled. "It's just gravel. We have a few trail runners in the club, and they're...interesting. They'll run right up the side of a mountain, tree roots and all."

On his back, Aria shifted position. The frame took all the girl's weight so it was a lot more comfortable than holding her. When she'd been small, she'd ridden around in a cloth sling that he adjusted with rings on his shoulder, but then Olivia had gotten this from a friend who'd gotten it from another friend after her kids outgrew it.

Charlie said, "Will the lighthouse be open?"

"I doubt it. The lighthouse operators don't let you in except on special occasions. Like if you've been elected governor."

Charlie sighed. "I forgot to mention this, but I haven't been elected governor."

Brandon mimed slapping himself in the forehead. "I wish you'd told me sooner."

Out on the water, or what should have been the water, the wind picked up. Brighthead's lighthouse stood at the head of a cove, and you walked to it from the north where the sand spit naturally occurred. Every spring, a commission would assess the drift and erosion, dump new gravel, and then make any necessary repairs before vanishing for another year.

Far out to sea there were boats. Brandon said, "You should do a whale watch this summer."

Charlie said, "I remember something like that."

Eleanor and Gregory didn't own a boat. Something they had in common with Brandon's family, at least. "Can you see the lighthouse from your window?"

Charlie nodded. "It's gorgeous at night. The waves sparkle ahead of it."

The further they walked out onto the ocean, the more nervous Charlie seemed. They were the only ones walking right now, giving the place an eerie feel. *Imagine if it were foggy,* Brandon thought of saying, but she'd probably turn right around. It was a little more than a mile to the lighthouse, maybe a twenty-minute walk. They'd gone about that distance to Farnsworth's yesterday and then back, but a mile straight out into the ocean felt a lot further than a mile down Sky Ridge Drive and taking a left onto Ebbetts Road.

When they got to the island, the causeway pitched up into a gravel path encircling the island. He led her to the lighthouse, then set Aria free of her harness. Charlie stared up at the white building while Aria played with the pebbles.

"No rock in the mouth," he told her. Aria pouted but put down the rock that had been en route to her lips.

Charlie quipped, "Some things you shouldn't have to tell people."

"I've had to say quite a few things I didn't think you'd need to tell people." He followed her gaze up to the light at the top. "Awesome, isn't it?"

"The run doesn't come all the way up here, does it?" Charlie sounded winded. "Because that's insane."

"We go around the base of the island and then back out." He paused. "It's maybe, what, a tenth of a marathon?"

She brightened up. "Totally easy! What was I thinking?" Her eyes gleamed while the wind tugged her hair, and he noticed all at once her long legs, her amazed smile, and the way she carried herself.

Heat flushed through Brandon, and he forced himself to look away. Sure, bring the recently dumped rich girl out to the island and then start daydreaming about how cute she was. Great idea.

Charlotte mused, "It would be a nice place to bring a picnic."

"Not sure we'd have had the time today." Brandon kept his gaze on Aria. "We need to be off before the tide comes back."

Charlie took a thousand pictures, then got a picture of Brandon and Aria. It was enough time for him to get a grip on his thoughts. Lastly, she took a selfie of all three with the lighthouse in the background.

"Whether you get service out here depends on how the wind is blowing," Brandon warned.

Charlie's nose wrinkled. "I'm pretty sure satellites don't work that way." She sent the photo to her aunt and one to him, then said, "Oh, I should send one to my mother too." She took a solo selfie and sent that.

Her smile in the picture was so pretty, her eyes lively. But he remembered yesterday, the tears and the forced smile when she talked about a marriage destroyed without ever getting the chance to become a family. But here they were, out in the middle of nowhere, a man and a woman and a baby.

Don't think that way. Seriously, don't think that way.

He said, "We ought to go." It came out raspy.

Brandon bundled Aria back into the carrier. The water was visibly higher.

"Freaky," Charlie whispered. "It's undetectable how it's coming in, bit by bit. By the time you realized, you'd already be underwater."

The notion sent chills through Brandon as he watched her walk with the wind tugging at her clothes. "Yeah." His throat felt thick. "It could sneak up on you if you're not careful."

Chapter Seven

On Saturday morning, Charlotte let Pepper out while she brought her coffee and her phone onto the cushioned wicker chairs. Last night had been Anna's baby shower.

Pepper bounded up the porch with a Frisbee, so Charlotte threw it and settled down onto the chair...only to have to get up again when Pepper brought back the Frisbee.

"I'm supposed to be relaxing," she told the upraised eyes and wagging tail. "See, it's early, and I have a nice cup of coffee."

Surprisingly, Pepper did not care. Charlotte had to leave her coffee and stand barefoot in her pajamas on the wet grass, throwing the Frisbee until her arm ached.

"I need to get better distance on the toss," Charlotte told the border collie on the millionth throw. "If I could make it go a mile, I'd get a reprieve in between."

The Pelletier landscaping truck appeared on Sky Ridge Drive, and Charlotte dashed into the house, leaving Pepper on the lawn. Up in her room she grabbed last night's discarded clothes and yanked them on. When the doorbell rang, she almost had sandals on both feet, and she ran her fingers through her hair.

Downstairs, Mr. Pelletier was tossing the Frisbee to Pepper. He didn't send it out in long arcs. Instead he waited until Pepper crouched, staring at the Frisbee, then sent it spinning upward. Pepper would take a tremendous leap, snatch the Frisbee mid-air, then snap her head and throw it back at him.

Charlotte stepped outside. "What's up?"

"I wanted to get an early start on the lawn, see if I could get it patched up from the horses." Mr. Pelletier tossed the Frisbee again for Pepper, who looked delighted. "I'm also going to trim the bushes and fix up the flower beds on the southern side, mow the lawn, and maybe prune the decorative cherry trees."

This was in line with what Uncle Gregory had said would happen. Pepper stood on her hind legs with her paws on Mr. Pelletier's jeans, and he rubbed the dog's head.

Brandon's grey Ford pulled in behind his father's truck. Charlotte told Mr. Pelletier, "Let me know if Pepper's a bother."

"Doesn't bother me."

Brandon came up the driveway with a wave, too energetic for so early in the morning. She said, "Do you work for your father?"

Mr. Pelletier laughed. "Him? He's got his head in the clouds."

Charlotte glanced at Brandon, who looked pretty darned sturdy in jeans and an Imagine Dragons T-shirt.

"Thanks, Dad." Brandon sighed. "Actually, I thought maybe since you don't know anyone around here yet, you might want a grand tour of Brighthead."

Mr. Pelletier roughed up Pepper's head. "She's living in Brighthead's grandest part."

Brandon gave a shy smile. "But I've got a full tank of gas and the morning off, so if it's lonely not knowing anyone around here, I'll take you for a ride."

Charlotte glanced at the wicker chair and her abandoned coffee. As Mr. Pelletier revved up the riding mower and backed it off the trailer hitched to his pickup, she bid farewell to any hopes of quiet. "Come inside, and I'll get ready."

She put her coffee in the microwave, then asked what blend coffee Brandon preferred. Momentarily she had the single-brew coffeemaker chugging away while she went upstairs to get changed. A few minutes later, her coffee was in a travel mug, and she'd poured Brandon's into a travel mug of his own.

Brandon backed out onto Sky Ridge, looking amused. "Thanks for the coffee."

Charlotte chuckled. "So what's open at eight o'clock in the morning?"

"Nothing. Even during tourist season there's nothing, so I figured I'd take you for a joy ride."

They drove with the windows down and the radio on. Brandon took her back to the lighthouse and parked at a scenic overlook.

"The causeway's gone." Charlotte put on her sunglasses against the glare on the water. "You wouldn't know it was ever there. How deep does it get?"

"About six feet, I think." Brandon shrugged. "Deep enough that you could take a motor boat. I never tried to swim it."

He led her to a statue of a woman holding a lantern in one hand and shielding her eyes with the other as she gazed out to sea. "Behold," Brandon said. "Brighthead's most amazing claim to historical fame."

Charlotte gasped. "I remember her! We used to climb up on the base and look at the ocean just like she was doing!"

At the statue's feet was a plaque headed by a quote: "Build your lighthouse against the storms of life." Beneath that, it read, "Alice Brightman, 1823-1895, founder of the Brighthead Point Lighthouse. The mother of five children, all of whom worked the sea, Mrs. Brightman single-handedly raised funds for a lighthouse after her husband's sudden death during a storm. Brighthead is named for her noble sacrifice."

Charlotte said, "It sounds like she used her tragedy for everyone else's good."

"That's very much *not* our claim to fame." Folding his arms, Brandon shook his head. "Our claim to fame is how every part of the monument is wrong."

Charlotte recoiled. "What?"

Brandon ticked the points off on his fingers. "First, her name was Alicia Brightman. Secondly, she was born in 1825. Thirdly, her husband was a state senator and not a fisherman. Pretty sure he died of tuberculosis."

Charlotte started laughing. "Wait, what?"

"And you thought I was going to point out the 'Missus' as the error? No, we're not even started. The statue is based on a photograph of her sister because of a clerical error. She had four children, some of which may have been or married fishermen, but who even cares at this point? And I think she petitioned the statehouse for the funds, which isn't exactly fundraising." Brandon's brow furrowed. "Oh, and Brighthead isn't named for her. We've got documents from before Maine was even a state calling this place Brighthead, so she may have been named for the town."

Charlotte ventured, "Is at least her death date correct?"

Brandon was shaking with laughter. "Who knows? Maybe she's still alive."

Charlotte started laughing too. "If I can ask...why does this exist?"

Brandon wiped tears from his eyes. "Because our historical society isn't all that awesome? To mess with the flatlanders? I have no idea. It's noble and tragic and beautiful, and tourists come to take their pictures, buy souvenirs, and go home energized to fill their own lives with glorious lighthouses in the storms."

Charlotte tried to stop giggling long enough to take a picture of the plaque. "No one ever told me the statue was erected on a pedestal of myth."

"That's what we call it." Brandon went helpless again with laughter. "Myth Brightman!"

They picked a trail to a different part of the beach, then hunted for shells among the rocks. Charlotte relaxed with the regular sound of the waves. "When the tide is out, you can do this thing called tide pooling," Brandon said. "We could have done it yesterday with Aria, except she'd put gross things in her mouth."

A family was on the rocks some distance away. Charlotte felt a pang when she thought of the family she'd intended to start with Hunter. And how Brandon had just suggested coming out here with a baby. And how Anna was going to have a baby. Everyone was living their lives and leaving her behind.

No, don't ruin the day. Just enjoy the waves and the breeze.

They were returning to Brandon's car when her phone rang. She glanced at the screen, then exclaimed, "Anna!"

Brandon turned, beaming. "Baby time?"

"Hello?" Charlotte was breathless. "Anna, what's up? Is she here?"

"No." Anna sounded stern. "We have to talk because I cannot accept that gift."

Charlotte stopped still. "What? Why not?"

"Because I'm not stupid." Anna's no-nonsense tone could have sliced a tin can in half. "That's not a beaded christening blanket. That's the shawl you crocheted for your wedding."

"I want your baby to have it!" Charlotte could feel Brandon's eyes on her, and she pivoted toward the sea. "Why shouldn't the baby have it?" And then, "How did you even know? It's square."

"I recognized it from the pictures you'd been posting on Instagram." Anna sighed. "This isn't right. It's a gorgeous piece of artwork, and you made it for yourself. Just because you're not marrying Hunter doesn't mean you don't deserve a beautiful shawl."

"It's not bad luck." Charlotte's pulse quickened. "Are you saying that just because the wedding failed—"

"The wedding failed because Hunter is a jerk. The shawl is gorgeous, and everyone gushed over it. But it belongs with you."

"It belongs where I sent it." Charlotte sounded urgent. "Please keep it. Use it for the christening."

"You should have heard the gasp when I opened it up." Anna was softening. Maybe she'd relent. "I wouldn't pass it around because I didn't want cake all over it. But you do realize that babies spit up on things, and worse."

"It's cotton and silk. It washes. I'll even re-block it for you afterward." Brandon was being patient, and she felt bad about answering now that there was no baby to report. "Really, keep it."

"I'm sending it back."

"If you send it back, I'm pulling out the corner and frogging the whole thing, so you might as well keep it." Charlotte tried to sound stern. "I'll tell your mother if you send it back. Besides, everyone saw it. Now you have to use it."

"This isn't going to work," Anna said. "You're emotional, and I'm emotional."

"Then you need to keep it. At least for a few months until we're both less emotional." Charlotte paused. "Look, I'm not somewhere I can talk longer, so I'll call you tonight," and a minute later she'd extricated herself from the conversation.

Brandon looked intrigued enough that he deserved an answer. Charlotte opened her phone's photo album. "Anna wanted to return my baby shower gift. I'd made...wait, hang on." She found the photos Aunt Eleanor had texted of Anna holding up the shawl/blanket thing. In retrospect, Anna did look a little stunned.

"You *made* that?" Brandon touched the screen to enlarge

it. "That's gorgeous! Why would she want to get rid of it?" He paused. "The beads? Choking hazard?"

Choking hazard? "It was supposed to be my wedding shawl. Maybe she thinks it's cursed."

He kept moving the photo over different parts of the shawl. "Maybe she thinks it'll get ruined, but I think it's wonderful."

They reached his car, but he kept studying the picture. Then he handed her phone back and dictated into his own, "Shelly, where do you get your yarn?"

His phone beeped with five incoming texts in two minutes, and he laughed. "Ah, I've found the next stop on our tour. Hop in."

He drove Charlotte through downtown Brighthead. A number of the businesses had changed. Sparrows, where the running club had met Tuesday night, used to be a pizza place. The green in center Brighthead was new; they'd bulldozed something in order to make that. Brandon noted, "The statue in the center is, sadly, factual. We won't bother." He pointed out the library and the post office, and then they were on the other side of town. He stopped in front of a tiny store called Bright Stitches.

A woman ran up to the car. "Charlie? I'm Shelly. We met for a few minutes at the running club. I had no idea you were a knitter!"

"Crochet, actually." Charlotte got out of the car. "But I don't need yarn right now."

"You *might* need yarn. That's enough reason to show you where you can nip off to in an emergency." Shelly led her into the store.

Cubbies of rainbows lined the right-hand wall and the entire back. The left wall had the counter and an assortment of needles and hooks, notions, pattern books, yarn bowls, and a million other necessities. At a central table, four women sat with projects, and one of the four stood. "Shelly! How's the cardigan going?"

"I'm going to murder the individual who invented the buttonhole," she said, "but I brought you a sacrifice! This is Charlie. She crochets, and she's here for the summer."

The ladies at the table greeted Charlotte with an enthusiasm that left her embarrassed. The shop owner mentally calculated exactly how much yarn a crocheter could consume in eight weeks of leisure, and she immediately led Charlotte to a cubby of gorgeous hand-dyed silk-wool blends produced by a local farm, followed up by shelves of fingering weight from an independent dyer.

Brandon was stroking a skein of tonal brown worsted merino wool. The owner said, "Are you going to ask her to make you something?"

Brandon's eyebrows shot up. "I could never afford her work!"

Every woman in the store picked up her head and looked right at him.

Brandon said, "Charlie, show her that shawl! It's a work of art. Her level of craftsmanship is way beyond my budget."

Charlotte said, "Actually—"

"Don't *actually* them." Brandon turned to the owner. "She's a professional textile conservator."

Charlotte made a mental note to decapitate Brandon at her first opportunity. "I just finished my fellowship," she managed, bringing the photo back up on her phone. "But textile preservation isn't really about crochet."

One of the women said, "How much do you charge to restore heirloom quilts?"

Another woman said, "I have my mother's bridal gown that my daughter wanted to wear for her wedding, but there's insect damage. Could you fix that?"

Brandon said, "She can't give an estimate until she's seen the piece, but how often are you here?" He turned to Charlotte. "Actually, you're on vacation, so it's not fair to take up your time that way."

In that moment, she realized what he'd done: she'd said she would be looking for contract work, and he'd walked her into a place where clients would abound.

That wasn't what she'd meant by contract work. Usually the contract would be with a historical society or a museum, not with someone's grandmother's mothballed quilt at the bottom of a cedar chest. But the summer days would stretch long, so she agreed to take a look at both projects.

Forty-five minutes later, Charlotte exited the store with half a mile of a cobweb yarn that meandered from a deep-sea blue to a granite off-white. She didn't need yarn, but in her hands the yarn had spoken to her: *Make a shawl of me; crochet me for Aunt Eleanor.*

Shelly stayed behind, working on her button band. Brandon said, "One more stop, and by then Dad should have finished making noise."

On the same stretch of road were three antique stores, dusty and cluttered, two in little houses and one in a barn. They wandered through all three. The products weren't for the most part antiques. Sure, there was the occasional sterling silver button hook, but Charlotte would have dated this as "Early Garage Sale Era." Nevertheless, it was fun. The books were crumbly and some of the dolls creepy; the furniture wobbled, and overhanging it all was a sweet musty scent that reminded her of time.

In the third shop, while Brandon stayed at the front looking at obsolete electronic game systems ("antique") Charlotte rounded a corner and encountered a cardboard box of wood with a giant wheel sticking out of the top.

Charlotte took a step forward and extended a hand, more tentative than Sleeping Beauty.

Alongside the wheel was a forked object, each of its arms lined with hooks. In the center was a spool. And all these other pieces were one by one recognizable as legs, a tabletop, a pedal, a whorl.

A spinning wheel. She'd found a disassembled spinning wheel.

Kneeling beside the box, she picked up one of the whorls. It was quite definitely worn, the grooves shiny where the drive band would have passed. The wheel had drips of varnish on some of the spokes, but the surface was smooth.

How many miles of yarn had been spun on this wheel? What sweaters and hats and mittens came from that yarn, worn day and night by family members who never took into account all the hours behind their warmth? Had the spinner sat alongside her fireplace, spinning while her children read out loud and her husband perused the newspaper?

And then, at the end of the spinner's life, or maybe when her eyesight failed, the family members had disassembled her instrument, stuck it in a box, and dropped it off at the junk shop.

She poked through the parts she could see. It had a reeling pin. It seemed to be missing a distaff. There wasn't an orifice hook, but that was pretty much to be expected.

Brandon approached. "Oh! Now that's interesting."

The box of wheel pieces carried a price tag of three hundred dollars. She glanced toward the front where the proprietor sat with a magazine. Brandon said, "Are you buying it?"

It sat there, unacknowledged as a prince among junk. Did the donors even realize what they had discarded?

She'd never spun before, let alone on a wheel like this.

"No. It's just pretty." She set the whorl back in the box alongside the flyer and the mother-of-all. Pretty, useful, practical—but ultimately, rejected by whoever had used it and didn't need it any longer.

Chapter Eight

Sunday morning, Brandon turned up on Charlie's porch wearing running gear. "I'm taking Pepper out to burn off energy."

Charlie looked unnerved, but Pepper jumped up behind her. "It's fine," he said. "That dog needs exercise, and I'm a runner. This is a natural pairing."

"I just feel...bad making you do this." Maybe she was unnerved because she was still wearing whatever she'd slept in. Granted, it was a T-shirt and yoga pants, but her sleepy look meant he'd better text before trying something like this again. Charlie reached for the leash behind the door, and Pepper went wild. "Are you sure?"

Brandon looked around. "I got up, put on running clothes, and drove over here to ring your doorbell. What about that seems unsure?" Brandon took the leash. "Come on, Pepper! Time to burn off some of that energy!"

Out on the porch, Pepper leaped around until he got her to sit, and then he clipped on her leash and removed her electric collar. "How far can a dog like you go? You're not wearing sneakers."

Pepper bounded along at what seemed like a slow pace for a dog. She ought to be chasing down sheep, but instead she contented herself with circling to the back of him to run on his left side and keep him out of traffic. Brandon disliked that: his own instinct said to keep the dog on the edge of the road, but there was no arguing with a border collie who'd found someone to herd. Brandon was, for now, her flock.

Sky Ridge Drive traced the coastline, and Brandon knew which houses his father took care of versus the ones that hired the rival landscapers. "Rival" being a relative term, of course. They all pitched in to help one another when times got tough. Last summer, when Johnson of Johnson's Landscaping had broken his leg mid-August, two of his clients hadn't even realized it wasn't Johnson mowing their lawn. Come wintertime, his father plowed these ridiculously long driveways for the houses set way back on their multi-acre properties. He'd raised two kids doing this, while his wife worked inside the houses doing the cleaning.

Brandon had been ten the first time his mother had brought him and Olivia to Eleanor's house for a piano lesson. He hadn't realized back then that his mother was trading services: one hour of housekeeping for one hour of piano. But then the next summer, he'd visited the house a lot more often. He and Anna would dig pits in the woods, covering them over with twigs as if they were deadfalls to trap bears. They'd play on the rocks, finding buckets of crabs and mussels that they sent back into the sea when the sun set.

In late June, Charlie would arrive, freckled and skinny, with mousy hair and a penchant for scraping her knees. Eleanor would produce a bicycle for her or rent a pony for the summer, and Brandon would ride over in his father's truck or pedal his bike over there. *Mrs. Boucher, are Anna and Charlie home?*

Eleanor was strict when teaching grammar school, but she didn't structure the girls' summertimes. Once Charlie started coming, there was no more summer camp for Anna. There were dance lessons for both girls, though, and horseback riding and day trips to destinations that filled Brandon with envy.

When Brandon was twelve, Mr. Boucher had joked, "Are you in love with these girls?" and Brandon had said, in earnest, "No, sir!"

He was in love, but with someone else.

Kelty Duncan came to the house with him on a regular basis. Anna knew her, of course. They were all in the same grammar school, and Kelty already shone as an athlete. An athlete? No, she'd been a goddess. Long-legged, happy, pretty, funny, quick-witted—what better could exist? Anna was fun to dig with in the woods, but Kelty was someone to admire and hope that someday she'd notice you.

Her coming to Anna's house had started precisely because she'd noticed Brandon. "Where are you going?" she'd asked one day, and he'd said, "Anna's house. Want to come?" Kelty had turned around on her bike and biked with him up Sky Ridge Drive. That happened on a regular basis, that they'd meet on the route and she'd join him biking up to the rich houses. The same road he was running now with the dog.

Pepper's sides heaved, and Brandon slowed for her. She panted, but her tail wagged. "You needed this run," Brandon assured her.

Sky Ridge Drive dipped and rose like a lazy roller coaster, beautiful but without traffic. You only came up here if you lived here or if you'd been hired by the folks who did. Or if you'd been invited by two girls and you were bringing a girl on whom you'd had a lifelong crush.

Kelty and he would ditch their bikes on the driveway and ring the doorbell. Miss Eleanor would give them lemonade and called down the girls. Kelty and Anna would talk like crazy, but Charlie always hung back, and Brandon would listen with her.

One day, Anna had said to Kelty, "Are you going to join track?"

Brandon would sooner have joined an underwater bowling league. He was clunky and slow, and whenever they made him run in gym, he came in at the back.

"Well, yeah!" Kelty had pushed Anna. "I'll totally leave you in the dust."

"As if." Anna turned to Brandon. "What about you?"

Kelty was doing track? "Sure!"

Kelty and Anna had taken off, their tan legs whirling as they careened down the hill in a race to the bottom that would just as likely end up in a tumble. Brandon took two running steps, then turned. Charlie was standing, hands around one another.

"Come on," he urged.

"I don't like to run." She looked nervous. "You go. I'll catch up."

"It's fine. I'll walk with you." He wondered how he was going to deal with a whole year of finishing last in track meets. Would the coach even let him stay? Did the girls do track at the same time as the guys?

If Kelty was running though, he'd make it work. He'd leave the bike at home and jog to Anna's house. In fact, for the rest of the summer, he did run most days with Anna and Kelty. Charlie never ran with them. "I don't like sports," was all she'd said. She'd said that to her aunt, to her uncle, to her cousin, to her friends. *I don't like sports.* It was only once she'd slipped and said, "My mother doesn't like sports."

Brandon didn't enjoy running until college, when he'd discovered distance running. Once it no longer mattered whether he could outrace a cheetah, he found joy in the rhythm and the endurance. He relished moving through places rather than circling a track. It had been he, Kelty, Julie, and Shelly who started the Brighthead Running Club, and he'd designed their web page and their logo, and then he'd regularly taken photos for their Facebook page.

At the top of the next hill, he stopped. You couldn't see the Boucher house from here, but it was a little over a mile. "Time to reverse course, Pepper."

The collie waved her tail, and he turned back. Kelty. He'd

run after her, but in too many ways, he'd never overtaken her.

When Brandon got close to Eleanor's house, Charlie stood from the wicker chair on the porch, dressed in shorts and a T-shirt. "Can you take me wherever you're running so I know where to take her tomorrow?"

Startled, Brandon revised his plan to quit for the day. "How far do you want to run?"

"How far did you take her already? I don't want you to drop dead of exhaustion." Charlie looked him up and down. "You don't look like you're about to die. It's just that it took me this long to get awake."

"We did a couple of miles, so you'll need to go easy on her." Pepper was panting but still bright-eyed and pleased. If she weren't leashed, she'd probably be flushing birds out of the bushes.

"I'll give her a drink from the garden hose." Charlie grinned. "You'll need to go easy on me anyhow."

They jogged along Sky Ridge Drive, the same direction he'd gone before. "I let her walk some of the uphills. Also, you're going to want to be careful about her feet and the pavement because once it's hotter she could get burned if she's not on grass."

Then he pointed out the neighbors, which houses had been sold, which ones were the same they'd known back then. As they jogged, he realized she looked different than she had even last Tuesday—not as pale, her head higher, her eyes brighter. Come to think of it, this used to happen every summer. She'd arrive skinny and wilted, and within days she'd be nutty and limber. Mainers had claims about the benefits of ocean air, as if it were an elixir to cure everything. Maybe it did.

But New England had so many of those claims. Hard work,

for example. Apple cider vinegar was another, for reasons Brandon could never explain. Head cold? Apple cider vinegar. Acid stomach? Drink apple cider vinegar and somehow the acid makes it less acid.

Maybe it was like goose grease over in England: you made remedies out of anything you had too much of. Were there any home remedies involving snow? Not that he could think of, although some remedies involved chopping wood.

"Did they show you how to use the fireplace?" Brandon asked.

Charlie laughed. She looked happier too, and the laugh didn't sound as forced. "Did we just go from scorching pavement to burning things to make it warmer?"

"Long train of thought. Some nights it does get chilly."

"I'm reluctant to set a fire in the living room."

"It's not a big deal. I can show you."

She wasn't a trained runner, but she had the body to become one. Long legs, good form, a sweet smile. Hunter was an idiot to have lost her, especially to have lost her the way he did. Why hadn't Hunter thought this woman was worth living up to his promises? Why hadn't Hunter valued Charlotte enough to put her first instead of breaking her generous and sincere heart?

Then Brandon caught himself in his own thoughts, and he dropped to a walk. At his side, so did Charlie. "Thanks," she breathed. "The hill was getting to me."

What was he thinking? She'd broken up with her fiancé a few weeks ago. But at least she hadn't been listening to Brandon's thoughts. She hadn't noticed his gaze lingering over her body.

At the highest point on Sky Ridge Drive, Charlie stopped to absorb the view. Pepper dropped to sitting, keeping her head eye and her eyes straight ahead.

"It's so pretty here," Charlie whispered. "There's so much of the world."

The wind picked up the edges of her hair, and she shielded her eyes from the sun as she watched the waves. Brandon was watching her. "Yeah," Brandon said in a low voice. "Beautiful."

Text:

Brandon, 7:50 p.m. "When should I come by tomorrow to give Pepper a run?"

Charlotte, 7:55 p.m. "You don't have to. I can take her."

Brandon, 7:56 p.m. "I know I don't have to. What time?"

Charlotte, 7:56 p.m. "You're pushy. How about eight? You said you work in the afternoon?"

Brandon, 7:56 p.m. "I'll see you at eight."

Brandon, 7:58 p.m. "Also, Tuesday night is the running club. You should come again, just to hang out."

Brandon, 7:58 p.m. "Shelly is usually there too."

Charlotte, 7:59 p.m. "I guess."

Brandon, 7:59 p.m. "Think about it. I'll see you tomorrow!"

Chapter Nine

Doreen met Charlotte at the door of Sparrows on Tuesday night. "Hey! How's your first week in Brighthead!"

As Doreen grabbed a menu and led her to the back, Charlotte said, "Kind of overwhelming? The dog herded three horses into my front yard, and that was a problem. We went antiquing, and I've started running. Oh, and I'm supposed to be writing a manuscript. I did serious damage at a yarn store, and..." She paused, wondering if that was far more information than Doreen needed, wanted, or ever intended to have. "I think that's enough for now."

"Sounds like a great start!" Not looking like a woman with information overload, Doreen gestured to the Sparrows function room. "Wherever you want, just sit. Have you ever had Moxie?"

Charlotte's eyes widened. "I remember Moxie!"

"It still exists. I'll bring you one?"

"Sure." It was more sugar than Charlotte required at this time of night. Or ever. She didn't have to keep to a schedule though, so if she stayed awake until three o'clock in the morning, it wasn't that big a deal.

She went to the corner table she'd been at last week. From the next table, a dark-haired, dark-eyed guy with a laptop studied her. "You're Eleanor's niece? Charlie?"

She nodded. She hadn't been *Charlie* since...wow, for years now. In high school her mother had overheard her friends calling her Charlie, and Mom had reacted as if Charlotte had gotten a tattoo on her forehead. In disgrace, Charlotte had notified everyone that she preferred not to use that nickname any longer. Hunter had called her Charlotte or "Shar." ("Char" looked like something left after a fire, which in some ways was how she felt in Hunter's aftermath.) Dad, who once upon a time had called her Charlie, had likewise changed his ways. "Charlie's" sudden resurrection at the hand of Brighthead was more than a little startling. Or rather, at the hand of Brandon.

The man turned back to his computer. "I'm Cashman." He had a smooth baritone. "No reason you'd remember me."

Feeling dismissed, Charlotte pulled out her crochet bag. Doreen returned with her soda, and Charlotte sipped.

Yes, this flavor! How could she have forgotten? Sweet soda with a bitter aftertaste, almost like cream soda but more astringent.

Abruptly she recalled tree-climbing and ocean breezes and a smell she couldn't name at all. Grass stains and loose earth. And right on the heels of those memories, an emotion without a name.

She relaxed into it. Whatever sensation that was, it was good. Something she hadn't felt in a decade, but something she hadn't realized she'd ever missed.

Cashman said, "I hope you're not disappointed. A lot of people complain Moxie's not as good now that they're using high-fructose corn syrup."

"It's fine." Charlotte half closed her eyes and let the last wisps of a nameless emotion fade through her spirit. "It's just like I remember."

With her crochet pattern on the table, Charlotte hooked while Cashman pecked away at his keyboard. French onion soup sounded fantastic right now, but before it arrived, Julie and Shelly entered with the first wave of runners. They disappeared into the ladies' room and returned in less-neon clothing.

Julie exclaimed, "Hey, look who's here!"

Shelly said, "It's a virus!"

Julie looked horrified, but Shelly took the seat next to Charlotte. "Let me see! Crochet patterns are insane. How do you read this?"

"Don't try to think your way through it." Charlotte spread out her project on the table. "Just follow the next instruction, and don't worry about the one after that."

Cashman chuckled. "Now that does sound like running."

Julie said, "Virus?"

Charlotte looked up. "She wasn't calling *me* a virus. The pattern name is Virus."

"Then no wonder you're not offended." Julie looked at the shawl-in-progress as if afraid to touch it. "That's wicked pretty."

"Could you read that?" Shelly said, pointing to the chart with its arcs and slashes.

"No, but I can't read a knitting chart either." Julie gave a hand-wave and sat diagonally from Cashman. "So does your presence here mean you've started to run?"

"It's the dog," Charlotte said. "She needs a workout every day."

Cashman looked up. "Greyhound?"

"Border collie."

He laughed. "Good luck with that. The dog's smarter than all four of us combined."

Julie side-eyed him. "At the very least smarter than you."

Cashman said, "Better looking, too," and Shelly nearly spit out her water.

By the time a dozen runners were hanging out, Charlotte's soup appeared, so she put away the shawl. Brandon arrived shortly after the soup, his hair dark and his eyes bright. "I'll be back in a minute." He took up his gym bag. "Save me a seat."

She reached across the table to set her phone in his spot.

Shelly said, "Not the project bag, I notice."

"I know which is more important." Charlotte looked up. "Oh, I had a question. If I'm running alone, how do I carry my ID?"

Shelly said, "Why?"

"You know, so they can identify my body if they have to."

It was a perfectly normal question. There was no reason for such an awkward silence to follow.

Julie said, "You're not in the city, you know. No one's going to murder you."

Charlotte said, "Cars don't ever hit people? People don't collapse on the side of the road with heart attacks?"

From his seat, Cashman rolled his eyes. "Sure, you've only been here two weeks, you might as well start mentioning that too."

Shelly waved him off. "It's never occurred to me that identifying my body was a felt need."

Well then. She'd have to trade on luck, wouldn't she?

Charlotte's phone vibrated. "Hey!" She showed the screen to Shelly. "Aunt Eleanor says Anna's in labor!"

Everyone responded with excitement, and when Brandon returned, he beamed. "Keep us posted!"

Cashman started a betting pool on when the baby would be born. "I'll pay the winner's tab next week. Unless it's Julie because she has terrible taste," which earned him mock derision, laughter, and a withering look from Julie herself.

Aileen, the librarian, joined them late, accompanied by a tall guy who grinned like a big kid and said, "Sorry we're late."

"Translation," Aileen said, sitting at a nearby table. "Trey's not sorry we're late. Trey's sorry that I'm irritated at being late." She asked Doreen for a lemon tea.

Brandon said, "Eleanor's grandbaby is on the way."

"Oh! Very exciting." Aileen turned to Charlotte. "I'm glad you're here tonight. Since you're around for the summer, is there any chance we could convince you to offer a presentation at the library? The director, Nicole Hartnel, said textile preservation is one of those niche areas that would be perfect for a lunchtime talk. You'd tell us what it entails, answer questions for a while, and then we pay you a speaking fee. Not a huge speaking fee," she amended. "But you do get paid."

Brandon said, "You can't pay what she's worth anyhow."

"Brandon," Aileen scolded, "they don't pay *me* what I'm worth."

He turned to Charlotte. "Even if it's a pittance, make them pay you. Don't work for exposure."

"Speaking of which," Julie said, "what's going on with the Lighthouse logo?"

Brandon shook his head. "They're being stubborn, and I'm being stubborn right back. If they want graphic design, they should pay for graphic design. They want a free design with payment in 'exposure' and the promise that eventually, sometime in the future, before the sun burns out, my business might possibly score them as a corporate account."

Cashman said, "Are you willing to lose your job? Because that benighted 'at-will state' designation could come into play."

Brandon sat back. "I'm hoping it won't get that far."

Cashman shook his head. "They're not going to let it *not* get that far. Think about it: it's not a question of *either* exposure *or* money. If they publicize their own logo, it gets exposed. You get exposure either way. They aren't doing something special by putting eyeballs on the work they commissioned for viewing by the public."

Brandon shrank. "When you put it that way..."

Trey said, "You did Kelty's logo for free."

Brandon said, "That's different."

Charlotte asked, "Kelty's logo?"

Aileen said, "The one I showed you, for the race."

Well, that cleared up everything.

Brandon said, "I'm a part of this group, and I'm loyal to it.

I'd design my father a logo for free if he ever wanted one. But the gym is a business, and there's no loyalty." He looked back at Cashman. "You just said they'd fire me if they can't take advantage of me. If that's going to happen, it might as well happen sooner rather than later."

Cashman's face hardened. "Then you need a contract. Hand the guy a document stating that you'll design his logo *for exposure* with the expectation of certain conditions. Say that you expect six referrals from their 'exposure' in the next six months, and if those clients fail to make it to your door, they'll pay five hundred dollars."

Brandon's eyes widened. "Are you kidding?"

"Not anywhere near as much as they're kidding about *exposing* you. You could also contract for the future design business they're promising, with a fifty percent down payment due on signing, with the Lighthouse Run logo bonused in as a freebie." Cashman tapped his temple. "Be smart about this. Since you don't object to getting fired, pretend corporate is not lying right to your face and present a contract taking them at their word." He grinned as he picked up his mug. "You'll learn in one hot minute just how honest they are."

Julie said, "You're brilliant and evil."

Cashman arched his eyebrows. "Don't I know it?"

Brandon waved his hand. "Wow, the night got smug all of a sudden," and Charlotte beamed.

It wasn't about the running, she realized as she picked up her shawl and hook. It was about the runners.

Text:

Eleanor, 1:21 a.m. "Charlotte, there are complications. I'll keep you posted."

Eleanor, 2:35 a.m. "They just took her for an emergency C-section because the baby's heartbeat kept dropping."

Charlotte, 2:51 a.m. "I just saw this now. What's going on? Is Anna okay?"

Eleanor, 2:51 a.m. "I don't know. We're not getting any information. I'll let you know as soon as I can."

Charlotte, 2:51 a.m. "Okay."

Eleanor, 2:52 a.m. "Don't wait up."

Charlotte, 2:52 a.m. "Just let me know."

Text:

Charlotte, 3:10 a.m. "I'm sorry to bother you now, but I can't sleep. If I text you, maybe I'll get it out of my head. Anna's baby had complications, and I don't know what's going on over there."

Brandon, 3:12 a.m. "Oh no. What happened?"

Charlotte, 3:12 a.m. "I'm so sorry. I didn't mean to wake you up."

Brandon, 3:12 a.m. "Not a big deal. What happened?"

Charlotte, 3:13 a.m. "I don't know. She had a C-section, and no one's telling Aunt Eleanor anything."

Charlotte, 3:14 a.m. "And now I can't sleep because I'm worried."

Charlotte, 3:14 a.m. "I can't even crochet because my hands are trembling. The hook won't go in the right places."

Brandon, 3:15 a.m. "I'm sorry."

Charlotte, 3:16 a.m. "Except now you're not going to get any sleep either."

Brandon, 3:16 a.m. "What can I do for you?"

Charlotte, 3:18 a.m. "I don't know."

Brandon, 3:18 a.m. "If you want to talk, call me."

Text:

Eleanor, 4:21 a.m. "They med-flighted the baby to Children's Hospital. Anna is still here. Eric and his parents went with the baby."

Eleanor, 4:22 a.m. "We're not sure what's wrong. The baby wouldn't breathe and there's something about her heart."

Eleanor, 4:22 a.m. "They named her Violet."

Charlotte, 4:22 a.m. "Oh my gosh, I'm so sorry."

Charlotte, 4:22 a.m. "Violet is a gorgeous name. I don't know what to say."

Eleanor, 4:23 a.m. "Get some sleep. There's nothing you can do from there."

Chapter Ten

Brandon drove to the Boucher house armed only with a box of donuts and a text message indicating Charlie was awake.

He met her on the porch. She flung her arms around him and crammed her face into his shoulder. "They're just donuts," he joked, but it was all wrong. She was upset and he was helpless, and Anna's baby could die. In the face of all that, the best he could do was stop at the donut shop.

"It's her heart." Charlie's fingers clenched into his shirt, tightening the fabric around his shoulders. "They're trying to get her stabilized, but she's going to need surgery. Only she's so little. She's six pounds. Human beings shouldn't be six pounds. How are they going to operate when she's only six pounds?"

Brandon squeezed her closer. "I don't know. They do it, though."

"Aunt Eleanor texted me a photo. Violet has all these tubes and a breathing mask, and she looked so banged up. I don't understand." Charlie looked up into his face. "How did this happen? Anna took such good care of herself!"

With no answers, Brandon said, "I'm sorry."

"Yeah, well—" Charlie wrapped her arms around her chest. "I did this, didn't I? I gave her that shawl. It's cursed. My engagement went down in flames, and now this. Anna must hate me. I don't understand."

She walked back inside, Pepper at her heels. Pepper looked just as worried as Brandon felt, her tail low and her head down.

Brandon set the donut box on the counter. "Tell me what you need me to do. If you want to fly out there, I'll get you to the airport in ninety minutes."

"What would I do out there? They've *got* people." Charlie flung herself into one of the kitchen chairs and rested her face in her hands. "Eric's whole family is out there. Anna's in the hospital so it's not like she needs someone to take care of her, and even if she did, both her parents are with her. Someone's got to be with the baby, but Eric's doing that. And I can't just leave Pepper alone."

"Pepper can stay with me. If you want to fly out there this morning, say the word." Brandon stood awkwardly in a huge kitchen that felt larger with every passing moment. "We'll make it happen. I could even stay here for a few days if you want someone in the house."

Charlie put her face in her hands.

"Can I at least make you coffee?"

She nodded.

The single-serve coffeemaker took a little figuring out, but Brandon extrapolated from a similar one at the gym. He found a mug and a plate in the cabinet, then got the half-and-half container out of the fridge. "I don't know what kind of donuts you like." He sounded tentative. "So I got an assortment."

She looked bloodshot and rumpled and just stared at the box without comprehension.

That look. He'd felt that same decision-paralysis after learning about Kelty's death.

It had been Julie who let him know. *Hey, you got a few minutes?*

The text had sounded innocuous, but for months after—well, still, it was *still* only months after—whenever someone opened a text convo with those words, Brandon went numb.

He'd replied to Julie, "Sure, what's up?" and fifteen seconds later his phone rang because she didn't want to text him the news.

He'd been at work. Michael had found him at the desk in a thousand-yard stare. After dragging the story out of him word by word, Michael sent him home. Five minutes later, Brandon had come to himself in his car, idling in the gym parking lot, unsure how he'd gotten there and incapable of remembering how to drive.

The inability to decide anything had been unexpected and unparalleled. Some people went into high alert after a crisis, thinking clearly and making life-saving judgment calls. And then there'd been him, unable to remember the half-mile route back to his house, and Charlie unable to remember what kind of donut she preferred.

Without pushing her to eat, he made a second cup of coffee for himself.

She checked her phone, but of course nothing else had come in.

"Her name is Violet." Charlie swallowed hard. "How do you name a baby who may die?"

"You give her the name you picked out." Brandon swallowed hard. Gosh, if Aria had died... No, he couldn't even imagine. "You give her everything you possibly can."

"Including a cursed blanket."

"It's not cursed." Brandon spun to face her. "You made it with love, and you gave it with love. With all that love, how could it be cursed?"

She pressed her fingers into her forehead and temples. "My love is a curse."

"It's not. I promise you."

"If Violet dies, maybe Anna will bury her in the blanket."

"Stop it." He rushed back to the table and crouched where she could see him. "You're trying to find a way this is your fault so you're in control of the situation, and that's not right. You already said this isn't Anna's fault, so you need to accept this isn't your fault either. Babies have surgery all the time. This is scary right now, but we don't know what's going on. They found the problem right away. They med-flighted her to a hospital where they specialize in this stuff."

Charlie couldn't reply. Behind him, the coffeemaker beeped.

Pepper broke the stalemate, pushing her nose between him and Charlie, her tail in a slow, concerned wave. Charlie wrapped her arms around Pepper's neck and put her face in the dog's fur. Displaced, Brandon got his coffee.

"Pepper stayed with me all night." Charlie gave a rueful smile. "She can't be on the bed, but the minute the first text came in, she got right into her guard pose at the doorway. I don't think she slept afterward."

"She knew you needed her." Brandon pointed to the donut box. "Eat something. It doesn't matter which one. Whatever happens next, you need fuel."

She stared dully at the box and finally grabbed a glazed donut. Brandon took a chocolate, amused that Charlie didn't just bite into hers. She broke it in pieces, then one at a time dunked the pieces. Back when they were kids, she'd done that too. With cookies. With grilled cheese and tomato soup. With chips and dip.

He caught himself before he raced too far down memory lane. "You'll want to stay where Eleanor can reach you, so I'll take Pepper for a run. Take the time and decide whether you want to fly out to Michigan."

Charlie braced herself. "I think I do."

He didn't want her to go. "Then tell me how I can make that happen."

"Thank you." Charlie looked up. "I'll run with you and Pepper. Just to get my head clear."

The day had dawned clear and hot, with temperatures

predicted into the nineties later. If Eleanor had air conditioning, they'd have to seal the house and get that started before much longer. He and Charlie started in a walk alongside Sky Ridge Drive, but Pepper kept tugging at the leash. Charlie shook her head. "Let's run, at least until I drop dead of exhaustion."

"Or a little before, maybe?" They jogged at an easy pace, and Pepper settled down. When they reached the path to the beach, however, Brandon suggested they descend to the rocks. Charlie didn't object.

Alongside the ocean, Brandon tossed a tennis ball to Pepper while Charlie climbed a boulder well above him. Pepper plunged into the water after the ball, came up with it in her mouth, then swam back. She'd scramble onto the rocks and shake, redistributing the ocean all along the shore, then cheerfully return the ball to Brandon. It was all so simple to Pepper: ball in the water, ball out of the water, water on Pepper, water off Pepper.

Ten minutes into this, Brandon noticed Charlie arguing into her phone, distressed.

No, please. No bad news. Nothing bad for Violet. Please.

Leaving Pepper to play in the waves, Brandon climbed back to Charlie. She wasn't in tears, so hopefully that was a good sign.

When he got close, Charlie mutely handed him the phone, shaking her head. Frowning, he took it. "Hello? Who am I talking to?"

"Brandon? This is Eleanor."

"How's Violet?"

"I'm not getting straight answers from anyone. Charlotte wants to fly out here. She can't come. Please, tell her not to come."

As if Brandon had anything approaching the right to tell Charlie what she was or was not allowed to do. "Why not?"

"Because her mother is a menace, that's why. If Charlotte

comes, her mother is going to demand to know why *she* wasn't notified immediately so she could sweep in and make this entire situation about herself. So far the only saving grace has been that everyone here is one hundred percent about Anna and Violet." Eleanor had never spoken so stridently. Never, not even once. Brandon had spilled grape juice on her cream-colored carpet, and he'd knocked a baseball through her picture window, and he'd left an open can of mandarin oranges in the living room where it attracted a black river of ants...and not once had she used this tone.

"We have plenty of people here, and there's nothing for anyone to do. Anna's doctor won't discharge her from the hospital, and Violet is in the children's hospital NICU. There is literally not one thing to do other than add more people to an already-confusing situation."

Charlie buried her face in her hands.

Brandon said, "Is this about...the shawl? I mean, the crocheted blanket?"

"What?" Eleanor's vocal double take was genuine enough that Brandon had no doubt, not even one, that no such thought had ever crossed her mind. "This is entirely about the overbearing Margaret Fletcher and the fact that it's a waste of Charlotte's energy to come here when there's nothing for her to do. When Anna's feeling up to it, I'll have her call so they can commiserate, but this is not the time."

Brandon said, "Because if it's a matter of the house-sitting, I'll manage things."

"I don't care about the house! I'd burn the house to the ground if it made Violet healthy." Eleanor's voice cracked. "There's nothing Charlotte can do here. Make sure she doesn't come. Put her back on the phone."

Brandon handed back the phone, and Charlie hit speaker. "I'm back."

"Charlotte, you're a love, but please stay where you are. I'll text you updates all the time, and I'll tell Anna you want to be here. If she needs you, we'll let you know and book a seat on the next flight out. That's a promise."

Charlie whispered, "Okay."

"I love you, sweetie. I'll talk to you later."

"Love you too." And she ended the call.

Chapter Eleven

Charlotte sat with her knees to her chest, phone warm in her hand, aware that it was already hot on the rocks but too stunned to move.

Brandon sat closer and put his arm over her shoulder. Pepper was trying to herd sea gulls (who, for the record, did not want to be herded).

She and Anna used to play on this beach. Down to the water's edge you go. Out on the rocks, wearing beach shoes to protect your feet and give you a grip on the slippery rocks. Waves in, waves out. This cove was protected by the curve of the land, so only the Sky Ridge Drive residents ever came down here. And their guests. Brandon and Kelty had ventured down here with them.

Brandon's arm felt strong around her shoulder, and she slackened into him. "This stinks."

He didn't respond. Of course it stank. Everything about this stank.

Charlotte added, "Did she rant about my mother?"

Brandon said, "What was that all about?"

"My mother takes over. She's used to running the show because she thinks about things a lot. I've never heard Aunt Eleanor go off about her like that. She's just upset. But she's right that if I go and my mother finds out, Mom's going to be upset that they didn't tell her right away about the baby."

Brandon sounded tentative. "You haven't told your mother?"

"I figured Aunt Eleanor would have messaged her, but that's why she called: to make sure I wouldn't. Then I asked about flying out, and she lost her mind."

Brandon said, "It's got to be stressful."

Maybe that was it. Maybe Charlotte didn't have to worry about some decades-long rift between her mother and her aunt.

Brandon added, "Anna's not angry at you, so that's a relief."

His shoulder was so comfortable. The waves, the warmth, the feel of a man's arm and chest. The last time she'd been with Hunter had been a lifetime ago, both of them working different shifts and him putting in so much time as a resident. She hadn't seen Hunter for three days before the phone call when she'd ended everything. He'd begged to see her again, and she'd agreed to hear his explanation over dinner. Instead she'd stood him up, blocked him on everything, and snuck around like a fugitive for the last weeks of her fellowship.

She'd had his schedule. Working sixty to eighty hours a week, he was easy to avoid. There'd been no last hug, no final kiss, no long cuddle on the couch that made the pain resolve into the closure of something worthwhile.

Most of all, no talking. If he talked to her, he'd loop her back in. He'd convince her the truth wasn't real. He'd persuade her (as he nearly had) that she owned half of his infidelity and if only she'd been better, smarter, more available, prettier, he'd have been able to stay faithful. His charming voice would have undone her, as it had in the past.

By contrast, Brandon remained silent. He spent no energy belittling her feelings, mocking Aunt Eleanor's reasoning, or planning ways around the decision. He didn't tell her to get on the plane anyway, nor did he tell her it was best to stay put.

His quiet left Charlotte lacking a rudder: head to his

shoulder, attention on the waves, and heart aching for her cousin.

By noon, they had a little more information about Violet, and they sat on the porch swing while Charlotte read everything she could Google up about the baby's condition.

Brandon had a sweating glass of ice water in his hand, and the ocean breeze picked up stray strands of his brown hair. "It doesn't sound good. Anna's got to be beside herself."

"I feel so bad for her." No matter how many times Charlotte said that, she couldn't make the words or the thought big enough. *I feel so bad for her.* What was the right word? Gutted? Eviscerated? Torched? If having a fiancé and then not having one was terrible, having a baby and then not having one had to be ten times more excruciating. A hundred.

Charlotte could blame Hunter. Violet had done nothing wrong. Violet was innocent. Anna was innocent.

Aunt Eleanor forwarded them pictures sent by Eric at the children's hospital. Even his brief explanations sounded like he was being drawn and quartered: his wife in one hospital, his baby at another. His sister had offered to stay at the NICU while Eric returned to Anna, so he'd taken a thousand photos for the baby. Nevertheless, Charlotte couldn't really see the baby, only the tubes and the medical tape.

"I'm sorry," Charlotte said.

Brandon said, "I'm sorry too."

"I mean, I'm sorry I dragged you into all this. There isn't anything we can do, but I woke you up, and then I gobbled up your whole morning." She checked the time. "You have to be at work soon. Right?"

"I can call off."

"I'll be all right." Charlotte mustered a smile. "Thank you."

Half an hour later, that bravery was gone, and Charlotte wandered from room to room to room with nothing to do, no aim except waiting for the next text.

Eventually she gave up and sent Pepper out into the yard (where Pepper immediately charged to the pond, scaring the geese with her huge splash). She got into the car.

The Audi's air conditioning blasted her as she pulled out of the garage. Where to? What to do?

First the grocery store, with its Antarctic blast the moment she stepped inside. There she picked up a six-pack of Moxie as well as a cartful of comfort food. That all went into the cooler in the trunk. From there she wasn't sure what to do, so she was about to head back home when she thought about the yarn store.

Yes, because on a thousand-degree day, that's just want you want: wool. Maybe that was why there were spaces right in front: because everyone else in Brighthead was sane. Charlotte went inside Bright Stitches to find only one lady at the table plus the store owner.

The owner grinned. "I knew you'd be back."

Charlotte looked at the yarn lining the walls, waiting for any of it to speak to her. The colors she normally favored didn't jump out at her. Instead everything felt like dread, like disillusionment. She shouldn't even be in here.

The owner let her wander, touching the skeins, comparing prices. This was an expensive habit, but fortunately (or unfortunately) Charlotte was on the slow side with her crocheting. During her fellowship, the only piece she'd completed had been that shawl.

Her hand landed on a skein of cotton-bamboo yarn, plump with softness, and she turned to the owner. "Do you have any pattern books for babies?" She paused. "I mean, about making things for babies."

"Yeah, I didn't think you wanted Baby's First Pattern Book." Chuckling, the owner ran a hand over the book shelf until she pulled out the right volume. "You're a crocheter, right? Most of these are for knitting."

This book showed a baby, old enough to sit on her own, clutching a crocheted stuffed animal, with a crocheted blanket draped over her lap. Charlotte paged through, her heart aching at all the chubby, happy babies with their bright eyes and early smiles. None were newborns with tubes and wires. None looked wrinkled and bruised, their skin vaguely blue and their eyes covered to protect them from the lights over the plastic bassinet.

Charlotte hadn't crocheted a single thing for Violet. She'd spent whole days on preserving antiques but never once made something for the new life being knitted in her cousin.

She found a pattern for a teddy bear. She checked the list of materials. "DK weight cotton."

"Follow me," said the owner.

At Charlotte's speed, a blanket would take months. A bear would take weeks. A duck-headed lovey wouldn't take form until well past the end of the summer. But as if from a distance, Charlotte watched herself lose her mind. Two skeins of yellow, another two skeins of blue. Five skeins of the purple-blue speckled bamboo-cotton that would become the blanket.

At the register, she showed the owner a photo of Violet.

"If you get home and you realize your stress bought all the yarn," the owner said, "just save your receipt. I'll let you return it if you bought enough for ten babies."

Charlotte choked on a laugh. "You think?"

It struck her that the owner hadn't said, "Just in case Violet dies."

The owner gestured to the entire shop. "How do you think I ended up starting a yarn store?"

As Charlotte handed over her credit card, she noticed a fiber braid on the wall. Several fiber braids, actually—unspun sheep fleece dyed and coiled, priced and awaiting a spinner to purchase them. Also on the wall were hand spindles.

The owner noticed her gaze. "If the crocheting doesn't help the grief, I'll teach you to hand-spin. It's hypnotic and soothing."

"I know how to hand-spin." She took back her card and hefted the bag of too much yarn and one pattern book. "I just never saw unspun wool braided that way."

In the car, she sat with the windows open and the air conditioner blasting hot air out of the car. But then she turned it off and dealt with the heat for three blocks before parking at the antique store.

Toward the back of the store, she again found the cardboard box full of the remnants of the Spinning Beauty. This time, Charlotte shifted all the other junk to create space on the floor, and one by one she removed pieces and laid them out in a rough approximation of how they'd all fit together.

She felt the proprietor come up behind her but didn't turn. Yes, this wheel was very well-used. The treadle had indentations from the previous owner's (owners'?) foot, and there was notable wear on the axle.

He said, "All the pieces are in there."

"Just making sure." She fit the bobbin onto the flyer, then fit the whorls onto the end of the bobbin. The bobbin rotated freely within the flyer, a little noisy but nothing that couldn't be adjusted. The flyer whorl sat snug against the bobbin whorl. "It's missing an orifice hook," she said. It looked like the tension system would work just fine.

This was what, upright Saxony style?

She inspected everything, noting the non-critical crack in the flyer arm and a notch on the wheel.

He said, "Do you think you can reassemble it?"

"I can restore it." She did have a degree in restoration, after all. Restoring wood was, obviously, different from restoring fabric. But she'd covered this in her coursework, and she'd listened to the other students and later to the experts at the museum. This wasn't in her (pardon the pun) wheelhouse, but it was immediately adjacent.

There, on the floor, lay the entire skeleton of the Spinning Beauty. Definitely a Saxony. There were faint markings on the bottom of the table that would once have indicated who'd made it and when.

This was wild. She'd never encountered a mystery piece before. Always it was this thing in a museum or produced by a collector, the item's history known ahead of time. Then her only challenge was identifying the problem and figuring out the solution.

"Well, then." The proprietor huffed. "I guess you know what you're doing." He left her alone.

Maine was so weird. In Philadelphia, the guy would have been breathing down her neck, swearing that someone had just put a hold on the thing and would be buying it as soon as he returned from the ATM—unless she sniped it first.

Charlotte picked up the pieces one at a time and made sure they'd all fit one another. "This is going to need some work," she called to the owner.

The owner replied from behind his newspaper, "You do know where you are, right?"

She stood. "Three hundred for that is a rip-off."

He looked over the top of the paper. "But I'll let you rip me off."

She laughed. "Really? You're that generous?"

"More than generous. Next week there's an antique crawl, and I'm raising the price to four-fifty." He returned to his paper.

Restless, she replaced the pieces in the box one at a time, noting every single one of the wheel's flaws, every slight crack in the wood, every unevenness in the finish, every worn-out part that needed rejuvenating.

She didn't need a spinning wheel. She certainly didn't need a spinning wheel requiring repair when she'd never spun with a wheel before, plus had no fleece, plus had already bought far too many balls of yarn. She didn't need weeks of working with antique wood, and then afterward, she didn't need to figure out how to ship it home.

She didn't need to plan on where she'd be putting it, when she wasn't even sure where she'd be living at the end of the summer. A one-bedroom apartment wasn't the best place to keep a Saxony wheel.

Three minutes later, the whole thing was back in the box, and Charlotte stood. Goodbye, Spinning Beauty. May it find a lovely, rich, vacationing owner next weekend during the antique crawl.

As Charlotte turned to step out the door, the proprietor said, "Two twenty-five?"

He helped her load it into the car.

Chapter Twelve

Brandon stopped at his apartment before heading to the gym. As early and as quickly as he'd left to get Charlie some donuts, he hadn't taken everything he'd need. It was a shame he'd been away, actually. The apartment had natural air conditioning in the form of being underground. As long as he kept the windows curtained and shut, it stayed cool all the time.

He'd lived here three years, unconcerned with whether this setup were exactly legal. He'd needed an apartment, and his sister's family needed rent. He wasn't exactly a tenant, and they weren't exactly his landlord. But it was exactly what all three of them needed. Four, if you counted Aria.

Brandon started the coffee, a four-cup Mr. Coffee rather than a super-specialized single-cup rapid-brew contraption that frothed your milk and launched the space shuttle. While it hissed and dripped, he packed his backpack, threw in some snacks, and tucked in a change of clothes. Five minutes later, he was out the door.

It was ninety-two degrees, but the gym would be air conditioned. It was only half a mile's walk. This far from the coast, you didn't get an ocean breeze. Well, that's the difference between a half-million-dollar home and what you could afford when your husband owned a moving company and you worked part-time for a flower shop.

Inside the gym, Brandon worked out for an hour. Lunges, squats, leg extensions, deadlifts, the works. His gym membership came as a job perk, so that was nice.

He glanced at himself in the mirror. He could lift weights all day every day and still not be built like his brother-in-law. That man looked like he could toss a couch over one shoulder and a refrigerator over the other. Then he'd ask if there was anything else you wanted brought downstairs, since he was going that way anyhow.

Brandon showered, toweled off, and changed into fresh clothes. At the front he clocked in.

Leaning against the desk was Corporate Alex.

"Oh, great," Brandon lied with enthusiasm. "I was hoping I'd see you today!"

Alex fake-smiled as though he'd expected a fight. "Good to hear it. You've thought about the logo?"

"Absolutely!" Brandon opened his computer sleeve and pulled out the papers he'd printed off last night. "Here's a contract outlining everything we talked about."

Alex gaped, not taking the papers. "What?"

"Last week, when we talked about the logo?" Brandon kept his voice smooth. "You said Lighthouse Athletics would hire me as a freelancer if I did the Lighthouse Run logo, so I drew up a contract based on your terms. I inserted my rates and a timetable. You should have your lawyer look it over, and then we can discuss changes."

Leaning against the wall, Michael watched with folded arms.

Alex tried to blow it off. "We don't need a contract."

Brandon tried to sound sincere. "I don't fly without a contract. It's better for both of us if we outline our expectations about what we want and when to expect everything to happen."

To his credit, Alex skimmed the contract.

Four years ago, Brandon had bartered for his boilerplate

with an attorney who wanted an updated website. But Brandon had also done as Cashman instructed: he specified the exact terms of exposure. He'd come up with an estimate on his first sixty billable hours, then thrown in five free hours to design the Lighthouse Run logo and two rounds of changes; he'd come up with a deposit, then deducted a certain percentage from the balance for each referral received.

It sounded very legal. There was no way the club would sign such a document.

The key now was to keep silent. Alex's response, pure and unfiltered, would tell Brandon everything about the corporate office's intentions. Unfortunately the phone rang, and Brandon answered. Yes, they had a spin class. Yes, it was included in your membership, but you needed to arrive early so all the spin bikes weren't taken. No, they didn't have a reservation system for spin bikes. Yes, he was sorry for the inconvenience.

Another member came over as Brandon hung up. She said, "I don't think you're turning the air conditioning high enough. It's wicked hot in the cardio room."

He stood. "Let's go check it out."

So much for getting a clean-catch sample of Alex's response. By the time Michael was done with Alex, and by the time Brandon was done with every gym member who needed something, Alex would have diluted his initial response into bureaucratic pablum that meant nothing.

Half an hour later, as Brandon replaced a stack of towels in the weight room, he finally had Alex in front of him again. "I'll give this to the owner, and we'll talk early next week."

Brandon gave him a thumbs-up. "No hurry. And you got the logo I already designed, right? Those are the full-size files, so you can run with them and then not worry about signing anything."

Of course there was a hurry. The club had six weeks until the race, so if they wanted their logo on the signup site, they needed that thing in the can. But that was another reason to give the gym a contract: with any luck, a lawyer would take long enough that they'd run out of time and use the mockup. Or just call whatever designers they normally paid.

You know, paid with money rather than promises and starshine.

When Michael met Brandon again at the front desk, he was frowning. "I'm not going to fire you. I'll make them do it themselves."

Brandon said, "Much appreciated."

"That wasn't your best move."

Brandon opened his hands. "You were the one who told me to stand my ground."

Michael shrugged. "A contract makes it seem adversarial."

As if it wasn't adversarial already.

Michael was shaking his head. "I happen to like working with you, and I don't want to train your replacement. If you could manage this without losing your job, I'd appreciate it."

"My bank account would appreciate it too. Look," Brandon added, "they want a logo without paying someone to do it. If they fire me, they still don't have a logo. But if they force me to do it on the clock, when I'm being paid to fold towels and mop floors, then they're just going to tell me to do it again. And again." He opened his hands. "This looks like a little thing, but it's actually huge."

The fall after they'd joined track together was when Brandon first realized how bad Kelty had it at home.

He knew Mr. Duncan had bugged out, something Kelty never made a big deal of. Whenever she mentioned the man, it was always more like, "as if I care," but she didn't even mention him much. But that year was the first time he realized her family had no money.

Brandon's family shopped the secondhand stores and Walmart, so he knew how it went. You want that new trendy thing? Tough.

He didn't have a game system, and while they did have a computer, it wasn't new. His parents both worked a lot of hours, and once his sister was old enough, she found part-time work as well. But his family did have clothes, food, and a working car for the family as well as a working truck for his dad's business. During snow storms, Brandon got awakened in the middle of the night to ride in the cab of Dad's truck and shovel out people's walkways while his father plowed their driveways. Half the time Brandon got a tip, and he'd leave all that money in a heap for his mother to count in the morning. They did okay.

Kelty's family didn't. Her clothes were notably shabbier. She didn't go on the class field trips. She brought a lunch every day, but it was usually a jelly sandwich and an apple, plus a plastic bottle of water. The track coach told Kelty over and over that she needed better sneakers, but Kelty never got them.

One day after practice, Brandon asked why she didn't just get the sneakers. "I bet you'd run a lot faster."

Kelty said, "I can't ask my mom for that. We need to eat."

Instead Brandon told his mother, who said, "I'll see what I can do."

The next week, Kelty had new sneakers. Apparently the school had an award for an up-and-coming young runner, and she'd gotten it this year. "But you can't tell anyone," Kelty said, stuffing the award certificate back into her bag. "I'm not allowed to find out who got it last year. I shouldn't even be telling you."

Brandon said, "But that's good!"

Kelty nodded. "I know, right? Now I don't need to ask Mom."

Brandon's mother started packing him larger lunches. "I

can't eat all that," he protested, and she'd said, "See if anyone else wants some." He offered extras to their whole friend group, and Kelty usually took them.

Mrs. Boucher (nowadays, Eleanor) knew Kelty, and she knew Brandon's parents. In later years, looking back, it became obvious that his parents had brought Kelty to the attention of the school administration. Teachers would find spare somethings-or-other, and they'd end up with Kelty. Class trips would be paid for; a track jacket arrived with her name due to a clerical error. Brandon only met Kelty's mom from time to time, but his own mother "found" a number of Olivia's outgrown clothes in the attic and sent them over to her instead of bringing them to the consignment shop, in case Mrs. Duncan could use them for her girls. "They're only going to rot if I keep them," Mrs. Pelletier assured Mrs. Duncan.

Years later, the same small town machinery swung into motion when Olivia got pregnant with Aria. Olivia would come home to find a bag of secondhand (or thirdhand) newborn clothing on the porch with a note attached. "Thought you could use this." Aria's crib was on its fifth occupant, her high chair on its third.

Only as time went on did Brandon begin learning the subtle art of helping someone without being detected, as well as the fine art of accepting a helping hand when you needed it.

Dad asked Mrs. Duncan if Kelty would come on their midnight shoveling ventures. "We could do driveways faster if I had more help. Brandon can't shovel forty feet of walkway as quickly as I can plow a hundred feet of driveway." Kelty had crammed into the front of the truck with them on those midnight plowing runs, and they'd drunk thermoses of hot chocolate while driving from one property to the next. The next morning, Brandon's mother would split the tips and bring them over to Mrs. Duncan.

Was she splitting it fifty-fifty?

"You've got to understand something," his father said one

night after they'd dropped Kelty back at her house. "This is Maine, and it's not a land that loves us being here. The snow and the ocean would swallow us up if we didn't fight hard. We're all in it together."

Kelty had a huge rivalry going with her kid sister. They never interacted at school, so Brandon never saw her. But he did look out for Kelty. Within the friend group, she and Anna both thought of him as a big brother.

Before he got up the nerve to ask her out, Kelty found a boyfriend. Brandon backed off and waited.

Chapter Thirteen

Charlotte had Pepper leashed and ready to go as Brandon's car rolled into the driveway. Before he was even out of the car, she was alongside his open window. "How far today?"

He looked her up and down, startled. "Well, then. Two miles sounds good?"

"Two miles sounds great." She bounced on her toes. "Let's do this."

Charlotte didn't want to unleash the dog even though no one would drive through here. Pepper tended to run right at any cars that came into the Boucher driveway, but she also veered off at the last second—about two seconds after Charlotte had a heart attack. She'd averted that this morning with the pre-leashing.

As they ran, Brandon said, "Any word about Violet?"

"Doctors are being 'conservative,' whatever that means. They want her to get bigger before they open her up, but surgery's inevitable."

Brandon said, "That rots. Poor kid."

"I know. Where's the post office?"

"Downtown," Brandon said, as though "downtown" meant something in a town of five thousand people. "If you remember the town green and where the school is, it's nearby. Also the library."

She'd just have to GPS it. A post office should have a flagpole, at least. Should make it easier to spot.

Her side started burning. Baby Violet. So sweet, so small. And Charlotte, trapped here.

"Did you talk to Anna?" Brandon said.

"For about five minutes." It was harder to speak this morning, probably because she was tired. Charlotte sifted in her mind for what was important. "She sounds exhausted. The doctor doesn't want Anna to leave. Because she had surgery. She's going to force him."

Brandon said, "If you leave without the doctor signing off, don't they not pay?"

"Not true." She was having much more trouble speaking, actually. "They'll pay. It doesn't matter."

"I'd always heard you couldn't do that. I think they call it AMA?"

"Yeah." Charlotte gulped down air. "Not true."

Her legs felt leaden, but she kept pushing. Anna was pushing. Anna had gotten a checklist of everything that needed to happen before she could get discharged, and she'd vowed to work through the whole gamut today so she could get over to Violet's side.

Anna had cried on the phone. Her cousin, so strong and happy and with her whole perfect life before her, had cried on the phone.

Weeks ago, Charlotte had sobbed about Hunter. It wasn't the same. It wasn't anything like the same. Anna's sobs had come from way down within her, helpless and furious and driven. But goal-oriented. Hold the baby; nurse the baby; talk to the baby; touch the baby; be with the baby. With every part of her oriented toward that, Anna was tackling each obstacle one at a time, and she'd hurdle over them all like a long-legged runner at the track and field championships. First, get out of the hospital. Second, get to the new hospital. Third, help Violet stay calm so she could grow. Fourth, feed Violet so she could be well enough for surgery.

How long would it take? Days, months? Meanwhile, what could Charlotte do? She could go running with the dog.

Charlotte missed a step and stumbled, but didn't go down. Brandon put a hand on her arm. "You okay?"

"Fine." So hard to talk. So hard to keep going.

She was halfway up that huge hill. Her head swam, and she stumbled again. This time she stopped.

"Keep walking." Brandon's voice was low. "Don't stop right away or you'll get dizzy. You're really pushing the speed."

She yielded to Pepper's tug on the leash.

"You need a pacer," he said with a cajoling tone.

"Which is?"

"A pace group is set up to keep you from outrunning yourself. You figure out how fast you want to finish a race and then stick with that group. If you get ahead of them, you know you're messing up."

Her legs felt heavy.

"Don't drive yourself into the ground." Brandon wasn't touching her, but he was very close. She kept staring at the pavement ahead of her, head bowed. "You can't make things right for Violet."

"I have to. Do something." Charlotte felt disconnected from the ground, on her own space-time continuum. "I feel so useless."

Brandon said, "Are you running for her?"

"What?" Charlotte focused on the hill, on her feet. "Raising money?"

"Well, yeah, people do that. They run for a cause, sometimes to raise money or raise awareness, but I mean just as a motive. Aileen joined the running club to run the 5K race for her sister. I think you make it a goal to run a race, and you do it for them." His voice was forming something like a trail guide for Charlotte to follow in her brain and take her mind off her body.

"The Lighthouse Run?"

Brandon said, "That race is a thorn in my side, but sure. I'll run it with you if it helps."

"It's two and a half miles...?" Over rocks, with waves all around you. You couldn't run in a huge crowd. Actually, the last runners would be sharing the causeway with the fastest runners en route home. That might put you in the ocean if you got jostled. But it seemed nice. There would be wind, so maybe you'd get blown faster in one direction. Maybe you could put up a sail and just fly home.

Maybe she really had pushed too hard and her brain wasn't functional.

At the top of the hill, Charlotte said, "I should keep running, if I'm doing it for Violet."

"Well, if you're doing it for Violet, let's make sure you don't injure yourself." Brandon took Pepper's leash. "Let's turn back. It's hot, and you're really flushed."

She hadn't brought a water bottle. Why would she? She was walking the dog. She turned around and they jogged down the hill at a slower pace than she'd tried going up it. In the house, she sat at the table while Brandon made the fridge door produce ice and cold water, and she gulped it down. He also gave her apple juice. "Get some sugar in you."

"It's lame if less than a mile did that to me." She resting her head on her steepled fingers, but then she popped up again. "Oh! I wanted to show you!"

She struggled with the gate across the parlor entrance to retrieve her project. She was loopy, so loopy, but she'd had no one to show last night when she'd stayed awake, bleary-eyed with the pattern book on her bed, a ball of yarn in her lap, and a yellow bunny lovey growing in her hands. She'd made something, and now she needed to share.

Brandon exclaimed over it, and she let him admire the floppy ears and the little bow tie around its neck before it morphed into the ripples of a blanket-like body.

"You did this last night?" Brandon said. "How fast do you work?"

"I was up until three o'clock," she admitted.

"Maybe that's why you feel lousy this morning...?" Brandon's voice had a teasing tone. "Not that I'm your dad, but some people run better if they're awake."

"I bought a book. I'm going to make Violet every single thing I can and stitch her right into wellness." Charlotte flushed. "Also, I lost my mind yesterday. Want to see?"

She flipped on the overhead lights in the garage. Uncle Gregory's Audi inhabited Aunt Eleanor's spot, and in the spot where Uncle Gregory's car should have parked was the reassembled Saxony wheel.

"You got it!" Brandon rushed forward. "Amazing!"

"It needs some love." Charlotte swallowed hard. "I'll need to sand it down, oil it, refinish some parts, repair it, replace the drive band—but it looks like it should work without me having an emotional breakdown."

Brandon looked afraid to touch it. "You can give it a whirl," Charlotte said. "It's seventy years old. I'm sure it's gotten beaten up plenty."

He pushed on the wheel so it rotated. The footman raised the treadle in a slow motion while the bobbin turned inside the flyer. "Is this part of your fabric restoration training?"

"I learned about restoring wood products, and I know how wheels ought to work. In theory." She pulled over a stool and sat alongside the wheel the way she'd seen in videos, then pumped the treadle. The wheel turned, and the bobbin rotated. It was stiff. "There are also videos all over YouTube, so I was watching them last night while I finished off the bunny. I was out here early looking through Uncle Gregory's tools. I need a few things, but I should be able to get started."

Brandon shook his head. "That's...phenomenal." He waited a beat. Then, "I thought you said you don't spin...?"

"I don't. I also said I lost my mind. I nearly walked out of the store without it."

"But he cut you a deal?" Brandon offered. "Man, he's savage at reading a customer. I wish I were half that good."

She smiled. "Everyone would have a website?"

"A website *and* a logo! I'd be your next-door neighbor up on Sky Ridge." He touched the wheel again and listened to the creaky sound of wood on wood. "Instead I'm probably going to lose my job because I can't close the deal." He shrugged. "Well, if I get fired, you can have me come out here and sand this thing down for you."

She shook her head.

"No, I get it, I get it." He followed her back into the kitchen. "It takes a specialized touch and a licensed conservator."

"More like I'd rather ruin it myself." She sat at the table. "Can they really fire you for not doing something you weren't hired to do?"

"Maine is an at-will state. They can fire me *for* doing something they hired me to do. But I'm not going to make it easy."

She logged him into her laptop, and he opened up the Lighthouse Run website, still featuring last year's information. The photographs and the write-up made it sound like a lot of fun: a hundred people running the causeway, entry fee to benefit the historical society, T-shirts for all finishers. Afterward they had a party on the beach, and the lighthouse operators gave a presentation on its history. Maybe they'd even talk about Myth Brightman.

"I couldn't raise money for Violet this way." Charlotte paused. "If the gym took over the race, does that mean the historical society doesn't get the money either?"

"I'm sure the historical society gets something. The corporate overlords will find a nice way to spin it because they need good PR."

"Sure would be terrible PR if anyone found out they weren't paying their graphic designer..." Charlotte murmured, and Brandon laughed. "They think they can wheedle it out of you because you did the 5K logo for free. No good deed goes unpunished."

"Yeah, well, but you get it. You wouldn't charge your cousin for the bunny, right?" Brandon stood to go. "Speaking of which, do you want me to take it to the post office?"

"I'll head downtown with it later. I haven't written a note yet."

After Brandon left, Charlotte took the pieces of her next crochet project out to the porch where she could work in the morning light. Crocheting for Violet or running for Violet both would have no effect on health, but it was kind of esoteric to run for someone. If you crochet "for" someone, you made the thing for them. But running "for" someone didn't mean you were running "for" them the same way, not like "washing the dishes for them" would be.

He said Aileen had run for her sister. Maybe Charlotte should ask Aileen how that worked, whether you were supposed to think about the person the whole time you ran.

And then, although it was warm, goosebumps covered Charlotte from head to toe.

Aileen's sister.

Kelty's race.

No. *No.* That couldn't be.

It could be. It was.

Charlotte was an idiot, an idiot, an idiot. She should have put it together the moment they said it, but all the pieces were lying around like a spinning wheel disassembled in a box. She should have realized from the strewn-around sentences the same way she'd recognized the connections between a flyer and a bobbin and a mother-of-all.

Google turned it up in a heartbeat. The Brighthead Running Club's first annual Kelty Duncan Memorial 5K.

The Kelty Duncan Memorial 5K website led her to a chain of newspaper articles. A head-on collision last January with a distracted driver. An arraignment, a "no contest" plea. An obituary.

One sister: Aileen.

Back to the race website Charlotte went, and there were Kelty's photos. These were so much more emotional than the newspapers', but maybe the emotion came from the viewer. Sitting on the porch, Charlotte struggled to remember Kelty from those Brighthead summers, if there were any hint of Kelty's destiny to die tragically, but no, there was just a girl alive, a girl climbing trees, a girl finding turtles and chasing Anna around with a turtle extended in her hands.

Brandon had been in awe of her. That much Charlotte remembered. He'd been nice to Charlotte and Anna, of course. He had to be, since his parents worked for the Bouchers. But he'd carried a torch for Kelty that was visible from space. When Kelty was there, he'd moon over her. Any joke she'd said was the funniest joke ever said, and Kelty's thoughtful comments were the most thoughtful and perceptive observations anyone had ever made. Kelty's suggestions were commandments, and wherever she'd led, he'd followed.

Had his infatuation lessened over time? Or had her death killed part of Brandon too? Had he ever had a chance with her? Had she ever fallen in love with him?

Tucked up on the wooden steps, Charlotte went through the whole memorial site, all of it stamped at the bottom, "Designed by PacerStudios." Brandon had created all this for Kelty, not just the logo (which was, for the record, a gorgeous logo). Aileen treasured that logo. She'd kept it on her phone, minus the lettering.

All the pieces, lying around. Charlotte just hadn't known to reassemble them.

It wasn't only Aileen who had run for Kelty. Brandon ran for Kelty too: Charlotte had been there the day Kelty had sold him on the track team. It hadn't been a hard sell. Kelty could have made him join the cheerleading squad if she'd tried.

Anna had laughed that no, it wasn't like that, that Brandon wasn't in love with Kelty. She'd said they'd just always been friends. But to Anna, Brandon was just the gardener's son who got the occasional piano lesson as gesture of noblesse oblige. Charlotte observed people all the time. She'd realized Brandon thought of her and Anna as "just one of the guys." She'd also noticed that with Kelty, he hadn't.

Brandon had been so supportive of Charlotte about Hunter, steady and strong and thoughtful. He'd been there when she'd struggled not to cry about Violet, and at Charlotte's most fragile moments, he hadn't said a thing that might push her right over the edge. But who'd been there for him? Or was he being so strong for Charlotte because he knew how much it hurt to grieve alone?

On the runner's club website was a memorial page for Kelty, only a couple of sentences but a dozen photos. Photos taken with care, cropped, adjusted, filtered, laid over one another in a collage that showed a woman alive and brilliant and loved.

If Brandon had assembled this, then he'd loved her right to the end. If they hadn't been dating, then he'd been waiting for her.

Among the solo photos were pictures of Kelty with Julie and Shelly, Kelty with Aileen, Kelty with the whole club. No photos with Brandon.

Maybe he didn't have any. Maybe Brandon was always the one taking the pictures, not the one with his picture taken.

Or maybe those photos were too special. Maybe some things you didn't put out in public for just anyone else to remember.

Chapter Fourteen

Saturday evening, Brandon returned with Aria from the park. She lay across his shoulder as he carried her up the porch steps, and he contorted to get the door unlocked without waking her. The door popped open before he could get it all the way, and Olivia let him inside. "Oh, no. You wore her out."

"It's a delicate balance, getting her tired without conking her out." Brandon carried Aria to the bedroom. "I failed."

"I'll have you sit up with her tonight," Olivia whispered. She dropped the side of the crib so he could lower her down without breaking his back. Aria tensed, then returned to sleep. They snuck out of the room like thieves.

In the hallway, Brandon said, "I'm not working tonight, so if you need me to stand vigil for you, that's fine."

"We'll see. I'm making spaghetti for dinner if you want to stay."

"Thanks." Brandon hesitated. "Actually, I need to talk to you and Dale."

"Uh-oh." She turned. "Don't quit the babysitting."

"Never," he promised. "I'll drive her to prom and embarrass her in front of her date."

"Good. That's why you get paid the big bucks."

He got paid zero bucks for childcare, big or small, but they'd negotiated that while figuring out a fair price for the rental.

Before dinner, he went downstairs. Corporate Alex hadn't replied yet to Brandon's generous contractual offer. Lately Brandon had tensed every time he checked his email, awaiting the moment he didn't want. The longer it went, the less he knew what to expect. An immediate response would have been, "Are you kidding us?" but this delay and delay and delay (well, four days of delay) felt interminably long. Was it possible they actually meant to pay him?

That was weird. Given what he knew of corporate, that would be very weird.

His business address did have a few other inquiries, which he answered with additional questions as well as his rates. One of his clients requested a very small change to their ad (they were apologetic, but hey, they were paying for it), and another client had dumped their quarterly assignment into his inbox. He'd start that tonight. If Aria's nap kept her awake later, then maybe he'd finish it tonight too. Might as well impress the client with his turnaround time.

An hour later, Olivia texted that dinner was ready, and he went upstairs. Dale was already at the table. Spaghetti, garlic bread, cheese, green beans. Dale drank a cola, but Brandon preferred the tap water.

After they were eating, Olivia said, "What did you want to talk about?"

"I'm about to get myself fired from the gym." Brandon sighed. "Whatever happens next is either going to be really good or really bad, but I'm planning for the bad."

Dale swallowed. "That's the better way to budget, but why are you getting yourself fired?"

As Brandon explained about the logo, Dale reached for another chunk of garlic bread. "I get that all that time." Dale sounded annoyed. "Yeah, I got a truck, and I own a moving company. That doesn't mean I want to spend my Saturday hauling your grandfather's best friend's piano out to his lake house."

Olivia shook her head. "They can't fire you for that, can they?"

Dale said, "Hon, they can fire him for anything they want."

Brandon said, "They'll say I'm being insubordinate. I looked into filing for unemployment, and it's not going to work. You know they'll contest it, and anything my business earns is going to come straight off the top of any payment the state would give me."

Olivia said, "Yeah, I get that. But you'd find another job. It's summertime. Every single tourist trap needs people."

Dale said, "Heck, you're strong. In a pinch, I'd hire you if you don't mind lifting furniture."

Working out wasn't the same as the actual daily grind that Dale's men went through. Those guys understood at a glance things Brandon wouldn't be able to master for months. Things like what went first into the truck so an entire household could fit, or how to get an armoire down a stairway with a ninety-degree bend. "I'm thinking maybe what I need to do is work harder on launching my own business."

Olivia nodded. "To be honest, I'm not sure why you aren't doing that already."

Brandon stared into his spaghetti bowl. "It's not easy to get clients."

Dale said, "You know about advertising."

Brandon laughed. "It's different."

"It's not different."

Olivia swiped around the inside of her bowl with the bread. "The gym is holding you back. That's forty hours a week you could spend hustling on your own work. You make these savage designs."

Brandon turned aside. "Yeah, but I'm not clearing enough with just my business to do everything. The rent, car insurance, food, and all the things you spend money on. Like if I blow the transmission or need a new computer."

Olivia glanced at Dale. Brandon reassured, "I'm going to

prioritize the rent."

"Look, you don't even know yet if you're getting canned." Olivia tried to relax. "I guess if you don't have that job, you could take over all Aria's daycare, and that would save us a bunch of money."

That wouldn't make up the rent. Not by a long shot.

Dale said, "Watching the kid is time you're not getting clients."

Brandon rubbed the bridge of his nose. This whole thing felt overwhelming. "It's not steady income. Money comes in sporadically. It's all at once, or it's nothing for weeks."

Dale said, "The gym hasn't even fired you yet. They may come back with another offer and you can keep the job."

"They're taking advantage of you," Olivia said. "Any other company would have you managing a location, not mopping the floors. Some of these things they have you doing, they weren't part of the job when you started. It was answering phones and refilling the soap dispensers." She leaned forward. "But once they saw how good you are, they loaded you up with other things to do and tossed you an extra fifty cents an hour when they felt like it. You're worth more."

Brandon clenched his hands. "If I had more clients, I'd feel better about this."

Olivia said, "And because you have this job sucking away your time, you don't have more clients."

"I have money in the bank to cover next month's rent. After that, it starts getting tight."

Olivia said, "Give yourself one month to figure it out before you find another job."

Dale took more garlic bread. "Sounds like a plan. You do what you have to. We're not going to evict you."

Brandon raised his glass. "You couldn't rent out that apartment if you did."

Olivia said, "I'm sure we'd find some college student who didn't mind living like a rat," and Brandon choked on his water. "We'll figure it out. You're not in it alone."

Chapter Fifteen

Through the whole weekend, Charlotte couldn't stop thinking about Brandon. About Brandon and Kelty. The grief thrummed in her throat, behind her eyes, over her heart. She focused on his heartbreak while throwing Frisbees for Pepper or crocheting for Violet or refurbishing her sweet Saxony wheel.

Every single thing Charlotte had ever heard about stress told her she wasn't actually fixated on Brandon's pain as much as distracting herself from her cousin's pain and her own feelings of betrayal. She couldn't bear to Google stories about babies getting cardiac surgery, so instead she Googled every single thing she could about the Brighthead Running Club, about Kelty, about the memorial 5K. She even searched the driver who'd plowed into Kelty.

On Sunday, she worked on her wheel with Murphy's Oil Soap and a soft toothbrush, scrubbing the grime from the grooves and wishing she could scour the grit from her heart. Scrub hard enough and maybe she could brush Hunter into oblivion. Maybe she could clean Violet into health.

Kelty, though. Kelty had been one of the founders of the running club, along with Julie and Shelly. The Facebook page hadn't updated with weekly meeting photos for two weeks after Kelty died. When it resumed, the voice was different and all the photos were tagged.

Had Brandon been the one to suggest the 5K? Or was a memorial race just something runners did when they lost a friend?

Paraffin wax was the best lubricant for wood of this age. Charlotte would need to replace the leather flyer bearings as well, but those could wait. Maybe Farnsworth could sell her bits of leather.

Maybe she could ask at the running club. Maybe they'd disclose the rest of the story between Kelty and Brandon. *Hey, Doreen, I was wondering if I could get a Moxie, and also I want all the dirt on Brandon's heartbreak.*

Dirt. She went back to work on the wheel.

One of the websites on refurbishing a wheel said each wheel needed a name, but the dirt and wear marks on this wheel meant it already had a name. What the name was, Charlotte would never discover. How do you make something talk? You can't just Google search its obituary and find the name of its mother and sister, but no names of boyfriends or fiancés.

If Hunter had died, whose name would have been on the obit? *Hunter leaves behind his parents, three sisters, his fiancée Charlotte, and his side dish Vanessa.*

Vanessa was the main course now, and her promotion had created a job opening.

Charlotte's phone beeped, and she found a message from Aileen. "Have you thought about presenting at the library?"

She dried her hands and dictated a text back. "It might be fun. What should I talk about?"

Aileen replied, "What are you working on right now?"

Charlotte sent a photo of the floor of the garage. "I'm restoring a spinning wheel."

"That sounds so cool!" Aileen's replies came stacked right on top of one another. "Is it Eleanor's? Can you spin?" And then, "I would love a spinning wheel demonstration."

Charlotte's phone rang while she was composing a text

reply. Aileen said, "I figured I should just call rather than blowing up your phone. A spinning presentation would be really amazing for everyone if you did a Wednesday lunchtime feature."

Charlotte stretched where she sat on the cool concrete of the garage floor. "I don't even know if I'll be able to get the wheel working."

"That might be a problem. What else are you working on?"

"I'm writing a book-length publication about preservation of antique furniture coverings."

"That might work too," Aileen said. "We have a few people who come no matter what we present, of course, but I really think the antique spinning wheel would be much more of a draw."

"Pun intended?" said Charlotte.

Dead silence.

"I guess not," Charlotte said. *Drawing* was when the spinning wheel was pulling in the spun fleece. "How much lead time do you need on the subject?"

"A couple of weeks."

Charlotte rubbed her hands on her jeans. "You know what people do seem to be interested in? Restoring antique quilts."

"Oh! Goodness, yes. Except you'll have twenty people bringing in paper bags stuffed with quilts and asking if you can just patch this little bit here..."

"Someone already tried that in the yarn store."

Aileen laughed. "If you want to talk about quilts, I'll set you up with a time slot. We usually start at noon on Wednesday, and I'll block off the next thirty-six hours."

Charlotte exclaimed, "I hope not!"

The day Aileen suggested was three days before the Fletcher/Mattingly wedding would have taken place. It was better that way. Charlotte could spend the weekend before it planning the talk to give herself something else to think about, and the weekend after it cringing at every verbal gaffe she'd made.

"We aren't much of an antique town, but we're definitely cheap. If we can glorify cheap by saying something's an antique, more the better." Aileen paused. "Okay, so I need to inform you that there's an honorarium because you're a professional, but it's not exactly a professional pay grade if you get my meaning."

"Meaning gotten. I won't call my tax attorney to ask her advice."

"Yeah, save the call for the police when they arrest you for jaywalking because you ran across the street to escape fifty library patrons with old quilts." Aileen giggled. "You know where the library is, right? Stop by next week to get a look at the community room. If you have a good time, you could maybe do it again after you get the spinning wheel working. So, any questions?"

Charlotte said, "An apology, actually. I didn't make the connection that Kelty was your sister."

Aileen sounded subdued. "Oh, I didn't figure you should have. But thank you."

"Brandon said you were running for Kelty, and it was only then that I put it together. I'm sorry for your loss." Charlotte touched the box containing the spinning wheel's uprights and the table. "My niece, Eleanor's granddaughter, she's having a lot of problems right now, and Brandon said I could run for her."

"Yeah, Brandon told Julie, and she posted to the rest of the group. It sounds awful."

Charlotte said, "How do you *run for* someone?"

There was a long pause. "I don't know how to explain it, but it made me feel closer to her. Kelty was a good runner, but I never ran with her because I just...didn't."

Charlotte said, "How do I run for Violet, then? She's never been a runner."

"I don't think there's one way to do it, is the thing. Maybe it's just that when you do it, you think about her? Not that what you're doing is useful to her, because it's not. But thinking about her gives you a reason to keep moving." Aileen was talking slowly, as though grappling with her thoughts. "When you don't want to do it anymore because it's too hard, you think about the person you're doing it for, and you find motivation. Does that make sense?"

"I think so." Charlotte tucked up her knees. Okay, into the breach here. "I think Brandon started running because of Kelty, back when she decided to join track."

Aileen said, "Yeah, but that's a different kind of running for someone."

"Were they dating?" Charlotte asked.

"I don't think so. But I didn't really...we weren't close when I was growing up. I didn't pay attention to her friends. I mean, apparently you knew her back then, but I never met you."

"Yeah, that makes sense." Brandon had just orbited Kelty, never coming in close. "So when I run, I should use that time to think about Violet and the way she's struggling?"

Aileen said, "If that helps, sure. When you talk to Eleanor, tell her everyone's pulling for her."

"Will do."

Aileen said she'd run her topic by the library director, and then Charlotte found herself face-to-face again with a disassembled antique wheel.

Chapter Sixteen

When Kelty was seventeen, Brandon finally asked her out.

It was September of senior year, and she'd broken up with her boyfriend during the summer. Brandon had slid right into place and made sure he had her attention, and when the time was right, he asked. She accepted.

After five years, he'd asked and she'd accepted. It was amazing.

They went out a few times, and it was fun. He could be with her without the fear of revealing too much and without the concern that he'd scare her off. They watched the high school soccer teams, hung out at the library, and of course ran track together. It was perfect.

Until the day it wasn't. Mid-October, Kelty came to school distracted. At lunch she hadn't wanted to look him in the eyes. After school when they sat in the bleachers before the JV basketball game, she finally said, "Am I your project?"

Brandon squinted at her. "What?"

With her hands clasped between her knees, she stared at the bench below them. The guest team was warming up while the Brighthead High School coach was giving his guys a pep talk.

"Last night, my mom told me to be careful. She's worried that I think I owe you something, so I kept asking questions." Kelty bit her lip. "She told me that your family was like our charity sponsor all these years, that they were arranging stuff because we couldn't afford anything after my dad abandoned us."

Brandon wanted to say, "Yeah, you needed help." The wispiness in her voice left him cold, though, the thready uncertainty. She knew they'd needed help. That is to say, she knew it now. But not back then. Back then, everyone had worked so hard to keep from her where the help was coming from. His mother and her mother had made it seem like a series of coincidences or awards or just things that happened. Oh, we need another person to shovel driveways. Oh, my sister gave me this bag of clothes. Oh, there's no cost for this field trip because she's on the track team.

"Always protect people's dignity," his father had said. "Not their fault they can't make it on their own."

The help dried up when they didn't need it any longer. Last year, Mrs. Duncan had finished her nursing certification and gotten a job at a skilled-care facility. But that's what help was supposed to do: set the family to get back on their feet. Give a single mother enough clothes and she could pay for education instead. Talk to your friend's brother who sold used cars and she'd have a reliable vehicle to get to those classes. Then someday, when another family needed help, these folks would step up to help them.

We're all in it together in this part of the world. The weather and the ocean don't want us here, so all we have is each other. How many times had Dad said this?

Kelty wrung her hands. "Mom was worried. She didn't think you were using me or anything, but she didn't want me to feel like I owed you my life."

Brandon said, "We didn't do that much."

"You were the ringleaders though. Your mother organized an army. She circled the wagons. I'm not ungrateful," she added quickly. "But now I'm wondering about everything, all the little things that happened that made stuff turn out right, if those things were just orchestrated or if I actually earned them."

Brandon turned away. The referees were coming onto the floor.

Kelty tensed even more. "I always felt like I lived a charmed life, like that was how the universe was making up for giving me such a crappy father. I felt like I mattered."

"Of course you mattered!"

"Not like that. I mean, like the world around me—I'm not making sense." She blinked hard. "But that's beside the point. My mother was afraid I would stay with you out of obligation. Like I'd sacrifice myself to you as payment of a debt for saving my sister and my mother."

"No." Brandon reached for her hands, but he would have had to pry her apart like a twisted bit of metal. Instead he rested his fingers overtop hers. "Nothing like that. I love you, Kelty."

He'd never said it before. He hadn't planned to say it now.

"I love you," he repeated. "You were in trouble, and my mother said she'd see what she could do. She talked to the people she worked for. None of that was me. If you ever felt any obligation, I'd...I'd want you to go. Because that's not right."

Kelty was blinking hard. "But you see, now that I know what you were doing—"

"You weren't supposed to know. That was the point." Brandon squeezed her hand. "No one did it to be thanked. My parents weren't planning your betrothal, like some kind of volcano god demanding the village throw in a young girl."

Kelty laughed in surprise. He put his arm around her. "See? It's just what people do."

The ref blew the whistle to start the game, and they watched in silence. There weren't many people watching from the bleachers, and Brandon didn't have it in him to cheer or comment or really even to watch the game.

During a break, Kelty said, "You didn't answer. Am I your project?"

"Never." He squeezed her. "You're a lot of things to me. You were never my project."

"I feel like your project. Like something you did in Boy Scouts to earn a badge."

The Boy Scout troop had sponsored the Duncan family for Christmas one year. Brandon kept his mouth shut.

He could read her mind. He'd known her for a decade and a half. He'd been infatuated with her for five years. They'd worked together, played together, run together. She'd sat with him waiting for his mother after he'd fallen out of a tree, bleeding like crazy, talking to keep him from freaking out. He'd listened to her heartbreak over her deadbeat father. He could read her mind.

He didn't want it to happen, the thing that would happen next.

The game went on. Kelty was gripping his hand hard. Brandon wanted to leave the game and take her somewhere else so he could maybe explain, but there wasn't anything to explain. She hated that she'd been the charity case. She hated that she wasn't who she thought she was, the universe's golden child, and she hated that all along, she'd had a benefactor. It didn't matter that she was getting thirdhand Walmart clothes instead of secondhand name brands—a patron was a patron. And she was proud. It was one of the things he loved about her, along with everything else.

At halftime, he almost asked if she wanted him to get her something from the concessions. Almost. Even at seventeen, he wasn't quite that stupid.

She withdrew her hand as she turned to him. "If we keep dating, if we got married, I'd never know if I could make it on my own."

There it was.

Brandon said, "None of us can make it on our own."

She shook her head. "I'd feel forever like everything I'd done, I'd only done it because of you. I would be charmed, but like those princesses in stories where they're guarded by someone and then claimed by them, and then it's happily ever after. It would never have been me doing these things. It would have been me going through the motions because you made it happen."

She'd set this up so the worst possible outcome was that their romance went the distance.

Brandon said, "You're selling yourself short. No one ever ran for you. No one studied for you. No one made your sense of humor for you. The only thing we did was get the obstacles out of the way so you could do those things for yourself."

"That's not how it feels." She doubled forward. "I'm the punchline of the biggest joke, and everyone in Brighthead was in on it but me."

You're not supposed to break up with someone because it works too well. You're not supposed to break up with someone because you love them or because they've been too good to you. But you also aren't supposed to scream at someone that their gut-level revulsion is wrong.

"We're all in this together" had never prepared Brandon for the moment when the recipient of that togetherness uncovered how deep it had gone.

"My mom relied on my dad." Kelty looked like she was fighting nausea. "When he left, she had nothing. Literally nothing. I'm not going to let that happen."

"You're going to college," Brandon said. "Five years from now, you're going to have a degree and a career. No one will ever abandon you the way your father left your mother."

"I'm going to make sure of that." Her gaze hardened. "But that means I can't just hang onto you, hoping if I hitch my chariot to your star that you'll keep everything safe forever."

"I agree. Because even when the guy isn't a total jackwagon, he might die. He might get injured and not be able to work." Because Brandon could read her mind, he knew this was the only argument that might give him a chance, the slightest sliver of a chance with her. "It only makes sense to protect yourself. I would never tell you not to get a degree or five degrees or not to get a job. If you were going to marry someone who thought that, I'd tell you not to."

She offered a smile. "Do you see what I'm getting at?"

"I don't think you're making the right conclusion. I want you to do all the things you want to do."

Kelty tightened her fists. "I need to do them alone."

Brandon shook his head. "We're all in this together."

"Not me. You've all been in it for me for far too long." She swallowed hard. "I need to get my own feet under me."

She broke up with him then, but Brandon put conditions on it. He laid it out for her, nice and logical the way she liked.

WHEN she got her degree...

WHEN she had an established career...

WHEN she had her own house...

THEN he would come back to her. She would be successful on her own, and then she would date him again.

"That's at least six years," he told her. "But you're the one who brought up marriage and going the distance. A lifetime together would be a lot more than six years."

Kelty thought about that, and finally she agreed.

She finished college. She got her first job. She got a better job at the law firm. She bought a townhome.

And then she died.

Chapter Seventeen

Monday morning, Charlotte was up early with her newest project, a purple-blue baby blanket with a pink border. She'd finished the purple-blue part (a very large patterned square) and had awakened at sunrise to start affixing the pink. Hello, 5:45 a.m. If she finished the border by three, she could express this to Anna as well.

Charlotte and the pattern book, the yarn, the project, and her hook all moved downstairs into the coffee-maker's domain. She let Pepper out, then let her back in five minutes later. It was raining, and she made Pepper shake it off on the porch.

With the dog cared for, Charlotte propped the pattern book and began hooking. Her first attempt ended in an uneven number of stitches, so she ripped back the entire border and started again. Midway through the second attempt, the coffee finally kicked in, and Charlotte had gotten more into the pattern's rhythm. She'd also begun to wonder if she should go back and buy more of the pink yarn. (Hah, what kind of question was that? Even asking such a question was akin to walking in Bright Stitches' front door with her credit card in her fingers.)

Her phone rang, and she froze at the Caller ID.

She answered, "Hi, Mom...?"

"It's terrible!" her mother exclaimed into the phone. "It is absolutely terrible! Do you know what I found out this morning?"

Charlotte set down her project and trudged to the coffeemaker. "Tell me."

There was no way she could possibly know what her mother had learned, except that obviously it could be exactly one thing.

"Anna had her baby!"

Exactly. There wasn't enough coffee in the universe for this.

"But the baby's terribly sick," Mom went on. "Eleanor didn't want to tell me because she knew I'd be upset. But I called this morning to ask if she'd had the baby yet, and Eleanor had to tell me then."

Charlotte glanced at the clock. 7:15. "You called her this morning?"

"Well, I just had to know!"

The coffeemaker was already spitting new coffee. Even so, not fast enough.

Mom's version of the story was oh-so-much-more dire than Charlotte's version, but she'd learned to reduce Mom's tales by a factor of three. It wasn't just that Violet had stayed blue after birth, but that she'd coded right there in the room. They'd done an emergency C-section because her heart must have stopped. While Charlotte added sugar and cream to her coffee, she endured a discussion of what Anna could expect if Violet had brain damage from oxygen deprivation and how awful it would be for Anna.

Charlotte debated starting the coffeemaker on its third cup while she drank the second. Instead she returned to the table, mm-hmming at appropriate intervals. Finally, when Mom wound down, Charlotte asked, "Did Aunt Eleanor say the baby had brain damage?"

"No, but how could she? To label her own granddaughter that way? This is because of Eric. His family is all sickly."

About to pick up her crochet hook again, Charlotte leaned back in the chair and rubbed her temples. Really?

Yes, really. Mom went on and on, and Charlotte very nearly put the phone on speaker just so Pepper would hear the hyperbole too.

After fifteen minutes, Charlotte had gotten onto the second border row when Mom said, "I'm flying out there."

"Oh, you can't!" Charlotte exclaimed. Her hook clanged to the tile floor. "It must be chaos!"

"I need to help," Mom said. "Anna is my niece!"

"But from what you're saying, you can't just bring chocolates and sit on the couch making small talk." Charlotte's pulse picked up as she retrieved the hook. "If the baby's in the hospital, there's literally nothing to do."

Mom said, "Then I'll go to the hospital."

Aunt Eleanor would call security and have Mom escorted right out of the hospital. In fact, she probably already had them on alert. "NICU doesn't work that way. Hunter told me about that," Charlotte said, making up her story as she barreled through it. "NICU doesn't have visiting hours. Only the parents get inside, and only for a few minutes."

She'd seen something like that on the news once.

"Think how awful it would be for you," Charlotte added, "if you flew all the way out there and couldn't even get in to see the baby."

Mom sighed. "But I should at least try."

"You could call the hospital and ask what their policy is about letting great-aunts visit patients in the NICU."

Mom huffed. "I don't see what the big deal is. I want to hold her. If the worst happens, at least I'll have held little Violet."

Charlotte blinked several times. "You just told me what the big deal is. Weren't you just saying brain damage and hemorrhages and the baby's heart stopping?" None of which had happened, but Mom had in fact said all those things. "That sounds like a big deal to me."

Mom said, "Then I should go."

Charlotte wanted to throw her phone at the wall, but instead she paced. "They need you back home pulling for them, not there getting in the way." No, that wasn't the right way to handle Mom. "Actually, maybe Aunt Eleanor didn't tell you right away because she didn't have the time to do it. I mean, she loves you and wouldn't intentionally snub you. Maybe you can take the weight off her by calling everyone else in the family and telling them her news about the baby."

Since the cat was out of the bag already, Mom might stay home if she thought of herself as an information spigot. She could deliver the same rant to all her cousins and extended relations. She could do it a dozen times a day and then start on Dad's relatives.

Charlotte forged ahead. "If you're the point person, Aunt Eleanor could text you every day with an update, and you could pass it along to everyone else."

Mom sounded awed. "Oh, that might be a good way to do it."

Yes, put Mom right in the center spotlight, but a center spotlight in Philly, not in Michigan. Aunt Eleanor could visit her later...assuming Aunt Eleanor didn't have to spend the next twenty years cleaning up misinformation about Violet.

"That would keep you out of the hospital too," Charlotte added. "Those places are full of germs, and I'd hate for you to get sick."

May fifty kinds of antibiotic-resistant germs inhabit Hunter's body any day now.

Mom said, "You're so sweet to think of me. I'd risk everything for the baby."

"I know," Charlotte soothed. "You're so generous to her, and I'm sure Anna will always think of you that way. But right now, the help they'd most appreciate would be to step up as Aunt Eleanor's phone tree."

Mom got off the phone fully empowered to shoulder her new role. Ten minutes later, Charlotte received a text from Aunt Eleanor: "THANK YOU SO MUCH."

She laughed, then looked outside at the rain.

She wouldn't go running today, not in this.

It was a shame. She wanted to see Brandon.

At eight o'clock, she did see Brandon.

The bell rang, and Pepper leaped in place at the door. Charlotte undid the security system and let him in, but he was (so help her) in running gear. "I'll just take Pepper. You shouldn't have deal with the rain."

"Neither should you! Get inside."

"I've run in the rain before," Brandon pointed out, but she tugged him into the living room. "I'm kind of drippy."

Pepper was dashing back and forth, tail going a mile a minute. Brandon dropped to his knees and roughed her up while she whined. "See? She wants to go."

"Until the minute she gets wet," Charlotte protested. "Then she'll want to shake water all over me."

"I won't shake water all over you." Brandon made a serious face. "I give you my solemn promise."

Charlotte laughed.

"Besides, running in the rain is good for you. It's got all sorts of health-promoting properties."

"It totally does not," Charlotte called as she raced up the steps. "Like, not even a little."

"It cools you off...?" Brandon called after her.

She shouted down at him, "I'm getting into running gear. I can use a few health-promoting properties."

It took a couple of minutes to get into everything, making sure to wear her darkest T-shirt after she realized anything light would become see-through in five minutes. Brandon shook his head anyhow. "No good. You need a gear upgrade. Do you have a waterproof jacket?"

Even at home she might not even have a waterproof jacket. "I could wear a sweatshirt. And you don't have a jacket."

"I don't own a running jacket. I figured you might." He shrugged. "Well, let's go get drenched."

"Healthy," she prompted as she clipped the leash to Pepper. "You said health-promoting properties."

"I was entirely making that up." Brandon broke into a jog. "Rain is wet, and it's going to be miserable."

"Wow, talk about bait-and-switch." She grinned as she kept pace with him. "Really, you just wanted to visit the dog?"

"I've been up-front the whole time that I'm running with the dog." He met her eyes, and Charlotte's body went warm. "At some point, *you* decided to keep the dog company too."

"She's my aunt's property. She'd be mad if someone broke the dog."

"So you're dog-sitter-sitting the dog-sitter?" He opened his hands. "Who's dog-sitter-sitter-sitting the dog-sitter-sitter?"

"I could tell you, but I'd have to kill you."

"Bummer." He looked amused. "I'm fantastically curious."

The rain was, in fact, miserable, and Charlotte mentally voted to turn around at around the top of the hill. If Pepper needed to run more than a mile and a half, Pepper could go out onto the property later and do it by her own darn self. Maybe chase those nasty geese who didn't seem to worry about the weather but also didn't relish the presence of a dog.

"Why are we doing this again?" she asked as water dripped into her eyes.

Brandon sounded resigned. "In case it rains the day of the Lighthouse Run. Also because running in the rain elevates you to a whole new level of awesome runner."

"I wasn't planning to run today at all," she retorted, "so I'm trading on your awesomeness."

Although she never broke stride, Charlotte's heart went off-balance. She wasn't just bantering with him. Suddenly she was flirting.

Flirting. *Quit that,* she scolded herself. *You have a broken heart, and he has a broken heart. There's a baby in an incubator a thousand miles from here, and you're both worked up with endorphins. This is not a recipe for a good time.*

But it was a good time. Brandon sounded stunned. "I wasn't aware I had any surplus awesomeness, but if it tops off your tank, go for it."

She decided not to quit at the top of the hill. "How can you be unaware of your awesomeness reserves?"

"It's not like I have a dipstick for it, and surely if I'd had a surplus of 'awesome,' someone else would have realized by now." His eyes met hers as they crested the hill. "You're really only detecting your own awesomeness."

"Then that's a problem because I'm not awash in it either."

"We're both awash in rain," Brandon admitted.

After the run, they stood dripping on the porch, and Pepper gave them a horizontal shower by shaking off a mini-pond of rainwater. "Thanks," Charlotte muttered, then dashed inside to grab a bunch of towels. She tossed one to Brandon, but instead of drying himself, he threw the towel over Pepper's back and then rubbed down her head and neck.

"I meant it for you," Charlotte said.

Brandon huffed. "I'm not going to shake violently and spray water on your aunt's cream-colored carpet."

Charlotte walked up behind him and draped a towel over his back, then rubbed around his neck and shoulders. "So, about your technique. Do it like this?"

He tensed under her touch. "Yeah, just like this."

She crouched behind him. "What next?"

Pepper walked away from Brandon, still wearing her towel, then shuddered it off. Brandon didn't move out from under Charlotte's hands, so she rubbed his hair, then his neck and shoulders. Her own arms were covered in goosebumps, partly from the cold and partly from what she was doing. She'd launched right past flirting and into "coming onto him" territory.

He pivoted toward her, and she kept the towel between them, pinning it over his chest with one hand. Her brain raced with some rejoinder about towel methodology, but he looked so startled, so...delighted...that all her words vanished. He guided her onto his lap, and then he kissed her.

She released the towel and let him pull her tight and close. The rain poured onto the porch roof, and she didn't care. No one was here; no one would see; no one mattered except her and Brandon. He kissed her again, then a third time, and she closed her eyes and let it happen.

It felt right. It felt wrong. It felt like everything every time he guided her lips to his. His hands in her wet hair, her doused skin against his.

Then he released her and let her lean against him, her sitting half on his lap and him leaning back against the porch post. Rain strafed them every time the wind shifted direction, but she relaxed against his chest. He'd been waiting for her to do that. He'd been waiting.

He'd waited for Kelty. He'd waited for her.

Kelty.

Violet.

Hunter.

Eyes screwed shut, Charlotte sobbed with new rain: salt water. It felt wrong. It felt right.

Chapter Eighteen

Brandon had no idea what to do.

Charlie had just jumped him with the most incredible turn-on he'd ever experienced in his life. Stunned, excited, reeling about what to do next, Brandon had given her the lead while he struggled to figure out how far she intended to take this...and then she'd started to cry.

With no idea how to proceed, he tried to be a comfort. But inside his brain, everything whirled like a protein shake in a blender. Was she crying because of him? Because of Violet? Was she remembering how Hunter betrayed her and wondering if it was too soon? They'd been teasing each other on the run, but now this. And to make matters worse, the clock was ticking. He had to get home to Aria.

Awkward. No matter how you sliced it, awkward.

"I'm sorry," Charlie whispered.

"Don't be sorry." He cuddled her closer, then tugged the towel over her shoulders so she would stop shivering. "I need to get you inside. You're freezing."

She didn't move, but she was too cold. He started sitting up, and she hugged him instead. No, inside. Get her in away from the rain. They dripped on the carpet on the way into the kitchen. Pepper stayed out.

"Does this thing make hot chocolate?" Brandon asked, opening the cabinet. It did, so he set it up for her. Then he pulled a chair near her at the kitchen table. She was still crying. He touched her cheek. "This isn't because of me, is it?"

She shook her head.

"Okay." He was shivering too, but he'd deal with that later. "I wanted to be sure."

He slid closer, and she hugged him again. Wow, it felt good. He hadn't even dreamed she'd ever look at him that way. Her doing this—being here—holding him—

Was it even real? Was she crying because she'd kissed him when she'd never meant to? No, don't let her have torpedoed any chance at friendship just because she was lonely and then felt ashamed. It would feel like Kelty all over again: someone crying, and it wasn't his fault.

He glanced at the clock. He had twenty minutes to get home. It was a ten-minute drive.

"Talk to me," he murmured.

She fit so perfectly against his chest. Her head nestled right into his shoulder. She still smelled like rainwater, and he tucked the towel over her shoulder.

Charlie whispered, "It's too much."

"I'm sorry."

Behind him, the hot chocolate finished dripping into the cup.

She jerked with a sob, then settled down again. "It's not your fault. I'm just overwhelmed. I just— Violet, and everything else, and you."

"It's okay." Nine minutes. He'd need to text Olivia that he'd be late but would definitely be there. "You're dealing with a lot."

Yeah, like a guy who'd broken her heart in the most humiliating way possible. Like every plan for the rest of her life upended in a matter of weeks.

She'd fallen fast for Brandon. He liked it, but he was stunned. He fingered her hair as she snuggled against him, and he brushed his lips over her forehead.

On the other hand... "Is this too fast for you?"

"Maybe?"

Well, that beat a yes.

He said, "We can take things slow."

"Yeah." She sat away from him. "You're drenched. I can look upstairs to see if Uncle Gregory has clothes you can borrow."

"Actually, I need to get home. I'm watching Aria." In seventeen minutes. He brought over Charlie's hot chocolate, then sat across the table because it would be tougher to pull her into his arms again with a table between them. He didn't trust himself.

"I have to be at Bright Stitches at ten." She looked into her mug. "Someone's bringing me her quilt. But..."

Her cheeks were bright red, not with the wet and the chill.

Brandon proffered, "You didn't mean to do that, did you?"

She shook her head.

He squeezed her hand. "But...are you sorry you did?"

Her answer took so long that Brandon was sure she'd say yes, she regretted it with every jot of her soul, only there wasn't a way to unkiss someone, to unhold them. She'd been hardcore flirting with him on the run, and no one could unflirt after something like that.

But instead of yes, she said, "I don't want to rush things. There's too many emotions."

His emotions shot straight through the roof. She didn't regret it? She *didn't*?

Charlie traced a finger over the table's woodgrain. "It's all so uncertain."

"Not everything." Brandon squeezed her hand. She didn't regret it. My goodness. She wasn't backtracking. "But we won't rush things. You're dealing with Violet. You've got so many situations up in the air. I get that."

Her eyes were red as she met his, her hair wet and wispy, her cheeks flushed, and she was the most beautiful creature he'd ever seen. All there, genuine and open and brilliant.

He could take it slow. He knew how to wait for something wonderful.

Charlie glanced at the clock. "I'm sorry. You need to go get Aria."

"I'm sorry. The timing stinks." He met her eyes across the table. "But I'll see you tomorrow. I promise. We can talk more then."

"We can talk more then" didn't account for the way Brandon had to spend the next four hours stopping himself from texting Charlie, calling Charlie, or thinking nonstop about Charlie.

He got home to an annoyed Olivia at the door, watching the clock. "I said I'd be here," Brandon protested as he swept in through the front door, still soaked from running in the rain, still in high gear from Charlie's kisses. Olivia thrust Aria into his arms and left.

Four hours later, after thinking of nothing but Charlie's kiss, Charlie's touch, Charlie's tears...Brandon handed Aria off to his mother so he could get to his own job. Not looking forward to a second soaking, he took his car.

Early afternoons were dead hours at the gym, the times he spent listening for the phone but instead checking up on accounts, making sure the place was clean, and refilling orders on everything that needed refilling. Also, thinking about kissing Charlie.

Olivia had a point about his ever-expanding duties. Only a few months after he'd been hired, he'd suggested someone update the website with their current classes rather than the classes from eight months ago. Michael had shrugged, so Brandon did it himself. Within six months, corporate was emailing him schedules for all the locations. He'd never thought of refusing because updating the calendar was more interesting than re-mopping the floor.

Not as interesting as kissing Charlie. He had to stop thinking about that or he'd start forgetting duties at work.

Anyway, now they had him managing inventory on the protein drinks, handling the linen deliveries, and sometimes calling folks who'd let their memberships lapse. None of that was in his job description. Brandon had counted it as filling his time at the desk. Now it seemed nefarious.

When you worked in reception, the company paid for your availability rather than your activities. If no one called and you didn't answer the phone calls that didn't come, you weren't doing something wrong. But you needed to be available in case someone did call. Yet some of these extra tasks actually took him away from the phones. (Thinking about kissing Charlie did not take him away from the phones.)

At the same time, it was fun. Brandon knew all the regulars and had conversation topics at the ready for each. He could work out any day he wanted, and he could grab a towel fresh from the dryer before doing so. He knew which were the good machines. On this salary he'd never own a yacht, but he probably wouldn't own a yacht no matter what job he had.

Corporate Alex walked in the front door at three o'clock while Brandon was refilling the soda fridge—another job that wasn't explicitly his. That was finally the thing to put Charlie out of his head.

Michael wasn't in the gym right now. For staff there were a couple of personal trainers and the janitor. In effect, Brandon was the senior branch employee.

Corporate Alex said, "I need to talk to you."

There was a method to stacking waters in the fridge. Shoving new waters in front meant some clients were going to grab a bottle and find it warm, so you made a path through the center of the shelf, pushed everything forward, and then filled from the back. Brandon didn't stop. "Go ahead."

"We're not signing that contract." Of course they weren't. "We talked it over at the main office, and we don't see why you aren't designing the logo for us already. You're an employee, and we are your employer. We've already lost too much time."

Brandon glanced up at him. "Then we're deadlocked."

Alex looked him dead in the eye. "You're willing to lose your job over a logo you could put together on company time?"

As pointless as it would be to review every one of his reasons again, Brandon felt the urge to do it anyhow. The exploitation. The disregard for art. The dyed-in-the-wool New England stinginess that seemed to fall in layers thicker than January snowfall.

Instead, Brandon said, "Are you firing me?"

Michael would have a fit when he got back.

Alex said, "Are you refusing?"

Brandon stood. "Yes. I'm refusing."

Alex said, "Then go."

Brandon let the fridge door shut and walked to the coat hook. For the last week, he hadn't been putting his belongings under the desk. He seldom left anything more expensive than a paperback novel in the drawer, but he'd taken even his small things home. Without bothering to put away the water cases or log out of the computer, Brandon picked up his jacket and backpack. "Thank you." He looked Alex right in his very startled eyes. Apparently it stinks to be called on an ultimatum. "It's been a pleasure working for the Lighthouse Athletic Club."

Brandon walked through the drizzle with his head high.

He'd be okay for two months. He could slice expenses to the bare minimum and watch Aria every day, and that would keep the rent paid. Two months—eight weeks—and he'd be able to land enough design work to survive.

He stepped over a rivulet of transmission fluid on the rain-glossed blacktop. Corporate Alex didn't pursue him, but Brandon hadn't expected he would. When Michael returned in half an hour, he'd blow a gasket. Corporate Alex might or might not stay to answer the phones. He wouldn't be wiping down the counters or mixing protein drinks, wouldn't reload the fridge. He'd probably leave the crates of bottled drinks right there on the hand truck for Michael to replace, fuming the entire time.

It occurred to Brandon that he'd been following that trail of transmission fluid for quite a distance, and he raised his eyes until he found its source.

Right to his car.

He started the engine with a feeling of dread, but it turned over. The car couldn't get out of second gear, but Brandon made it out of the parking lot and onto the street. It finally lumbered into third, but the whole way home it wouldn't climb over twenty miles per hour. In his driveway, it died for good.

Chapter Nineteen

She'd kissed Brandon. She'd kissed him a lot, and he'd kissed her back. He'd held her.

This was totally not Charlotte's plan. At no point in her scheme for the next few weeks had she thought, "I'll have a fling with the gardener's son that I used to know when I was a kid. You know, someone who grew up here and doesn't plan to leave. And then I'll go find a job in New York or Richmond and leave him behind."

This was *insane*. If she had the slightest bit of common sense—even a dose of common sense that would fit into a thimble—she'd never have done that. She wasn't the summer-fling type. She'd never dated like that, just for, "Hi, you're cute, let's go out, okay now bye." Never.

Hunter had done that to her. Actually, no, more like, "Hey, you're cute, I'll expect you to be faithful to me even though I've got no intention of being faithful to you."

Was she on the rebound? Was that what this was all about?

Filled with shame, Charlotte drove to the yarn store where a woman awaited with her grandmother's worn-out quilt. The woman's grandmother had probably been faithful to some man for like seventy-five years, growing old together and watching grandchildren and great-grandchildren enter the world. Not like Charlotte, recklessly kissing magnificent guys in the rain.

It was a pieced quilt in a cathedral window pattern. "It's in good condition," Charlotte said. She pointed out a few splits in pieces on the edge and one obvious tear in a center block. Next she examined the binding all the way around. "It's worn on the edges. It would be best to replace the whole binding." The backing was in reasonable condition, so she looked again over the pattern on the top, taking photos on her phone and jotting notes every time she found an issue.

The woman who'd brought the quilt said to the owner, "Watching her is worth the price of admission. I didn't even notice those little splits."

The owner said, "I thought the estimate was free," and the woman laughed.

Charlotte explained the different ways she could repair the split pieces. The tear through the center piece would be a relatively simple fix with silk thread. The splits were more troublesome, and she outlined a few different methods of repair. She could try to match with similar fabrics of similar age, if she could find them. She could lay a fine heat-sensitive mesh beneath the split areas and seal them back together.

Charlotte pointed out a yellowed stain along the sides. "I won't touch that. Trying to clean it will most likely damage the fabric. Tell everyone the stain gives the quilt character."

Then she traced a dozen seams that were loosening up. "Every one of these will need to be re-stitched. It doesn't make sense to repair those two split sections if every other seam goes in the next few years."

She assessed her client out of the corner of her eye while taking notes. Was this woman rolling in money? Or was she just curious about the cost of repair due to sentiment? With a museum you could spare no expense and expect the curator to sign a blank check. Here, though, how to proceed?

Instead of guessing, Charlotte laid out the possible charges for every method of repair, writing them down as she went along. She might be undervaluing her time, but it would be interesting just to get started on a commission. What was it Cashman had said about contracts? "I ask for a fifty percent deposit up front, and the rest on completion."

The woman said, "That sounds reasonable. How long do you think it will take?"

Charlotte fumbled in her head for a time frame. "Within the month. It will depend on how long I take to find appropriate fabric."

The next half hour consisted of a lot of decisions, a lot of dithering, and settling on a price. Right after, Charlotte found herself in her uncle's car with a trash bag full of quilt and a check.

"First thing we do," Charlotte told the quilt, "is find you a better container than a trash bag."

Her second stop was the library, where Aileen introduced her to Nicole Hartnel, the library director. "The community room isn't very big, but we have a podium and a smartboard for PowerPoint presentations."

Charlotte said, "How about a table where I can spread out fabric samples?"

Her third stop was a trip back through all the antique stores, where she picked up a quilted placemat in dire need of love, an appliquéd doll dress, and a terrible velvet cushion, all for five dollars.

In the car, with all this awesome fabric in bags (plus two skeins of yarn that had begged to come home with her), Charlotte whispered, "We're in business."

She'd need to put together a presentation.

She'd need a work space in Aunt Eleanor's house, something better lighted than the garage space occupied by the spinning wheel.

She'd need to finish up Violet's blanket.

She'd need to compile that publication for her fellowship.

She'd need to kiss Brandon again.

Text:

Brandon, 7:05 a.m. "I promised I'd see you again today, but I may be a little late."

Charlotte, 7:05 a.m. "Okay. Is everything all right with Aria?"

Brandon, 7:06 a.m. "No, my car blew up."

Chapter Twenty

The numbers did not work.

Actually, the numbers did work. Brandon's math was accurate. He just didn't like the result.

It would take forty minutes to walk to Charlie's house, and that was fine. It was humid but not disgusting, and he needed time to think. He could have run it in under twenty if he felt like it, but again he needed time. Right now, he had time in abundance, so he'd spend that.

The car was kaput unless he poured money into it, and he didn't have enough money to buy another car. He'd called the garage, and the mechanic had awarded him a good-natured chuckle along with a crushing estimate of the cost.

He'd get one partial paycheck from the gym when this period ended. He had one outstanding invoice for PacerStudios. The checking account currently had one month's rent plus one transmission job. He could handle those without going negative. There was one design job on the board right now, plus his quarterly work for the catalog.

He'd called all his regular clients. Anything on deck? No? Do you know anyone who might be interested? No? Well, talk to you soon.

People started businesses all the time. How did they do it? Or did they begin with ten grand in the bank to survive until the clients queued up?

Overwhelmed, Brandon concentrated on putting one foot in front of the next in front of the next, walking out of town, up the main route, up the hills, up Sky Ridge Drive.

The lighthouse glinted on the water, simultaneously beautiful and the source of all his trouble. But that wasn't really fair either. The lighthouse hadn't been taking advantage of him. The lighthouse hadn't been taking advantage of him for years.

Near the Boucher property, Pepper joined him from the opposite side of the invisible fence. Not wanting her to get used to breaking out, Brandon fell into a jog, and she bounded along with him, barking but keeping to her side of the border. At the driveway, he entered and she pounced all around him.

Charlie came onto the porch, ready to run.

Relief flooded through him. It felt amazing to hug her, holding her as tightly as he dared because of all the feelings of failure frothing in his throat.

She said, "You're not okay, are you?"

He said, "No. It's not a good story."

She kissed him lightly. "Tell me while we're running."

That way she wouldn't have to look at him, wouldn't have to see the inadequacy.

Now he wasn't being fair to her. She didn't even know yet, so how could she be judging him?

She took his hand. "If this is about the car... Wait, are you okay? Was there an accident?"

"No. That was just the final kick in the teeth." He turned toward the street. "Let's run. I'll tell you later."

She said, "You walked two miles to get here. You sure you're okay?"

He fought the darkness inside. "I've run further than four miles."

These numbers added up at least. He and she tended to run ten-minute miles. They would do two of them, one out and one back. By now they had something of a routine, although eventually he'd ask to change it up. Maybe go further. Maybe go a different way rather than just running along the top of a skyline where he could never afford to live but around which his childhood kept weaving in and out.

Half a mile in, he said, "Yesterday I got fired."

"Crud. They're jerks." Her nose wrinkled. "Are you getting a lawyer?"

"They didn't do anything illegal, I don't think." He'd spent time looking it up yesterday, the difference between exempt and non-exempt employees, plus discrepancies between job descriptions and actual job duties. A judge would take ages to sort it out, and an attorney would take money Brandon didn't have. The only consolation was that Michael had, according to Michael's text messages, told off Corporate Alex in vivid terms. Followed by, "I'm going to requisition three new hires to replace you."

Brandon had replied, "Maybe they should have paid me three times as much."

For that matter, he'd have done it for twice as much.

Charlie said, "It's annoying that your car quit on you the same day. That'll make it harder to look for a new job."

Brandon said, "Should I?"

They'd reached the hill, and Charlie dropped to a walk. "Should you get a new job? Versus what? Win the lottery?"

"Versus getting my own business in high gear."

"Oh!" She rubbed her shoulder. "Okay, so tell me: how do you get clients? Because I'm going to end up doing contract work too, and that puzzles me."

"It's all about networking. I think." He'd read a dozen web pages and half a book on networking last night until the combination of overwhelm and exhaustion finally snuffed his candle. "I started last night with some basic contacts, but I'm going to have to drum up business, ask everyone I know, and become more annoying than your second cousin who friends you on Facebook to ask if you've ever tried Amway."

Charlie squeezed his hand. "You can do that."

But what he couldn't do... He couldn't take her out to dinner. He couldn't treat her to a concert or a trip up the coast or delightful just-because gifts. Too much of romance was hitched to money. Especially for her, coming from a life where money peeled off the walls, how would this thing go anywhere if he couldn't even date her properly? Let alone provide for her.

Last week it had seemed so academic discussing it with Cashman. *Are you willing to lose your job?* Cashman had said. Brandon's cocky answer sounded so ignorant right now. *If that's going to happen, it might as well happen sooner rather than later.*

They ran again for a while, but Brandon kept churning up plans in his head about ways to get his name out there, ways to drum up clients, and in doing so drum up money.

By contrast, Charlie was doing great. Brandon was happy that she had a commission, albeit a little jealous. She needed his help carrying a folding table from the garage into the cordoned-off living room, but once they'd maneuvered it, she gated off the whole area and spread out the antique quilt. Talking the whole time like a tour guide, Charlie reviewed every minor repair to stabilize the quilt and keep it from disintegrating before the next generation got to use it.

"No, no one's going to use it," she corrected him. "This is for display. A quilt like this is a piece of art."

Brandon said, "Are you sure it wasn't functional? That must be how it got so worn."

She nodded. "Artistic and functional don't have to be in opposition."

True. Charlie was perfectly functional when she ran, but he'd become more conscious that her body was a work of art.

She brought in a bunch of supplies for her work, then showed him the three bits of junk she'd picked up from the antique stores for her library demonstration. "I need to write a presentation." Her nose wrinkled, and it was cute. "PowerPoint. My favorite."

Brandon shrugged. "I don't mind PowerPoint. If you want to dry-run your slides, I'll be your audience."

She needed more light, so they relocated floor lamps down into the living room. "Speaking of function," Brandon muttered as he moved a couch to reach the nearest plug, "this room isn't designed for working."

"I need a gated room so Pepper doesn't get to the quilt." She folded her arms. "When I came here, I thought I'd be bored. I figured I'd knock off that publication and then stare at trees for four weeks."

Brandon said, "Can I tell you how glad I am that you're not?"

At nine o'clock, Brandon's father pulled into the driveway with the Pelletier Lawn Care pickup truck and trailer. Pepper bounded up to him, and he bent over, saying, "Up!"

Up Pepper jumped onto his shoulders. Charlie rushed to the porch and called, "Pepper! Down!" and the dog sprang to the ground, tail wagging. Dad tossed Pepper a treat from his pocket.

Brandon called hi. Dad said, "Forty minutes," then backed the riding mower off the truck.

Brandon folded his arms and leaned against the porch post. "Sure, Pepper gets a treat, but I get a deadline."

Charlie said, "Forty minutes?"

"When he's done mowing, he's driving me home so I can watch Aria." He rolled his eyes. "It's a family operation now."

Charlie tilted her head. "When will you get the car fixed? Or are you just going to buy a new one?"

He tried to keep his eyeballs in their sockets. What was life like when you could choose to buy a new car the same way you'd think, "I don't feel like cooking tonight. I'll just order a pizza"? For that matter, what was life like when you could just feel like not cooking?

"I haven't decided." The car was fifteen years old. It had embarked on its first drive before Brandon had met Charlie for the first time. He'd only owned it three years.

With Dad on the property, even riding a mower and wearing ear protection, Brandon felt awkward, so there wouldn't be any more kisses. They called in Pepper so she wouldn't herd the mower, and Charlie showed Brandon the nearly completed baby blanket for Violet. "Oh, and my mother is in fine form. Did I tell you she called yesterday morning?"

Charlie had the best storytelling voice, and she led him through a hilarious, hyperbolic conversation with her mother, during which her mother proceeded to make Violet's life-threatening medical condition all about herself. Then at the last second, Charlie managed to turn that self-centeredness against the woman to keep her mother pinned in Philadelphia, tethered to the phone. "Brilliant maneuver." Brandon smiled, wondering how Charlie described him. "So now you're getting updates through her?"

"Yes, and therefore I have less information than I did before." Charlie rolled her eyes. "But it helps Anna, so I'll deal with it. Did I tell you Aunt Eleanor video chatted me just to talk to Pepper?"

He felt so much more relaxed with her today, other than the crushing tension of impending bankruptcy. Forty minutes passed too soon.

Brandon brought his own water bottle to Sparrows for the running club, on the grounds that if he intended to budget forty dollars a week for groceries, it didn't make sense to drop two bucks on a soda he didn't want. It was okay. Sparrows wouldn't kick them out just because he freeloaded a couple of times. Brandon also went for his second run of the day, on the grounds that if he exhausted himself, he'd sleep tonight rather than lying awake every other hour, wondering how one manages a grocery budget of forty dollars a week.

(Dozen eggs, two dollars. Gallon of whole milk, four dollars. Box of cereal. Box of pasta. Jar of sauce. Bag of potatoes. Bag of apples. Bag of frozen broccoli. Whatever meat was marked down for quick sale. Pound of butter. Loaf of bread. Package of bologna. Not very interesting, but that would yield enough calories to get him through a week.)

He kept the run easy, sticking alongside Aileen and trying not to wonder how you date a rich woman when you're simultaneously figuring out how to wedge a can of coffee into your budget. Also with no car.

When Brandon walked through the door at Sparrows, Cashman looked up from behind the divider as though alerted by radar. The man had a heat-seeking drama detector. "How'd it go?"

Charlie was in Eleanor's usual spot, so apparently she hadn't said anything. Brandon flashed Cashman a thumbs-up. "The good news is, they can't take advantage of me for free design work any longer."

Cashman's eyes darkened. "They canned you? Do you want an internet outrage mob?"

Brandon's eyes widened. "Are you kidding?"

"A couple of well-placed posts about rich companies forcing artists to work for free, and I guarantee you, exposure will be generated." Cashman's dark eyes glinted. "You know the Bright Hearts in Brighthead Facebook group? They breathe drama. I'm familiar with many such groups in towns where Lighthouse has locations."

"I'm not interested in getting hauled into court for slander." Brandon sat across from Charlie.

"They'd have to take *me* into court for slander, and they're not going to." Cashman smiled in a way that sent a chill up Brandon's spine. "I don't think Lighthouse will appreciate it, but since they wanted to pay you in exposure, it's fitting they get paid in kind."

"But I'd get exposed." Brandon's stomach lurched. "The kind of 'exposed' where people Google my name and discover I'm a whiner who got fired from a desk job."

Cashman leaned forward. "And whose website will they look at because they feel like they should help you out by maybe hiring you? This would only work in your favor."

Tempting as it might be to see Corporate Alex pilloried on the Brighthead Green, Brandon said, "Yeah, no."

Charlie said, "There's got to be a better way to work this out in your favor."

Cashman had an answer, because of course he did. "Tomorrow morning, walk into the main office of every gym in the area. Tell them what Lighthouse did to you, and ask if they were thinking of upgrading their website. Because as an insider, you know every single complaint against your former employer, and you'll be able to target their marketing toward exactly those dissatisfied customers."

Julie came over, downing the last of her sports drink. "Cashman, I'd ask you to remind me never to get on your bad side, except I moved in there a long time ago."

He pointed at Julie with two fingers. "I disguise it so well, you have to admit. I'm also irritated that you won the baby-betting pool. Go ahead: order twin lobster tails and a five-hundred-year-old bottle of scotch. It's on me."

"Hey, Doreen?" Julie called. "Cheese fries and a Moxie. Cashman's paying." She turned to Brandon. "They actually sacked you because they wanted highly skilled work that isn't anywhere near your job description, but that people do pay you for independently?"

Brandon said, "And then my transmission died, so this

week officially stinks."

Aileen's head picked up. "Trey knows a guy who'll fix that."

Julie said, "Oh, that guy on Route 1 who's on disability?"

Aileen nodded. "He did Trey's brother's car."

Charlie exclaimed, "Is that even legal?"

Brandon said, "I'm not going to pay too much attention to where the governor thinks I ought to get my transmission fixed."

Charlie flattened her tone. "Let me revise: is that even safe?"

Brandon's throat burned. "Look, even if it's not safe, I need a car. If the transmission explodes, I'm no worse off than I am now."

Driving a fifteen-year-old car was by definition not safe. Why not rub it in more that he didn't have a good enough job?

Julie said, "At least he doesn't rip you off like that guy on the corner of Main."

Aileen rolled her eyes. "Oh, please. The guy on Main would charge you seventy-five bucks to recline the front seat."

Brandon's gaze drilled holes through the tabletop. Money. Everything was about money.

Julie said to Aileen, "Speaking of Trey, where is he?"

Aileen chuckled. "Knowing him, he probably scored a one-time deal on paragliding lessons and he's about to text us pictures from overhead."

Charlie said, "And you believe that?"

Aileen nodded. "Trey's...how do I put this...?"

"A flake?" Cashman volunteered.

"Spontaneous!" Aileen said brightly. "Thank you, that was just the word I was looking for!"

Charlie wrapped her arms around herself, as if cold. "But...I mean, how do you know?"

Aileen said, "He hasn't given me a reason not to trust him."

Brandon could hear what Charlie was thinking: people didn't give you a reason not to trust them...until the moment they did.

Julie said, "Here's a practical question: the Lighthouse Run. Do we boycott it?"

Brandon looked up. "No. Why?"

Cashman balanced his knife on his first finger. "I don't give money to people who mess with my friends."

Brandon was Cashman's friend? News to him.

Cashman added, "The run's not benefitting the historical society anymore."

Julie said, "The gym is making a donation to the lighthouse preservation fund."

Cashman rolled his eyes. "My mistake. It's not *materially* benefitting the historical society. The gym is going to give the lighthouse some sliver of a percent of the registration fees. Did they even specify the percentage up front?" He opened his hands and raised his eyebrows. "Wow, so generous. We could, as a group, donate whatever we'd have paid in race fees directly to the historical society along with a nice letter stating that the gym can go twist in the wind. If the executives don't want to pay for talent, that's their choice, but then they don't get any of our talent. Or our payments."

Julie said, "It might be interesting to see what happens if one at a time we all cancel our memberships."

Brandon said, "That only works if you're billed monthly. If you paid the whole year in advance, they won't refund it." He nodded at Aileen. "You're stuck for another seven months at least. Cancelling won't hurt them."

"Fifteen negative reviews on their social media profiles will hurt," volunteered Cashman.

Julie raised a hand. "No social media mob. Brandon already said that."

Brandon said, "We shouldn't boycott the Lighthouse Run. Charlie's running it for Violet."

Charlie said, "Wait, no. Don't bring me into this. I'm just as mad at them as everyone else." She squeezed his hand.

"Violet doesn't care what I run. I'll run for her, but it doesn't have to be at the lighthouse."

Brandon's stomach lurched. The whole world was upended right now. Sunday morning, so much had been decided. Tuesday evening, everything was upside-down because of him.

Julie leaned back and folded her arms. "The lighthouse run normally gets about a hundred people. Just us not being there will affect turnout in a visible way. I can write a letter as president of the running club and state that as a group, we're not going to run the race."

Shelly said, "Co-signed."

Cashman said, "Triple co-signed. That's the whole power triumvirate."

Shelly gasped. "That sounds so much more fiendish than 'leadership team!'"

Julie continued, "We won't go on an active campaign to destroy the race, but we also won't keep our refusal a secret. I'll ask Cassidy over at Tempo Runs not to put up their flyer. There's plenty of other races."

Brandon pushed his chair back from the table. "It's not the lighthouse's fault."

Cashman said, "We've already established that this won't hurt the lighthouse. If it were a money-maker, the historical society wouldn't have quit doing the run."

Brandon got up and left.

It was still bright. At this time of year it would be bright until nine o'clock, and the sun would be back up well before six, but the breeze had shifted around. It was already cooling off.

Charlie stepped outside.

What was he supposed to say? That he'd just ruined everything for everyone? That her intention of running for Violet needed to be diverted to something else because he was incapable of supporting even one person in a basement apartment?

She slipped up alongside him and stayed there, leaning against the brick wall.

Tomorrow he should hit the pavement and forget about the graphic design business. How could he ever get enough clients to survive? He should have done the stupid logo and let them use him up and spit him out.

Charlie's voice was soft. "They're responding because they care about you."

"I don't know why." Brandon's hands clenched. "This isn't their fight."

"They made it their fight, the same way I made Violet's fight my fight." She tucked her arms around him. "It seems bad right now, but it's only been one day. Tomorrow you'll hit the ground running."

Tomorrow would be just like today: reaching out to his network and discovering that no one wanted any work done. Oh, and no one knew anyone else who did either.

But what did Charlie know about that? Charlie had just proven she could find freelance work without a second thought.

She kissed him. "It'll be all right."

He wanted to believe her. He just wasn't sure how it would happen.

Chapter Twenty-One

Charlotte didn't get to sleep until midnight. First she cobbled together the presentation notes for her slides, and then she opened the document for her fellowship publication. Because yes, this afternoon she'd received the loveliest email from her former employer.

Charlotte,

The director was asking me this afternoon if I'd heard from you regarding your manuscript. I wanted to check in to see how things were progressing and when we could expect to read your draft. I told her you weren't required to turn it in until the weekend, but if you have any questions, I can help.

Sincerely,

Evelyn Aldridge

Ms. Aldridge had been so...sweet...about not threatening Charlotte's future letters of recommendation or her network contacts. Fortunately, Charlotte could read between the lines.

By now she should have been further into the project. Nevertheless, she'd be able to get it all done if she pushed through. Up until mid-May, when the bomb dropped in her life, she'd been writing chapters and gathering images. She'd even created a few charts.

After Hunter's betrayal, that's when work stopped. The gears in her brain had locked up while sorting through the shambles of her life. She hadn't been able to figure out how to eat, let alone how to put together a manuscript the length of a short book.

It's too bad you can't restore a relationship the same way you can restore a quilt. You can remove the frayed edging and replace with a similar style cloth, using silk thread so the stitches disappear into the fabric. You can't do that with a betrayed heart. Those stitches were going to show, and the reinforced parts might still wear through and shed batting all over the place.

Charlotte spent the two hours after running club putting together the pieces of her manuscript. It shouldn't take long. It just had to be done. Five solid days was more than enough time, even with the presentation and the quilt. The quilt could wait. The presentation couldn't, but a lot of the presentation's material (pun intended) could come from the publication.

She also wrote back to Ms. Aldridge, *"Thanks for checking in on me! I am indeed progressing on the document, but if I have any questions, I'll reach out to you."* Because that was the dance her professional world had choreographed, all polite and constrained and with impeccable form to disguise the impatience and irritation.

Following that ultra-polite pirouette, she spent the next two hours pulling together all the random files and writing some connecting material for between the chapters. At midnight, with everything in the same document and in roughly the right order, she set the laptop on the nightstand and shut off the lights.

At five thirty, the sun woke her up, but she'd been editing all night in her head. *That* picture needed to go *there*. *This* caption ought to reference *that other thing*.

Well, wouldn't this be an awesome start to the day? She rolled over and stared away from the window, but Pepper trotted into the room. She wanted to go out. Of course.

The sun rose over the ocean with a breathtaking display of color, so while Pepper raced around the yard, Charlotte took a picture. She messaged it to Anna. "Maine says good morning." Then she texted a picture of Pepper to Aunt Eleanor, since that was all Aunt Eleanor would want.

Brandon...last night. It wasn't fair. But he'd be okay. He'd find clients. He was just shocked at losing his safety net, and she knew well what that was like. Right away was the worst, plus there was his car dying at the same time. Today he'd have his equilibrium back.

Anna texted her a photo of Violet. They'd decorated the crib so much that one more photo or sticker would send the whole thing imploding on itself like a black hole, transforming Violet into the world's first Star Child. In the crib was the crocheted bunny. Smiling, Charlotte texted back, "Something each of us made."

Anna replied, "Both cunning."

Cunning? Charlotte sent back a smile emoji.

She wished she could hear the ocean from here, but instead it was just the birds, just the wind. That was good too. It was harder to make out the lighthouse, with its white stone surrounded by sunlit waves, but it was there. Waiting.

Charlotte felt like that too: waiting. For now, her life was on hold. Maybe Brandon felt the same.

Pepper returned, happy but hungry. Charlotte brought her back into the house for breakfast. She needed to get the rest of the draft organized. Then she'd just format it and send it off to Ms. Aldridge. Knock that out of the way, and everything else would be easy.

She didn't look up from the computer when Brandon walked in the door, only growled, "I hate everything."

Brandon stopped. "Me too?"

She glared up. "You get a pass. I'm also okay with Pepper.

This," and she waved a hand at the laptop, "this has earned my eternal ire, and I loathe it with the brilliant fury of a hundred fiery suns."

He edged inside. "I take it you don't want to go for a run? I'll take Pepper on my own."

She shut the laptop as if closing the lid of a coffin. "Leaving the house will stop me from turning the oven to five hundred degrees and sticking Mr. Computer on the top rack." She yanked the leash from the hook. "Pepper, we've got to get out of here."

Brandon followed her and Pepper out to the road. "So—"

With that as permission, Charlotte launched into a diatribe about the stupidity she kept encountering as she tried to format anything whatsoever, and how pictures wouldn't stay where she put them, wouldn't move where she wanted them, wouldn't flow with the text, wouldn't remain the right size, or—her favorite—wouldn't show up as more than the bottom layer of pixels.

Brandon said, "I hate when that happens."

"I have to send it to my overseer at the museum, and I can't very well send it without the photos. The photos are half the documentation, and if I say, *now we reference figure five,* and there is no figure five, then guess what happens?" Charlotte huffed. "I need to get this done, but the computer's being an idiot."

Brandon said, "Sometimes when you dig about three levels down in the formatting menus, there's a 'Don't Be Stupid' button. Uncheck that and the application behaves."

She huffed. "I'll believe that in August of twenty-never."

Brandon said, "First give me fifteen minutes with the document, and then you can put it in the oven."

Charlotte muttered, "On the self-cleaning cycle."

In the house again, she logged him in, and half a second later, Brandon said, "Oh, I found your problem! You're using a word processor to do design layout."

She shrugged. "That's always what I use."

"You need a desktop publishing and typesetting application. I could download the free trial and get that set up if you want."

She folded her arms. "No. I want this thing over to the museum today. I can't go figuring out a whole new program."

Brandon said, "I've got all day. Like literally, I have all day. I'll get it done for you."

"Have you looked at the length of this monstrosity? The number of illustrations?" She folded her arms. "Really?"

"Yes. Really." He sighed. "I'll email it to myself and do it on my computer, then send it back to you. It'll be great."

Charlotte didn't budge. "Aria?"

"I can work while I'm watching her." Brandon gave a little roll of his eyes that was almost cute. "Charlie, please, I know what I'm doing, but I don't think anyone can do it in a word processor. If I use the right tools, this will be polished up before lunch."

She folded her arms. "Fine." She went to the cabinet and took down the travel coffee mugs. "But I'm bringing coffee."

Startled, he laughed. "You don't need to come too."

"I'll entertain Aria so you can get my project done. Fair's fair."

He flinched. "Will you be okay with that? Given everything that's happening with Violet?"

In the middle of setting up the coffeemaker, Charlotte paused.

Would she be okay? Or would it hurt like blazes being with one baby while her heart was with another baby in an incubator across the country?

"I don't want to make it worse," Brandon said.

"It's not like I've forgotten." Charlotte resumed programming the coffeemaker. "Besides, someone needs to be there to shield Aria's ears when the computer does its frustrating stuff to you too."

Then she remembered the insurmountable issue. "Um...but you walked here this morning, didn't you?"

Brandon said, "Yeah, my dead car's still dead."

Charlotte bit her lip. "I don't feel comfortable letting you drive my uncle's car."

Brandon laughed out loud. "*I* wouldn't feel comfortable driving your uncle's car! I'd barely feel comfortable sitting in it."

She glanced at him. Then, "You don't mind riding with me?"

Baffled, Brandon said, "You have a license, right? You haven't wrecked four cars in the last year?"

Hunter had never let Charlotte drive him anywhere. When he'd visited her at her parents' house, he'd driven her parents' car. When she'd picked him up at the airport, he'd driven the car home.

Was that odd? "You're all right with it?"

He was just fine with it. He didn't give her directions because she remembered the route. He didn't even mess with the radio.

The morning spun out leisurely, with Charlotte and Aria on the floor playing and Brandon at the table, talking to himself while formatting her document. For two hours, he worked with her text and occasionally sprinkled in questions about how she wanted things set up, more frequently telling the computer not to be stupid. Aria had a shape sorter, a box of wooden blocks, and a tube where she could push ten balls in one end and then uncap it to let them out the other. At noon, Brandon sat on the floor with them and started building with the blocks.

Charlotte blinked at him. "Is it done?"

He pointed to the table. "Go look."

On the screen was her publication laid out in columns, drop-caps at the section headers and fleurs on the top corners, page numbers on opposite bottom corners, and the photos brilliantly nestled into the layout.

Her voice broke. "Oh my gosh. This is beautiful. You did all this in two hours?"

Obviously he had, but she couldn't make the words form. Her document looked—amazing. Just amazing. Hers had been a nice word processing file. His looked professional.

Well, *he* was a professional.

Brandon said, "I emailed you the PDF file, so you can send that over to the museum. They'll ask for changes, and when you get me those, I'll drop them into the master document."

She turned back to the screen and scrolled through. He'd put her name in as well, as though it were a real book.

Well, it was a real book. The museum was going to publish this. He'd just...made it into a book.

She found herself blinking hard as she paged through all her work with the museum, the detailed write-ups of each project and the history of each piece, plus the care on each of them. She found a typo, so he showed her how to get into the text to fix it. "I'll generate a new PDF when you're done. If you find anything tricky, like you want to move a picture, let me know."

He'd even started every new chapter on a right-hand page. Then, on the very last page, she found her own photo and "About the Author."

"You pulled this from my LinkedIn?"

He was building a bridge with Aria. "I figured you'd change that before the final version."

In shock, she kept paging through. And then, still in shock, she pulled out her phone to send an email to Evelyn Aldridge. No need for the politeness dance this time. She had something amazing for her.

Chapter Twenty-Two

Charlie loved his work. That alone would have been enough to keep Brandon going for another week, with or without forty dollars in groceries.

From his perch on the floor with Aria, playing with blocks, he kept watching Charlie's eyes, her mouth, her whole expression as she flipped through screen after screen. She loved it. He loved that she loved it.

He shouldn't love *her*. Not yet. He'd promised they'd take it slow. For now, he'd just love that she loved it.

She took the laptop and sat beside Brandon while he let Aria stack blocks and knock down blocks and laugh and stack them again. Aria wanted to make the stack taller than she was, but then she couldn't get the next block on top, so she'd knock the whole thing over and laugh a big belly laugh. And she'd start again.

It was a good metaphor. Maybe he could be like Aria.

Charlie asked him a few questions, and within ten minutes he had the laptop back and was moving pictures for her. Could this go over there? Would that fit on that page? The nice thing about her as a pseudo-client was that when he explained why you wouldn't put this sidebar over there (if, say, it would draw the eye the wrong way, or because the colors looked better in that direction rather than this one), she either agreed or else gave a reason why she disagreed. She made suggestions that incorporated his thoughts but gave them her own spin.

By one o'clock, side by side on the floor, they had a finished document, she with her laptop on her lap and Brandon with his on the couch. Brandon's lap was taken up by Aria, sound asleep with her head on his thigh. He emailed Charlie the file, and she emailed it to the museum.

Charlie studied him. "You're pinned down."

It was way past lunch time. Aria usually slept about ninety minutes in the midday, but because Brandon had been bad and let her eat a bunch of graham crackers while he was working, her schedule was well and truly disrupted.

Charlie mused, "This is a dangerous situation for you. I could do anything."

She leaned over and kissed him, long and slow.

Brandon murmured, "I'm completely at your mercy."

"I'm merciless."

She was the last person he'd call merciless, and therefore she kissed him again. Oh, gosh. Yes, by all means, torture him.

"If that's what I get for formatting your manuscript, I'll work on your website next."

He waited, but she didn't kiss him a third time.

Instead she sat back. "I don't need a website."

"Actually, you do. You're going to be launching a job search, plus you're doing contract work. People will look you up. Speaking of which, we need to update your LinkedIn profile."

Charlie bit her lip. "I mean, eventually."

"I mean now, before you give that presentation. People are going to walk out of there thinking about every old thing in their house that could be restored, and when they get home, I want them able to find you." He shrugged. "It doesn't have to be a complicated website, but you need one."

When she still didn't move, he pointed to her computer. "I'll talk you through the setup. After that, I'll build the site. It won't take long."

Charlie opened the lid, muttering, "I should have just kept kissing you."

"Later," he promised. "We should get this done while we're thinking about it."

They were still working when Olivia returned from the flower shop carrying a wilted bouquet. She frequently decorated with past-their-prime flowers not good enough for their customers. This time Brandon didn't toss her his usual line: "For me? You shouldn't have!"

Aria rushed to her mommy, and Olivia lifted her. Brandon shifted on the floor because his lower half had gone to sleep. "Nothing weird to report. She napped until two and ate pretty well. Also, it's very, *very* funny if Uncle Brandon stacks up a tower taller than his friend Charlie."

Charlie said, "And even funnier when it falls over."

Aria laughed, and Olivia kissed her. "Good job. Did you get very tall while I was gone?" and Aria giggled again.

Brandon pushed up off the floor and onto the couch. Olivia said, "You ordered pizza?"

The box was in the trash. Charlie said, "Working lunch."

Brandon added, "Aria ate our crusts."

"Ah, a useful service." Olivia put Aria down, then went upstairs.

The pizza had been unexpected. Brandon had figured that at some point he'd make sandwiches, but Charlie had suggested pizza, then ordered it, then paid when it arrived. Talk about awkward. But Charlie didn't want to take a break to boil water or even get out lunch meat, so they'd sat at the kitchen table with pizza slices and her computer.

In exchange for a pizza, she'd gotten a simple website, plus a better LinkedIn profile, plus a rush shipment of business cards. "Just a small box," Brandon had reassured her. "You only need them until you land a job."

At about that point, he'd realized if she got a job, it wouldn't be in Brighthead. It probably wouldn't even be in Maine. So he added, "Or until you get a business license under your own name."

That felt better. Working virtually, he could move to follow his soulmate if it ever came down to that. His whole life was in Brighthead though. His family. His friends. His expectations.

Charlie had placed the business card order just as Olivia's car door had shut in the driveway. With that, Brandon could claim he'd spent the whole day working on marketing. Just not his own marketing.

She'd kissed him a few times too. Kisses and pizza—the perfect combination.

Charlie sat beside him on the couch, so he put his arm around her to draw her closer. Seeing that, Aria toddled over to share in the hug, getting on the multi-lap between them.

Charlie hugged Aria, her eyes tight.

Brandon said, "You're thinking about Violet?"

She nodded, her mouth quivering.

It'll be okay. He didn't say it. He didn't know if it would be okay, or if instead Anna was about to go through the unimaginable.

He couldn't claim he was close to Anna. They hadn't talked much after high school, when she'd gone to college in New Hampshire and he'd stayed local. You didn't have to still be close to someone to care about them, however, and if he hurt like this for Anna, then it must hurt twice as hard for Charlie.

Aria clambered down to pick up a plush dinosaur. Charlie shifted away from him. "I should probably get home. Pepper may have herded down everyone's farm animals by now and brought them into the strawberry patch."

Brandon said, "You got a lot done today."

She snorted. "Yeah, it was all me. I couldn't even get the

photos into the document."

Brandon gave her a mischievous smile. "We're not done yet. Tomorrow we dry-run your presentation."

"Oh, goodie. That means tonight I have an opportunity to write a presentation." She winked at him. "Thank you."

She bent over and kissed him quick. Then she was gone.

Gone, but everything about her lingered over him. Her words, her book, her business plan, and the warm feel of her lips.

Chapter Twenty-Three

Aileen introduced Charlotte to the Brighthead Public Library community, and they gave polite applause as she stepped to the podium. A couple dozen people had turned up to watch her talk. Plus Brandon, who sat at the back giving her a thumbs-up.

She'd been so nervous. She still was. She flashed him a smile, then clicked the remote to show her first slide.

Forty minutes later, Charlotte finished her final slide, and Aileen stepped to the front. Charlotte's hands were trembling, but at the back, Brandon was still smiling. It must not have been that terrible, despite her nerves and the occasional verbal flub, not to mention the way she hadn't anticipated how slowly a fabric sample would make its way around the room.

Brandon moved about the room, taking photos whenever she held up one of her props or to catch her showing a detail of the restored doll dress to an elderly woman. He'd warned her he would do that. "We'll set up a public speaking page on your website. And you always want photos."

Aileen said, "Wasn't that wonderful? I want to say thank you so much to Charlotte Fletcher for that great presentation about how to save our history and our heirlooms." More applause, maybe a bit louder now. "We've got some time, so let's bring on our questions!"

Hands went up all around the room. Aileen had warned

her this would happen. In fact, they'd banked on this happening, hence her hour-long talk being slated into fifteen slides and only forty minutes. The sheer number of tote bags had been the earliest indicator that Aileen might be right.

The first questioner wanted to know about restoring a wedding gown. Of course she did. Charlotte's own wedding gown lay in a box in her mother's house.

It was only fitting. (Hah, pun.) Her mother had picked out the ridiculous dress in the first place. Nice and modern, nothing Charlotte had restored herself even though that had been Charlotte's desire all along. The crocheted lace shawl had been Charlotte's attempt to wear something she'd made.

The second question was about a quilt the woman had right there with her in the room. They went back and forth for a few minutes, but then Aileen interrupted to say Charlotte would be happy to stay afterward and look at quilts.

Charlotte said, "Let's just go over this one first. That will give everyone an idea of what to expect."

The woman opened up her quilt, and Charlotte clasped her hands at her chest with a shriek. "A Baltimore Album quilt!"

Aileen said into her mic, "And that, folks, is why someone goes into fabric restoration."

Everyone laughed, and Charlotte's cheeks burned.

Aileen turned to Charlotte. "You should have seen me when I got my hands on a first edition of *The Great Gatsby*."

The woman holding the quilt said, "I squealed like a little girl when I found a vintage CorningWare casserole dish. Trust me, honey, you're not alone."

Flustered, Charlotte said, "Well, then. Now that we've established our various fetishes—" and the audience laughed.

She spread out the quilt on the table, then pulled out her phone to turn on the flashlight. "A Baltimore Album quilt is made of dozens of appliquéd blocks. From the back you can't see, but all the blocks are made of greens and golds atop a cream-colored background." Charlotte bent close, studying the fine stitching. "Alternating panels were intricate flowers. The remaining panels are scenes... This is a memory quilt?" Charlotte asked the owner. "It's telling a story."

The owner nodded. "That's why I want it preserved."

Then, in real-time, Charlotte showed her audience the things she made note of while examining a quilt and making an estimate about restoration. "You can inspect your quilt on your own ahead of time. Note the worn parts. Note any places where the stitching is loose. Keep in mind that sometimes the most visible problem is not actually the most worrisome problem, and that repairing one area may create stress on other areas."

On this piece was a torn corner, plus one square with damaged embroidery. She made note of the stains and the loose stitching. "This is overall in excellent condition."

The quilt's owner asked for her business card, and because of Brandon and express delivery, she had one to hand over.

Aileen said, "Do we have any questions that don't pertain to specific restoration projects?"

A man at the back raised a hand and stepped forward. "What brought you to Maine, Ms. Fletcher?"

She smiled. "I used to spend summers here as a kid, so I'm back."

He said, "Are you planning to live here in Maine long-term?"

The hair stood up on her neck, but Charlotte said, "I'd be willing to relocate permanently if your museums could use someone like me."

He nodded, then said, "What's your favorite thing about living in Maine?"

Charlotte said, "Moxie. Mainers have moxie."

He grinned at her. "Good answer," and then he stepped back again.

Brandon was looking right at the guy, surprised and a little pleased. That was odd. Did he know him?

When questions and answers had gone fifteen minutes over time, Aileen announced there would be one last question (how best to preserve leather), which Charlotte handled with ease. Aileen welcomed everyone to enjoy refreshments in the foyer, but please not to bring food and drink into the community room where Charlotte would be looking at heirloom fabrics. "It goes without saying," she added dangerously, "that you know better than to bring food into the book stacks."

Charlotte queued up a line to inspect the most amazing assortment of old fabrics (and hand out business cards). Brandon approached the man who'd had the intrusive, inane questions, and they exchanged business cards of their own. Then Brandon escorted the man right to the front of the line. "Ms. Fletcher, I want to introduce you to Mark Ennison, who writes for the Bar Harbor paper."

Ears ringing, she extended a hand. "Nice to meet you. Thank you for coming to the talk."

"I knew nothing about textile restoration and preservation before this I saw your press release," he said, shaking her hand. "Thank you for making it less boring than I anticipated."

"The pleasure's all mine," she said. What press release? And seriously, *less boring than anticipated?* Brandon should update her website to highlight that endorsement. Maybe a banner across the top.

Charlotte returned to the cornucopia of antiques and heirlooms: three quilts, a very old flag, a sailor's jacket, an Aran sweater that had sadly succumbed to moth larvae, and a rag doll that had been very, very well-loved. That last was simultaneously amazing and heartbreaking.

The last person opened a box, then parted several layers of tissue paper to withdraw a vintage leather purse with copper fittings and intricate beadwork. "My gosh," Charlotte breathed, barely wanting to touch it. The square purse was smaller than her fully stretched hand, and the frame was wrought with an elegant swirl design. The leather was worn from use, but the designs were still visible.

"It's very stiff to open," the owner said, "but if you can open it, the lining is completely torn up. I'd like to get that replaced, and the copper cleaned."

The copper was covered in verdigris, which in Charlotte's opinion made the purse even more lovely. It would be a privilege to work on this thing. She'd practically do it for free.

That's when it occurred to her that she didn't have to do it for free. She could love what she did and still earn money.

Charlotte handed the woman her card. "This is a work of art. Let's talk."

Chapter Twenty-Four

The day after the presentation, Brandon got ready walk to Charlie's house in the rain. He probably didn't need an umbrella. He wasn't even sure he owned one. In a backpack he stuffed a plastic bag full of dry clothes to change into afterward.

About two minutes before he'd have left, Charlie texted. "Don't bother walking. I'm picking you up."

He texted, "Rain is healthy."

She replied, "I'm going to call nonsense on that today. Pepper can run in the yard by herself."

He glanced out the window. Maybe it wasn't just drizzling. Maybe it was sheeting down rain with a nice ocean wind to back it up.

Thunder rumbled over Brighthead.

"Yeah, that settles it," she texted. "I'll be there in five minutes."

He tucked his laptop into his bag. "Okay." Maybe he could get some work done. She'd have changes for the website regardless, so he might as well come prepared.

Everything had worked out so well yesterday. Just so well. The sheer number of potential clients was one thing, but she'd also gotten her feet wet with the public speaking. He'd already updated her website to include pictures of the talk, and he'd taken the chance to check her stats. She'd had visitors.

Not a lot of visitors. But enough visitors to call it a success. You don't let clients pay in exposure, but exposure is a nice bonus after you've been paid.

The next thing would be to send letters to other local libraries and historical societies to get them to invite her. Even if she didn't stay in Maine, it would help to have a longer CV and a roster of public speaking engagements at her back.

Even if she didn't stay in Maine. But he wanted her to.

It thundered again. Maybe running wasn't the best plan for today.

Charlie pulled into his driveway, and in the fifteen seconds it took to reach the super expensive car, he still got soaked. She was wearing yoga pants and a T-shirt. "Even you wouldn't run in this slop."

His mouth tightened. "I'd probably have run at the gym, yeah."

She backed out onto the street, unexpectedly cute as she concentrated. He turned aside as she put it back into drive so she wouldn't think he was staring at her. "Do you still have a membership?"

Brandon shrugged. "I shouldn't. Since I'm the only one who would have thought to remove a former employee from the database, I probably do."

The wipers flipped at top blast as it thundered again, and Brandon wondered how well an Audi A4 stuck the corners when the road became a river. Charlie didn't seem concerned.

This was turning into a really nice summer.

Wait, what was he thinking? This wasn't a nice summer. He'd lost his job. Last night he'd overheard Olivia and Dale discussing money in the kitchen. (Actually, that would be *underheard*, since their kitchen was directly over his.) They'd kept their voices low, but still. Olivia, with that quiet self-possession he recognized as her alternative to a major freak-out. Dale, with his calm assurance. It would work out: Dale always thought it would work out, and to Dale's credit, it always had. Olivia had been panicked about daycare for Aria, and Dale had told her it would work out. Now Olivia was worried about the mortgage, and Dale had told her it would work out.

What was it like, to have someone you could dump all those anxieties on and hear that it would work out...and believe them?

Charlie pulled directly into the garage, and from there they went into the kitchen. Here she kissed him while the coffee brewed, and he held onto her. *It will work out.* It didn't feel like things would work out. He couldn't see any path forward, and all the most likely paths curled back around to end in the ditch of failure.

Pepper walked back and forth excitedly, so Charlie disengaged from Brandon. "Guess what Aunt Eleanor forgot to tell me she had?" She fastened a little coat around Pepper, kind of like a horse blanket.

Brandon watched the dog take off into the rain. That silly rain jacket would have changed things: after their previous run in the rain, Charlie wouldn't have ambushed him while he was toweling off the dog. He wouldn't have spent this morning hoping the rain would force him to towel off the dog again.

"You have to see this." Charlie unlatched the gate to the living room. She flipped on all the lights over the worktable, then showed him the thing she'd called a Baltimore Album quilt. "The owner said it belonged to her great-grandmother. Every one of these flower blocks is for one of her grandchildren, and she stitched their initials into the flower." She pulled on a pair of latex gloves and touched the blocks as she pointed out all the initials. "The larger squares are important moments in the family's history. This castle represents where they came from in Scotland. This book represents a family member who wrote poetry."

Brandon whistled.

Charlie nodded. "This is a treasure. She wants me to

rejuvenate the quilt so she can frame it. I'll need to re-embroider a couple of the blocks and tack down some of the others. Apparently her great-grandmother stitched the whole thing together with a number of the blocks blank, and then as important events happened, she removed the blank block and replaced it with a story block."

Three of the blocks remained blank, presumably due less to the lack of important events than to the lack of a living quilter.

Lightning flashed, followed a second later by the thunder. The storm was overhead.

Brandon said, "How's the spinning wheel?"

"Oh, she's gorgeous." She'd placed the wheel beside the piano, and she sat on the stool alongside it. "I'm not any good at spinning, but I think this is what I should be doing."

Her foot started the wheel, and the bobbin spun. She held the fleece with her hands so it twisted and fed onto the spool-thing that twirled in the middle of the fork-thing that was covered in hooks. Brandon watched for fifteen seconds before his brain decided this was more confusing than a transmission (since he never had to see a transmission at work) and instead he pulled out his phone. "For the website," he assured Charlie. It wasn't a total lie, only about ninety percent. He got pictures of her concentrating on the fiber in her fingers, again that very sweet frown and contraction of her brows, again that unbreakable concentration as she did something almost too hard for her to manage.

After the first few photos, he also took video. She was so beautiful when she worked. The video followed her hands, followed her rhythm. There was no other sound than the hum of the wheel and the hiss of the spool. He got closer for more photos.

She looked up, amused, and he caught a picture of her smile. "Caption: fabric artist who has no idea what she's doing."

She had no idea what she was doing to him, that was certain. Brandon sat on the piano bench and watched her hands as she held fiber and let go of yarn.

"Do you want to try?"

The fork-thing whipped through its rotation, all those hooks flying around. "Seems like a good way to lose three fingers."

She said, "I'll show you how to hold everything. Your fingers don't come near the flyer."

He declined.

All the lights shut off, and the house went quiet. The fridge silenced.

She let the wheel slow down. "Blackout?"

"Probably a tree limb came down. It happens out here all the time." There was only one power company for Brighthead, so he used the house phone and called in the outage. A computer voice promised someone would look into it.

He returned to the living room. "Usually the power's on again for fifteen minutes before they call back and say the power will be restored soon."

Charlie was back at spinning. "The wind is insane."

With this much rain, Brandon's bigger concern was his basement getting water, but there wasn't any use worrying. Instead he sat at the piano bench and opened the lid.

The wheel hummed at a smooth pace. "Can you still play?" Charlie asked.

He rested his hands on the keys and picked out the opening notes of "Für Elise."

"Never mind," she said. "Carry on."

She kept spinning while he worked his way through the piece, remembering as he did the way her aunt Eleanor would sit in a chair alongside the piano and close her eyes to listen better, occasionally stopping him for correction.

"My parents have a piano," he said. "I haven't played regularly since I moved out."

Rain blasted the side of the house, then let off. Charlie kept the wheel going. He transitioned into another of the pieces her aunt had taught him back when his mother cleaned the house in exchange for lessons. "Nocturne" something or other. Chopin?

Eleanor had included him with her normal students one December when she'd held a recital. He'd been practicing at home on the free upright piano his parents had gotten, always out of tune but with all the keys working. He knew these songs and had found sheet music online for a bunch of Christmas carols. Eleanor used to pass him sheet music at school too. "I think you'd like this," she'd say, and then he'd have to find the song online to hear it so he could translate the notes into something he could imitate.

At the end of the nocturne-whatever, Brandon stopped.

Charlie said, "Keep playing."

"It's been a while." He picked up the books on the music stand and found an early Hal Leonard volume. They were all little kid songs, but he picked through one of them.

Charlie and Anna used to go in another room when he was getting a lesson. Kelty had been there once for a lesson, but she'd left halfway through. Anna always said she got enough lessons of her own.

"You never learned to play, did you?" Brandon said.

Charlie said, "It didn't seem important back then. Anna always told me piano was boring."

Brandon started one of the other pieces he'd learned for the recital, "Jesu, Joy of Man's Desiring." It flowed so nicely, up and down, in and out. This piano was so much more sensitive to his touch than his parents' upright. That piano felt like it was either on or off, but this one graded its notes to his touch, and it responded differently to different pressures.

The lights flashed back on, and in the kitchen, the refrigerator whined to life.

"You need your own piano," Charlie said.

Yeah, but really, he needed a lot of things.

After driving him home, Charlie ruined everything by handing him a check for seven hours of work.

She seemed uncomfortable. "I tried to figure out your rates from your website, but everything requires an estimate. I looked up what other people were charging for formatting and web site design, and I tried to figure it out from that."

Water coursed down the windshield, down the side windows. Olivia was waiting inside for him to take Aria, and Charlie was holding that stupid check.

"I didn't do it for the money." The hair stood up on Brandon's neck. "You needed help."

"Look, just take it." Her voice rose in pitch. "The whole reason you left the gym was they were telling you to do work for free."

Brandon chilled. "Were you manipulating me in order to get design work?"

The thought had never occurred to him before that exact second, that Charlie would have known he knew how to use a desktop publishing application. Charlie would have known he could build a website. Had all that been a ruse?

She was privileged and urban. Was it just a matter of buttering up a working-class boy and paying him off with kisses and pizza?

The shock on her face was genuine. "*They* were manipulating you!"

"Right, but with you, I *offered*. If I'd expected you to pay me, there would have been a contract."

Charlie's face darkened. "You did a lot of work, and it's not work I could have done. This isn't any different than if a tow truck came up on the road and saw my car broken down. No, I didn't call it. Yes, I would have needed to get towed to the garage anyhow."

Right, and his car still didn't work. Brandon recoiled. "It isn't right."

"It's not right to steal someone's expertise." She unzipped his backpack on his lap and tucked in the check. "I refuse to take advantage of you."

Brandon said, "And if you sew a button on my shirt, should I whip out a twenty?"

She looked at him with a squint. "Not more than two dollars." Then she put a hand on his shoulder, trying to gentle him closer to her. "I want you to succeed. You know that. So let me help you launch."

His throat tightened. She fingered the top button on his polo shirt. "Please?"

"You're not being fair," he protested as she moved her face closer to his. His voice rasped a bit. "You're mixing business and pleasure."

"Maybe a little?" She put a hand to his cheek, and he looked into her eyes. "I had a good time working with you. But for you it was work."

And he needed his car repaired.

And Olivia needed the rent check.

And he'd like to live on more than forty dollars a week.

And he was weak. That was pretty much it: he needed the money.

"Fine," he said, and she kissed him.

It wasn't really fine. It wasn't fine at all.

Text:

Charlotte, 3:25 p.m. "They just took Violet into surgery."

Brandon, 3:26 p.m. "Now? I thought they were waiting."

Charlotte, 3:28 p.m. "I can't get a straight story from my mother. Anna thought she looked bluer than usual. The doctors investigated, and they couldn't wait any longer."

Brandon, 3:28 p.m. "I'm so sorry."

Charlotte, 3:29 p.m. "I'll let you know if Aunt Eleanor texts me."

Brandon, 3:30 p.m. "Do you want me to go over there?"

Charlotte, 3:31 p.m. "No, I'll be fine. I just wanted you to know."

Text:

Charlotte, 8:01 p.m. "Violet got out of surgery about half an hour ago. I think it went okay."

Brandon, 8:01 p.m. "You think?"

Charlotte, 8:02 p.m. "My mother is incoherent with drama. I cannot tell anything."

Charlotte, 8:02 p.m. "I'm talking her down so she doesn't fly out to Michigan tonight or convince my father to drive her."

Brandon, 8:03 p.m. "Should I text Eleanor while you're on the phone?"

Brandon, 8:03 p.m. "Also, I didn't realize your father was still around."

Charlotte, 8:04 p.m. "What? And yes, text her because I'm not getting anywhere."

Brandon, 8:05 p.m. "Done."

Brandon, 8:05 p.m. "You never mentioned your father, not even once. I didn't want to ask."

Charlotte, 8:06 p.m. "He's alive. I've already told him not to let Mom go to Michigan, but I don't know if she'll listen."

Brandon, 8:10 p.m. "Eleanor says Violet is really fragile, and it sounds like they'll need another surgery because they couldn't do everything."

Charlotte, 8:11 p.m. "Darn it. I was hoping it would be enough."

Charlotte, 8:12 p.m. "Well, at least if I keep my mother on the phone, she's not calling the airport."

Charlotte, 8:13 p.m. "It turns out, if I put her on speaker, I can spin."

Brandon, 8:14 p.m. "Spin away."

Charlotte, 8:25 p.m. "I need a sheep."

Text:

Brandon, 10:15 p.m. "Something awful just happened. I don't know if you're awake."

Brandon, 10:15 p.m. "PacerStudios' email account just got a message from Hunter Mattingly asking if I can meet with him tomorrow."

Charlotte, 10:15 p.m. "What happened?"

Charlotte, 10:15 p.m. "Wait, WHAT?"

Chapter Twenty-Five

No, this couldn't be happening. Hunter could not be here, not be in Brighthead, not anywhere near her. He could not have pursued her all the way to Maine, and he could not possibly still have the slightest interest in her.

They were done. Done. Hadn't she made that clear by blocking him, unfriending him, cancelling every vendor they'd booked, and then leaving Philadelphia? Hunter was a smart guy. He'd become a surgeon, after all. Stupid people don't become surgeons. By extension, stupid people should decipher those subtle cues indicating, "I don't want to talk to you ever again."

But he'd tracked her down. He'd tracked her to Brighthead, a place she'd never even mentioned.

Charlotte paced the floor, keeping one eye on the security system and Pepper near her side. Okay, think. Did he know her aunt and uncle's address? She'd handled the invitations, so probably not. She hadn't had a bridal shower, so his family didn't have the addresses either. Aunt Eleanor's last name was neither Charlotte's last name nor Charlotte's mother's maiden name, so he shouldn't be able to track her to the house.

But still: how had he tracked her here at all?

It was midnight. She texted Brandon, "I still don't get how he found me."

Brandon didn't reply right away. Maybe he'd gotten to

sleep.

No one would be awake now. She'd run down the list of every person she could think of texting, and every one of them should be sleeping. Aunt Eleanor, Anna, Uncle Gregory—all of them had gone through just the worst day today and should be conked out.

No, not the worst. Violet had survived the surgery, so it wasn't the worst.

"It's you and me," she said to Pepper, and she brought the dog upstairs.

Aunt Eleanor had trained Pepper not to sleep on the beds. Tonight, Charlotte patted the bed and got Pepper to jump up with her. "There's a scary guy out there. If he comes, I want you to bite his face off."

Unsure about this new protocol, Pepper sat tense on the bed, but Charlotte got in, pulled up the sheets, and put her hand on the dog. Once the lights were out, Pepper relaxed under her fingers.

"Why are you scared of him?" Brandon had asked before going to radio silence.

In the dark, Charlotte whispered, "He might talk to me."

She couldn't pin the fear down to more than that, and she sounded so lame. Still she felt hyperalert to the threat, terrified of his voice. Hunter would talk to her. His words would make her respond. Was he a snake charmer? Was she just his viper, easily manipulated by his eyes and his voice and then replaced in an airless clay jar?

Back in mid-May, she'd been fully charmed. Mom had "dropped by" for lunch one Thursday looking joyous. Charlotte had figured she was carrying another thousand pages of brochures and flyers for some wedding-related thing. Resigned to an afternoon of sifting through color swatches, Charlotte had asked Evelyn Aldridge for extra time. It was toward the end of the fellowship, so Evelyn agreed.

Instead, at lunch, Mom requested a booth and then spread

out a dossier on Hunter and his extracurricular activities. "I was just so worried about you," she'd explained. "I couldn't sleep worrying that my daughter was marrying someone I didn't really know. I had to hire a detective for my own peace of mind, and now I'm so glad I did."

The detective had gotten access to things Charlotte wouldn't ever have imagined it was legal to access, and yet there it all was. The other woman was a medical resident at the hospital.

Charlotte had met the woman at the holiday party. She was tall, slim, poised, and ever so friendly. By comparison, Charlotte was skinny, awkward, and uncomfortable among so many researchers and rich donors. Her competition for Hunter was the daughter of a researcher and philanthropist who had then become a doctor. Charlotte preserved textiles.

Charlotte had eaten nothing of her lunch while Mom had worked through her Cobb salad. Instead she'd sorted the evidence and then taken pictures of a few key ones. One at a time, she'd texted them to Hunter.

Mom kept saying, "This is going to be so hard, but at least you know now, not later," but Charlotte's brain hadn't been able to process anything. She'd drank a soda that tasted of exactly nothing; she didn't recognize her food when it arrived, and she ate nothing. Later on she'd call it the Cheating Diet: learn about the affair and lose fifteen pounds. While packing for Brighthead, it had been a struggle to find clothes that fit.

The wedding was six weeks away. She had a final dress fitting scheduled for the weekend. She was scheduled for a meeting with the florist, and they were supposed to talk to the DJ to let him know their first dance choices.

Well, she had a few choice songs right now.

Fifteen minutes later, Mom had finished her salad. The waiter hovered, wanting to know what was wrong with Charlotte's meal, but Mom soothingly ordering coffee and said just to box up Charlotte's lunch. Hunter chose then to text back: "Let me explain."

Her phone rang.

Mom said, "Are you going to talk to him?"

Accept the call? Send it directly to voicemail? Let it keep ringing?

She didn't pick up. Thirty seconds later, it rang again.

This time she answered. Hunter said, urgent, "What's going on?"

"What do you mean what's going on?"

"I mean what are you sending me all these pictures for?"

"You've been caught cheating," Charlotte exclaimed. "Those photos of you and Vanessa?"

"She's just a friend," Hunter said.

"A friend with whom you exchanged four thousand text messages in the last year?"

"I didn't do that." Hunter's voice dropped in pitch. "You are completely overreacting."

"How many thousands of dollars did you spend on your side dish?" Charlotte asked. "It looks like you flew her to Barbados for a weekend, that weekend you told me you were at a conference."

"It is not what you think," he said. "I can't believe you just leap to the worst possible conclusions!"

Mom was watching with a light in her eyes. She'd uncovered this. She'd suspected, and she'd been proven right. Now she was relishing the results of saving her daughter.

Hunter said, "You're always so negative and controlling. Why wouldn't I want to go with someone else? You never trusted me in the first place."

Charlotte said, "So you admit you were screwing around?"

Hunter huffed. "I'm not dealing with this right now. I'm at work, and if I mess up, patients can die. But do you care? No, you're always thinking of yourself."

In retrospect, that had been a mistake on her part. She wouldn't want a doctor examining her while distracted about the end of his engagement. She had just wanted answers right away, right then.

These weren't even answers though. There wasn't an explanation, nothing like an apology, nothing to hold onto. Hunter thought it was all her fault, and yeah, right now she *was* thinking just about herself.

Hunter's tone changed to encouraging. "I'll meet you tonight. We'll talk about it. We'll smooth things out and figure out where to go from here."

"Okay," she said. "Okay. Fine."

"At eight thirty, we'll meet at the Palm Tree Bistro and Cafe. I'll explain everything."

Her throat closed up.

"Don't be like that," he cajoled. "Don't do this to me. You mean everything to me. We'll get through this, and you'll see. We'll be stronger."

She agreed, and she hung up the phone.

Her mother leaned forward. "Did he admit it?"

He had, but he hadn't. He didn't dispute it. He'd only disputed that he was in any way guilty for lying to her, for taking another woman on vacations, for deceiving his bride.

Mom said, "You're going to call it off, right? What else can you do. This is a lot of trouble, but of course you can't get married."

Charlotte shook her head. At some point, her meal had left the plate and vanished into a box, kind of the way her heart had gone from being in one piece to being in thousands.

How do you restore something like that? Can you heat up a fine mesh and stick together a relationship torn apart?

Mom said, "Come home with me for the weekend. We can get everything settled out, although we'll lose a lot of money on the deposits."

At her apartment, Charlotte packed random clothing, unable to think about what she'd actually need. She emailed Evelyn Aldridge and said she was feeling sick and wouldn't return today.

When she left her bedroom with a stuffed duffle bag, she found her mother standing over the kitchen table where the finished wedding shawl lay on a rubber mat, a silky-silver square crocheted from cotton thread, airy as an autumn breeze, a design of leaves and vines, dotted with beads. Charlotte had soaked it and pinned it into shape this morning, the design stretched out to the point of torture so it would dry in the right shape.

Mom said, "You brought your work home with you?"

Mom thought it was something she'd restored for the library. Of course. Mom wasn't a handcrafty person. The only things Charlotte had ever crocheted for her mom had either vanished into a drawer or else gotten lost.

Charlotte said, "I'd just finished that," and let Mom think what she would.

Sitting in the car on the way out to Mom and Dad's house, Charlotte got a text from Hunter. "I love you, sweetie. You'll see. It'll work out."

She blocked his number. Then she went on all her social media accounts, one at a time, and blocked him on every one of those too. On Saturday, her mother came home with a stack of marriage announcement cards that said, "The marriage of Charlotte Fletcher to Hunter Mattingly will no longer take place." It was a mystery to Charlotte why Mom even bothered; she'd spent all day Friday and most of Saturday on the phone with anyone who would listen, gushing about how upsetting it was, such a surprise and such a heartbreak, but at least Charlotte was taking it well. Mom had all the cards addressed and stamped by Sunday night. By Monday, when Charlotte returned to work, Mom popped them in the mail. That was how Hunter and his family learned it was over.

What had he told them about her? Well, it didn't matter. Whenever she'd thought of one or another of his relatives, she'd taken a moment to block them too.

Charlotte had finished up her fellowship by working odd hours and commuting to her mother's house instead of staying in her own apartment. She'd left Philly without telling anyone where she'd gone.

So how had he tracked her down?

Worse, what did he want from her?

Text:

Charlotte, 12:07 a.m. "I still don't get how he found me."

Brandon, 6:32 a.m. "Do you want me to find out?"

Brandon, 6:43 a.m. "The more I think about it, the more I think I should meet him, just to get information."

Charlotte, 7:05 a.m. "I don't know. What are you going to tell him?"

Brandon, 7:06 a.m. "I'll act like I believe he wants to hire me for something. He'll want to know how to get in touch with you. I won't tell him anything."

Brandon, 7:07 a.m. "From what you say, he's unlikely to threaten me."

Charlotte, 7:08 a.m. "I'm not sure."

Brandon, 7:15 a.m. "I'm bringing my car to the shop now. Wish me luck."

Brandon, 7:17 a.m. "But I really think I should answer him. Tell me what you prefer."

Charlotte, 7:20 a.m. "Go ahead. Let me know what happens."

Chapter Twenty-Six

Brandon set himself up at a booth in the burger place and checked his phone. Five minutes until Hunter had claimed he'd show up for a "working lunch." The same words Charlie had used to describe ordering pizza for them while he put together her website.

Hunter had picked the time based on when his flight got in. Brandon had texted that right away to Charlie: "He's not in Brighthead. Not yet, at least."

She'd texted back her thanks, that she'd take Pepper for a run without worrying.

Charlie had already called the police and asked what to do if Hunter tried to get into the house. No, she didn't have a restraining order. It didn't sound to Brandon as though she even needed one, but the fear she'd expressed last night was so out of range that he wondered what else she hadn't told him.

If Hunter had hit her...? Brandon wasn't sure how he'd react. Charlie said Hunter hadn't. She was "just scared."

With a decent Wi-Fi connection, Brandon did a little more networking and checked his business's social media profiles. He ordered a burger and fries at the counter, took his little table number over to the booth, and joked with the manager of the cafe about updating the menus that had been designed while George W. Bush was still president. The manager took his card to give to the owner.

While Brandon was sending business emails ("Please? Do you have any work? Anything?") a message came in on his personal email.

Lighthouse Athletic Club.

Really?

Brandon opened it, and there was a polite request asking a question about the program he'd used to update the schedules and whether he could troubleshoot the calendar.

He hesitated.

No. They should know how to do this. He'd sent multiple emails to corporate documenting every step he took to keep the Brighthead online calendar up-to-date. Using calendar software they'd purchased before he'd been hired, in fact. They'd responded by sending him updates to every branch's schedule. If they couldn't read their own documentation, it wasn't his job to read it to them.

He deleted the email. Brandon had walked out the door because he didn't want to work for free. That included today.

Ten minutes later, a man walked in who matched the photos Google had turned up for Dr. Hunter Mattingly. Brandon waved him over, and Hunter slid into the booth. "Sorry I'm late."

"Tourist traffic?" Brandon said. "We hate it, but it keeps the state alive, so...yeah."

Brandon explained about ordering at the counter and having the food brought over. Hunter returned five minutes later with a coffee and a number stand of his own. Brandon put his laptop in his backpack and relaxed on the bench.

Hunter was handsome, tall and slender with a bearing that reminded Brandon of Cashman. What Cashman had in abundance though—the quick eyes and the air of analyzing everyone in the room—Hunter had substituted with charm. Hunter had style, and he knew he had style. The same with his education, and Brandon suspected Hunter had never budgeted forty dollars for a week's groceries.

Well, thanks to Charlie's check, Brandon could buy lunch in addition to getting his car fixed. Living the high life, right here in Brighthead.

Hunter made small talk while judging the cafe, and Brandon told him a bit about the area. *Oh, you're visiting? You should definitely check out the hiking trails over at Ingersoll Point. There's the LL Bean flagship store in Freeport if you want to take a drive. How can you leave Maine without seeing that?* None of these were places Charlie was likely to go, but each of the tourist traps would be happy to take Hunter's tourism money.

After he'd added sugar to his coffee, Hunter said, "Thank you for agreeing to meet me on such short notice."

"I was in town this morning for one of my clients." Brandon turned on charm of his own, a salesman smile. No need to mention he'd been leaving a trail of transmission pieces like breadcrumbs to follow back home. "It was easy enough to fit you in. What can I do for you?"

Hunter withdrew a tablet computer from his workbag, and he brought up a screen with Charlie's website. "I came across this yesterday, and it says PacerStudios designed it."

Brandon looked at the screen with a nod. "That's a standard low-end website design bundle, using a WordPress template on a hosting package the client purchases separately. The client provides the text and the graphics, but I set up the layout, the fonts, the links, the SEO, and so on, to match their branding."

Hunter had no intention of hiring Brandon, and Brandon knew it. Hunter said, "How long does something like that take to set up?"

Ah, so Hunter wanted to establish how long Charlotte had been in Brighthead. Brandon said, "I can get one of those set up in six hours if I have the availability and you want to pay a rush fee. What do you have in mind?"

Hunter said, "And would I have to consult with you in person...?"

He wanted to know if Charlie had been physically present in the area. "I work in a virtual world. Some of my clients have never been in the same state as me, so after you return home, we'd still be able to conference for website updates."

Hunter pointed to the screen. "For this website, did you meet with Charlotte Fletcher?"

Brandon recoiled. "Why would you ask that?"

"Because I want to speak with her. I've tried using the contact form on the site, and it doesn't work, which makes me question your website design skills. But also, it appears she gave a talk in Brighthead two days ago. Therefore I think she's local."

The waitress brought their orders and collected the number stands. Brandon's hamburger and french fries were nowhere near as elaborate as Doctor Hunter Mattingly's grilled chicken panini with curly fries. And yet, still enjoyable. Brandon paused the conversation to take a bite of his burger. Get some space. Keep cool.

When he swallowed, he said, "I'll go into the site later and test the contact form. It was working yesterday."

Hunter's eyes narrowed. "Does she live around here?"

"I'm not comfortable sharing any details about my clients other than what they decide to publish on their websites." Brandon shrugged. "If you want to ask her for a reference about me as a website designer, I can reach out to her and ask her to contact you. In the meantime, there are several endorsements on my page."

It was fun in a way, playing stupid. Pretending Hunter actually intended to use him for anything other than information. How long could Brandon continue being so dense that he never understood Hunter wasn't going to pony up the PayPal funds?

Hunter's face had darkened. "Look, I want to talk to her. It doesn't matter what I want to talk to her about. You need to put me in contact with her."

Need to? How interesting. Brandon himself felt no such need.

Doctor Hunter seemed like someone accustomed to obtaining the thing he wanted. He'd be a right old terror by the time he reached age sixty and had a few million in the bank, but right now he was just a medical resident, someone with a whole lot of useful skills and a wandering eye when it came to females.

Moreover, Brandon had what Hunter wanted. Brandon had (in fact) several things that Hunter wanted.

Hunter said, "Well?"

Brandon shrugged. "I guess I can send her your contact information and ask her to reach out to you."

Hunter said, "'Reach out' is smarmy business-speak for never talking to someone again."

Brandon paused. "Well, I won't disagree."

Hunter said, "Does she live around here?"

"I don't stalk my clients. If I can get the information right in my inbox, then why would I—"

"How did she pay you?"

"My standard terms are fifty percent deposit and fifty percent on completion." Perhaps he'd lessen the judicious stupidity and get to the point. "What's going on? Why do you actually want to talk to her?"

Hunter glared out through the window.

Brandon's computer was in the backpack. His phone was in his pocket. He'd paid when he bought his burger, so if things got heated he could just walk out. Hunter might follow him, but this was downtown Brighthead, where nothing was far from anything else. In this case, the police station was two blocks away. At least five officers worked out at Lighthouse Athletic Club and owed Brandon a favor. Hunter wouldn't be a problem for very long.

Hunter finally said, "Okay, look. She and I were engaged to be married. This weekend, in fact."

Brandon tried to look startled. "And...it didn't work out?"

"Obviously it didn't work out." Hunter stared at him as if he were a moron. "She panicked and got cold feet. Then she blocked my phone, blocked my email, and blocked everything. I need to talk to her and show her nothing's wrong."

Brandon gave a relieved smile. "Oh, that's why the contact form didn't work. If she blocked you, the filter would have caught any email sent through the contact form as well. I'm glad it wasn't a technical issue."

"That's not the point," Hunter snapped. "She made a huge mistake, and I need to talk to her."

Brandon dialed back his intelligence just a notch because it infuriated Hunter whenever he didn't read the subtext. "Ms. Fletcher only wrote that she needed a website. And she needed to be able to access it from anywhere."

Charlie hadn't actually done any of that, but it made Hunter look up.

Brandon rubbed his chin. "I got the impression she wasn't planning to stick around here. The website had to be up and running before her library presentation. That's all I know."

Hunter frowned at him. "So you *did* see her in person?"

Certain he hadn't said anything of the sort, Brandon tilted his head. "It doesn't matter, does it? You know she was at the library on Wednesday. Her payment cleared the bank, and that's the end of my involvement."

Hunter pounded a fist into the table. "Listen to me. Charlotte was very important to me, and she had a mental breakdown. I need to find her for her own good."

Yes, of course he did. Of course she was. Of course, of course, of course. Brandon said, "If it makes you feel any better, she didn't seem mentally distressed during the library presentation. Quite the opposite, actually."

"I read the write-up in the paper," Hunter snapped. "And you're an IT tech, not a psychologist. Leave the diagnoses to the doctors."

Brandon said, "Are you a psychologist?"

Hunter said, "Are you judging me?"

Brandon returned to his french fries. "Speaking of judging, you came in here with a low opinion of my town and the lie that you wanted to interview me as a potential freelancer. It turns out you have no intention of hiring me for anything, but you do want information. You've tried to cajole it out of me, charm it out of me, and now you're low-key threatening me. At every turn you've judged me for a dupe, but then you accuse me of judging you."

Hunter leaned forward, but Brandon shook his head. "Hear me out. Either you have a very super-secret project you want done, and you're making sure I would never betray your identity under any circumstance, or else you're a garden-variety bully with a medical degree. If Charlotte Fletcher really blocked your phone and your email, I'm not going to question her judgment. If you think she's a genuine danger to herself, it's your moral responsibility to go to the police and ask them to track her down. Police headquarters is two blocks from here, and in a town this small, they don't usually have a lot to do. I could have four cops in this diner in three minutes."

Hunter said, "What do you know about anything?"

"Almost exactly nothing." Brandon shrugged. "But despite that, you came to me."

Across the table, Hunter tried to stare him down. It was a good thing Brandon's conscience was clear.

On the other hand, he realized now why Charlie didn't want to talk to this man. Everything about his tactics was designed to leave you off-balance. The lies, the denial of the lies, the elaborate stories, the momentary revelations of vulnerability, the anger, the charm—minute by minute, it was difficult to tell which course he was going to take. For Brandon, since it didn't matter and since he'd walked in knowing he wouldn't give up any information, this wasn't effective.

For Charlie, who doubted herself and wanted to please, it

would be devastating.

Hunter said, "You know more than you're letting on."

Brandon kept meeting that stare. One of the nature channels claimed a level stare was a dominance thing with animals. Sure, why not? Because still, he had the thing Hunter wanted, and even if Hunter tried to beat it out of him, that would only result in assault charges.

Hunter glowered at him. "Well?"

"You wanted to talk to me about freelance work. It's clear you're not going to hire me, so we're through." He'd finished his meal anyhow, so he tucked a couple of dollars under the plate for a tip and got to his feet.

Hunter stood. "I'm not done."

Brandon was done. He walked out of the cafe, and Hunter didn't pursue him.

Chapter Twenty-Seven

Charlotte hadn't left the house until Brandon texted her that Hunter wasn't even in Brighthead yet. Then, a little safer, she took Pepper for a run.

"Would you rip out someone's throat for me?" she asked the border collie, who looked less murderous than excited to run. "Would you be a good girl and drive him away?"

Hunter couldn't charm a dog. Well, Charlotte hoped. Dogs can smell liars and devious people. Plus, Pepper liked Charlotte after these weeks. She still went mad for Aunt Eleanor whenever they video chatted, but last night Pepper had stayed in Charlotte's bed the whole time. Every hour, for every sound in the night, Charlotte had awakened, and Pepper had been right next to her, head up, keeping guard.

Sky Ridge Drive stretched around the highest elevation in Brighthead, and the wind raced up the hillside straight from the ocean. It really was a beautiful town. It had so many beautiful people. The shock had nearly killed Charlotte when her mother decided one summer that her daughter wouldn't go back there again. Instead she got Charlotte a job at the makeup counter in the mall. They'd gone on a cruise and a trip to Paris and a fashion show in Los Angeles. "Isn't this so much better than your aunt's house?" Mom had prompted as they nibbled on caviar and toast points at some gallery's opening night.

At the point where she'd normally turn around, Charlotte kept going. In her mind, the house wasn't safe. If Hunter could track her to Brighthead, surely he could track her to the house.

Brandon had offered to stay while she flew to Michigan. Maybe she should take him up on that now. Have him live here while she found a hotel in New Hampshire. Someone had mentioned the Mount Washington Resort as a gorgeous way to spend a week in a hotel filled with old carpet and beautiful draperies. She could go antiquing every day and bring restoration projects to occupy her nights.

When she reached the turnoff for Ebbetts Road, she and Pepper took it, heading downhill now. The farm had gone green and lush with summer joy, with portable greenhouses and rows of every vegetable Charlotte ever imagined. It felt like magic whenever she walked into the farm stand and saw the rows of tomatoes, the bouquets of basil, the fresh garlic stacked in the loft, or the bunches of onions tied together in the bins.

She walked onto the property to where a few cars had parked, hoping the animal smells masked her own sweatiness. Pepper had her eyes on one of the barn cats, but she knew better than to chase him. It took only one slash across the nose to convince her cats were sharp.

Jake Farnsworth turned from one of the bins. "Charlie Fletcher! What are you here for today?"

"I was wondering if you ever sell fleeces."

He brightened. "Absolutely! How many?"

"I'm thinking just one." Charlotte followed him into the barn. A horse whuffled at her from a stall, and she peeked over another stall at a goat-mom and twin goat-babies. "Oh, these guys are so cute."

"So much trouble too." Farnsworth picked up a garbage bag. "Here."

Well, that was easy. He walked her up to the front, filling a basket with things as they walked. "If you've never had fresh garlic, you need to. Your aunt is going to be so upset she missed out on it this year." He also gave her a bunch of garlic scapes, which she'd have to Google before she knew what to do with them.

Up at the front, Mrs. Farnsworth was stacking jars of homemade tomato sauce on the farm stand shelves. "Charlie! Good to see you." Then she paused. "What's wrong? You look upset."

She hesitated. "I do?"

"Is there anything you need, sweetie?"

Charlotte swallowed hard. "Actually...this is dumb, but you're right here. Can I have your phone number? In case I need help?"

Jake Farnsworth stepped closer. "What is it? Who's giving you trouble?"

Mrs. Farnsworth was writing phone numbers on the back of a business card. "If anything happens, you call. Call any time and we can be there in five minutes."

Farnsworth added, "You in need of a wood chipper?"

Charlotte nearly asked why on earth she'd need a wood chipper, and then she realized what he meant. She choked on a laugh, and Mrs. Farnsworth handed her the card. "That's my cell and his. If anything happens, you call. We'll get up there right away." She glared sidelong at Jake. "Not with the wood chipper. Nor the shotgun."

Farnsworth said, "Bonfire. Post-hole digger."

Farnsworth offered to drive her home, and Charlotte agreed because then she could get the cash to pay for the fleece and the veggies. It felt better having him idling in her driveway while she ran inside for her wallet. She thought about the wood chipper.

Hunter didn't need to be dead, of course. He just needed to leave her alone.

He hadn't wanted her before. Why would he want her now?

She showered, then spent the rest of the morning washing

a fleece.

Her phone rang at one, sending her stress levels right up to the top of the chimney. Brandon? Hunter?

No, Mom.

Brandon had texted half an hour ago, actually. "Met him. He's ticked off at me. Has no idea how to contact you. I left him thinking you moved on from Brighthead."

That was a relief. Maybe Hunter would decide to go on a whale watch, only it would be Moby Dick and he'd never come back.

"Hi, Mom!" Charlotte had a quilt spread on the work table, measuring the pieces that would need replacing. The speakerphone sat in the center of the quilt, an anachronism that felt comforting in a way she couldn't describe. History surrounded a palm-sized bit of tech that wouldn't last anywhere near as long as this collection of fabric and thread.

"I heard from Eleanor this morning. The poor baby girl! She died three times during the operation!"

Charlotte said, "Oh, that's horrible!"

Her mother's version and Aunt Eleanor's version of events didn't bear as much resemblance to one another as Charlotte would have found helpful. For example, she was pretty sure Violet hadn't coded during the operation or before it. Whether she'd had a crisis afterward, Charlotte couldn't tell. She'd have to wait for Anna to update Violet's Instagram story.

Mom said, "I can't stand being so far when everyone needs me."

The hair rose on Charlotte's arm. "You've been so good to Aunt Eleanor, taking over the phone tree like you have. I'm sure she's telling everyone you're a hero."

Mom sighed. "But if I were with them at the hospital, I

could do so much more."

Charlotte decided to play dirty. Literally. "I bet what they need is someone to take care of the house right now. They can't possibly have time to fold the laundry or mop the floors, with them spending so many hours at the hospital."

Mom hesitated. Then, "Your aunt always did have that woman scrubbing her house for her, didn't she? She doesn't like to clean."

No one liked to clean. For that matter, Mom had a housecleaner too, but that must have slipped her mind.

Brandon's mother had stopped cleaning for Eleanor after Brandon graduated college, on the grounds that it was too physically taxing. She'd found an office job where she didn't have to spend her days bending over.

Brandon had looked haunted when he'd admitted that. Maybe guilty. She'd kept the job because even with Brandon working part-time, they needed the money to make ends meet.

Mom said, "Does she still have that woman coming over to the house? The one with that skinny boy who got piano lessons? I wouldn't have taught him. I don't care how many toilets she scrubbed."

Charlotte frowned. "There's a maid service that comes in once a week. I don't give them much to do, but the place is shiny. They vacuum up the dog hair."

"I hate dogs too. So filthy." Mom waited a moment. "Maybe I'll just offer to pay for a housekeeping service. I'm sure they have those out there."

Hey, that worked well. "Such a great idea! Anna will definitely appreciate that."

With Mom's rundown of the past twelve hours as her background music, Charlotte continued taking measurements and making notes on everything she'd need. What she'd actually need was a field trip. She'd love to hit every antique store in the region and return with a back seat full of vintage fabrics.

She'd love to hit some of the local historical societies, for that matter. With Hunter in town, maybe she should plan a five-day road trip that would take her straight up the coast until she reached Canada, visiting every single antique-store-in-a-barn and hunting down fleece carders, niddy-noddies, lazy kates, and umbrella swifts.

When Violet's condition had been updated to as of an hour ago, Mom sighed. "Tomorrow should have been your wedding. How are you holding up, sweetie?"

Charlotte's stomach clenched. "I...it's not great."

"I'm so sorry I put you through all this, but I never trusted him. I could tell when I was near him that he was hiding something." There were sounds in the background. Charlotte couldn't tell what Mom was doing, although hopefully not driving. "I know you never appreciated my intuition, but I had to hire that detective to look into him."

This, again. "I'm glad you told me, even though it was bad news."

"I struggled for so long, thinking about what I was going to do to you, and whether I should keep it a secret."

Charlotte couldn't think of a single response to that. Well, not a single thing that wouldn't be unnecessarily nasty. Hunter's lies had undone her life and everything she thought about herself. She'd thought of herself as settled, as valuable, as loved. He'd thought of her as his game. Why would her mother willingly participate in making a lie of Charlotte's whole life?

"We should have been having fun tonight," Mom went on. "The rehearsal dinner, you and your bridesmaids having a final night out. And then on Sunday, you'd be leaving for your honeymoon."

Had they invited Vanessa to their wedding? Charlotte couldn't remember any longer which of Hunter's medical school friends had ended up on the guest list. He probably had, so proud of his ability to outsmart everyone in the room. What gift would Vanessa have selected off their registry? How about a pair of silver ice tongs, to go with her flash-frozen heart?

Mom said, "After you're done with Eleanor's house, I'll take you to Hawaii for a week. A mother-daughter trip."

Please, no. "I'd rather not. It would feel awful, like it was a replacement."

It struck her then, hard enough that she got tears in her eyes: her honeymoon.

Hunter was here now because he'd blocked off the time from work. He'd taken two weeks so they could spend time together before the wedding, then have the honeymoon, then a couple of days to beat the jet lag before he returned to the hospital.

She collapsed into the nearest chair. That was it, wasn't it? On his first day off, he'd been bored and felt outsmarted. She was a loose end he could tug. He couldn't find her through her social media or any of her friends, but she'd just given a talk to the Brighthead Public Library. He'd found her name in the news results and booked a flight to search her out. Her website was linked through the article, and at the bottom of each page was her privacy policy followed by, "Site created by PacerStudios."

Charlotte said, "Has Hunter tried to call you?"

Mom said, "I'd tell him to go jump off a cliff. No one hurts my daughter."

"Good. He's a monster."

A persistent monster. A monster who had his nose to the ground like a bloodhound and was searching for the tidbit he hadn't wanted when it fell off the dinner table...but for some reason wanted it now.

Text:

Charlotte, 1:55 p.m. "I'm beside myself. I just got an email from a museum in Bar Harbor."

Charlotte, 1:56 p.m. "They want me to make a presentation. They have a job opening and they asked me to consider applying."

Brandon, 1:58 p.m. "That's savage!"

Brandon, 1:58 p.m. "Presentation to the public or to their hiring committee?"

Charlotte, 1:58 p.m. "Good question! I can't use the same talk if it's to people who already know about textile restoration."

Charlotte, 2:25 p.m. "I just got off the phone with them. This is wild. It's an all-day thing."

Charlotte, 2:26 p.m. "I present to the public in the morning. Then I have lunch with the hiring committee. Then I make a second presentation to just the library board of trustees."

Brandon, 2:27 p.m. "Whoa!"

Charlotte, 2:28 p.m. "Would it be okay if you helped me again with the slides?"

Brandon, 2:29 p.m. "Absolutely. But don't pay me this time."

Chapter Twenty-Eight

If Charlie got a job in Bar Harbor, she'd stay in Maine.

That was Brandon's first awesome thought as he looked out the window at the driveway. His second awesome thought was to phone her.

Charlie answered with excitement. "Want to celebrate? How about dinner?"

Shame flooded through him, but Brandon said, "That would be great!"

Aria was fitting together big puzzle pieces. That was today's obsession. Puzzle pieces. If only Brandon could hand her the different parts of his finances and make her fit those together as well.

Charlie said, "I'll cook," and shame burned harder. He couldn't take her out. He couldn't take her someplace upscale, someplace she'd feel comfortable. Brighthead wasn't the culinary center of Maine, but there were a few places you could take someone for a really special meal. The jazz bistro had live music four nights a week. An old Victorian home about ten miles away had a maze of rooms with tiny tables and did a fixed-price menu with five separate courses (and a different wine with every course, including dessert). Afterward patrons could relax in the piano lounge until they were sober enough to drive home. Charlie would love that, and he couldn't afford it.

"Before we plan anything, tell me about meeting Hunter. What happened?"

"Pretty much what I texted." Brandon stretched. "He flew in early and drove out here from the airport. He saw your presentation in the news online and found your website through the paper. I designed your website, so he posed as a client to get information about you." He watched as Aria fit another wooden piece into its slot. "He acted like he wanted you to give him a reference, and he kept trying to work out if I'd met you and how long you'd been local. I told him you didn't plan to stay in Brighthead and I didn't know where you'd gone afterward."

Charlie said, "That's a lie."

"I wasn't sure *exactly* where you went after the presentation ended." Brandon leaned back on the couch. "And...you aren't planning to stay in Brighthead. Are you...?"

He wanted to plead with her to say yes. Yes, she'd stay. Yes, there was nothing for her back in Philadelphia. Yes, she wanted to endure the crushing brutality of a Maine winter on the oceanfront.

Instead she said, "Devious."

Brandon said, "No, he's devious. When he couldn't charm me, he tried to threaten me. That didn't work either. I also didn't trust him not to follow me, so after I left the cafe, I walked over to the police station. Did I mention I have friends there?"

Charlie said, "Oh! Did he actually follow you?"

"I couldn't tell." Brandon sighed. "I'd be a terrible action movie hero. But I know a few guys on the force, and I asked what you can do about him."

"And?" She sounded urgent. "Because Jake Farnsworth up the road offered me the use of his shotgun, a bonfire, and a post-hole digger. Oh, and a wood chipper."

Brandon laughed out loud.

"It's not funny," she said. "Jake Farnsworth got one look

and thought I needed him to murder someone."

"I get it, really." Brandon would have to indulge in shotgun fantasies later. "Typically what the cops would have you do is send a notice of criminal trespass. The problem is that in order to send it, you need to give the address he's not supposed to trespass on. Meaning he'd know then where you live. That would open you up to more danger than if he's not sure how to find you at all."

She went totally quiet on the other end.

"You can't get a restraining order because he hasn't done anything illegal other than be a massive jerk who won't keep his fly zipped. Nothing he did or said to me indicates he's a threat to you in the legal sense."

"Brandon, I can't talk to him again." She sounded terrified. "I just want him to go away. He didn't want me when he could have had me. Why would he come back?"

"I want him to go away too." Brandon closed his eyes, but he couldn't think the way that guy was thinking. How could a man have the love of a woman this perfect and then cheat on her? How could he not have done everything in his power to make amends right away?

Doctor Hunter had expressed a lot of things to Brandon over lunch, but not one of them had been remorse.

Quite the contrary. Hunter had told Brandon Charlie was psychotic and needed to be protected from herself.

"He thought of you as his property." Brandon kept his voice low, as if Aria would understand and be scandalized. "You escaped. He can't deal with that."

Charlie whispered, "I wasn't being abused."

"You were being lied to about reality. You were being led along by a guy who would risk your financial security and your health in order to indulge himself." Brandon swallowed hard. "That sounds like abuse to me."

Brandon wanted to be moving, so he paced the living room. Aria finished her puzzle, clapped at herself with a big smile, then dumped it out to start again.

Charlie sounded heartbroken. "I gave up on him."

Brandon said, "He'd given up on fidelity a long time before that happened."

Charlie said, "He's going to tell me I wasn't fair."

Brandon said, "Was he fair to you? When he was messing around with other women, was that fair?"

Total silence again. Finally she said, "Do you think there was more than one woman?"

Brandon didn't reply.

"What did he say?"

"He didn't say anything about other women. He told me you got cold feet and left him at the altar."

She laughed out loud. "Seriously? I'm just some flighty girl who scampered into the shadows with his flashy ring?"

Brandon wished she hadn't mentioned a ring. Another financial outlay he couldn't make. "What did you do with the ring?"

"It's at my mother's house. I should sell it and post pictures of myself online. Oh!" Her voice picked up an edge. "That's what we do. I'll start up a social media account for my business. You can Photoshop me into landscapes of all these terrible places. Have him go to all of them, looking for me."

Brandon laughed out loud. "Death Valley?"

She said, "Australia, where everything in nature is trying to kill you."

"How about that place in Russia where the reactor melted down...?"

"Too good for him. Farnsworth's vegetable stand on shotgun shell night. Do you guys have one of those axe-throwing bars? I bet a lot of painful things happen there."

Brandon said, "You probably have photos of yourself in Philadelphia. Post a bunch of them so he'll think you went home."

"Even better. I can put things online like, 'I visit Coffee

Calamity every Wednesday at one o'clock for my frozen hot chocolate! So delicious!' Then send the baristas twenty bucks a week in tips because they'll have to deal with him."

Brandon said, "The more important issue here is what exactly is a frozen hot chocolate? It's clearly not hot anymore, so it should just be frozen chocolate."

"That's such a good point, and it has nothing to do with anything." She sounded irritated, but Brandon didn't think it was irritation at him. "Are you sure I can't send him a notice of criminal trespass on behalf of the entire state of Maine?"

"Pretty sure."

"This is so not fair." She huffed. "I'm scared to leave the house. He might find me if I go to the grocery store. He's looking for me. I want to run away."

Brandon said, "You could stay at my parents' house."

Actually, she could stay here, but saying that felt way too far over the line. They were taking it slow. Granted, Dale would make Hunter pass out in terror just by squaring his shoulders. If it came down to that, Brandon's father was no wee slip of a man either. Neither of them had quite the finesse of Jake Farnsworth's shotgun.

Charlotte said, "I thought about it. I thought about leaving you in the house like you offered and taking off for somewhere he'd never find me. Except I thought Brighthead was a place he'd never find me, and here he is."

Brandon caught himself before saying, "I could stay there anyway." Because if suggesting she crash on his sister's couch was over the line, suggesting he sleep on her couch was so much further that you'd need a telescope to see the line.

She then explained about the dates and how he had time off from work for the honeymoon-that-wasn't. "I don't want to cower in terror for two weeks."

Brandon said, "You don't have to. He can't make you do anything."

She went quiet. Aria had finished her puzzle again and this

time left it, going over to the toy box and pulling out a box of plastic fruit you could cut apart with a plastic knife.

Brandon said, "Did he ever hurt you?"

Charlie said, "It's his voice. The way he talks to me. When he's talking, I believe him. It's only later that I wonder why I agreed. I was going to meet him so he could explain about the affair, but my mother was the one who said that was nonsense. She told me just to break it off. I didn't call him back or send him a letter or anything. I let him figure out for himself that he couldn't two-time me if I wasn't around."

Her voice broke at the end. Brandon said, "Don't be ashamed. He didn't deserve anything else."

"I stood him up. We were going to meet for dinner. My mother talked me out of it. I was in shock, so I went with her." Charlie swallowed hard. "What did he think after I didn't show up?"

Brandon said, "Based on today? I guarantee he was thinking about himself."

Granted, Hunter had no reason to express sorrow or shame to a stranger. When Brandon tried to imagine how he'd respond though...if he were trying to make things right with someone he'd injured... He wouldn't just demand a phone number so he could set that person straight on what she should believe. Brandon could almost hear himself: *Look, since you're in contact with her, just...tell her I'm sorry. Tell her I messed up everything. Tell her I understand if she can't forgive me, but I want to make it right.*

In Brandon, Hunter had a line to Charlie if he'd really wanted it. Instead the man hadn't even tried to lie about being sorry. Once he'd failed to manipulate Brandon, it had all been about coercion and self-righteousness.

Charlie said, "But he's thinking about me now. Brighthead isn't that big of a place. What if he starts ringing doorbells?"

"Gosh, I hope he rings this doorbell when Dale is home." Brandon laughed. "You haven't met my brother-in-law. He could bench-press Hunter, Hunter's car, and Hunter's massive ego all at the same time and never break a sweat."

"Jake Farnsworth still has that post-hole digger too…"

Brandon said, "So…dinner?"

"Yeah, maybe not tonight." She sighed. "My stomach is in knots. I'm worried about Hunter. I'm still worried about Violet, and now I'm just confused about everything else."

Moderately relieved that he didn't have to think about the intersection of romance and finances, Brandon said, "I understand. There will be other times to eat together. Just take care of yourself."

Text:

Aileen, to 26 members of the Brighthead Running Club, 2:30 p.m. "Who's free on August 1? Since we're not doing the Lighthouse Run, let's have a cookout at my place! Burgers, red snapper hot dogs, munchies, soda, bad jokes, cornhole, fire pit. Ice cream sundae bar after dark. 2pm to whenever, because everybody loves a good bonfire."

Cashman, 2:31 p.m. "Trey, you just show up whenever you want."

Trey, 2:33 p.m. "Very funny. But we'd love to have you arrive at 10 to haul tables around."

Cashman, 2:33 p.m. "No, I'm good."

Julie, 2:33 p.m. "Like Cashman can lift tables."

Cashman, 2:35 p.m. "By the way, everyone, if you'll check out the Lighthouse Run registration site, you'll notice the logo is the one they fired our friend Brandon for designing."

Cashman, 2:35 p.m. "And if you'll visit the Bright Hearts in Brighthead public Facebook group, you'll notice I just torched them in public. Feel free to pile on. Because everybody loves a good bonfire."

Text:

Charlotte, to Brandon, 2:37 p.m. "Um…did you see that?"

Brandon, 2:38 p.m. "Don't even."

Chapter Twenty-Nine

By Saturday, Pepper was getting restless.

Charlotte was getting restless too, but she didn't chew on the couch cushions when she wanted to escape, so her discomfort was of less importance than the dog's.

They ran on her aunt and uncle's property, since five acres gave them a decent lap to work with (even once she figured out a route that didn't take her into the pond or face-first into a tree). The lighthouse run would have been on terrain anyhow, so she counted that as good.

She sent a selfie with the dog to Anna. "Running for Violet."

Anna sent a selfie back with her looking intimidated by some equipment. "Pumping milk for Violet."

Her not leaving the house, plus Brandon not driving to the house, had resulted in a lamentable lack of Brandon. She could have driven to him, but every time she reached for the keys, she thought of Hunter. What if he was waiting for her? What if he was watching the house? What if he was watching Brandon's house, since he'd been able to find Brandon? What if he was just out and about and encountered her on the street?

She'd seen too many movies where the love interests met at random in a city of five million. With Brighthead one thousandth of the size, surely she'd crash right into Hunter the minute she went to the grocery store.

Brandon had texted her, "You realize I haven't come across him again."

No, but Brandon didn't have a bull's-eye on his heart. She stayed indoors.

Farnsworth's fleece was amazing. Saturday afternoon, she watched YouTube videos until she could work with the fleece carders and make the cleaned fleece straight and fluffy. She rolled the cleaned fleece into cigar-like rolls (the YouTube instructions called them rolags) and worked while the sunlight changed direction in the window and Pepper watched sadly from the gate at the living room entrance. The carder's pins stuck her every so often, but it wasn't too painful. At least she didn't start bleeding because blood would stain the wool.

Eventually she had a dozen sausage-shaped puffs, so she started to spin.

The longer she worked with the spinning wheel, the more the resulting yarn felt even. It took a while every time to get used to the motions, but her body was getting the hang of it. "It's like running," she told Pepper. "I need to get acclimated to it a little at a time."

Pepper's tail gave a lazy wave, and then she returned to looking pathetic at the gate.

About to finish the third rolag, Charlotte reached for the fourth, and a clump of unspun fiber slipped from her left hand through the orifice. Her hand shot out to stop the flyer—with all its hooks.

She didn't realize, not in time, not before a hook ripped into her hand, not without screaming. Fire coursing up her arm, she clutched her hand to her stomach, afraid to look and afraid to move and afraid afraid afraid. Hot blood soaked into her clothes. She curled around herself, wrapping her hand in her shirt and putting pressure where it burned worst.

Okay. Okay, think.

Think.

That's blood. The hand is still there. Direct pressure to

slow the bleeding.

Think.

Get into the kitchen and get the hand under the faucet. Look at it. Call 911 if you have to. But you have to move. First you have to move.

A whine...and then a warm muzzle by her ear. Pepper. Charlotte let Pepper nudge her, and finally she staggered upright. Blood streaked across the carpet, and the wheel was slowly rotating to a stop. She had to climb the gate because she wasn't sure how to let go of her hand long enough to unfasten it. Pepper just jumped back over. She could have done it any time, but Brandon said she knew not to go where she shouldn't. She also knew to go when she should.

Charlotte didn't even know where was the closest ER. Brandon. She'd call him, and he'd take her. Her phone was in her back pocket. First she'd get to the sink.

The cold water stung, but she finally braved a look. A slash jagged from her palm through the base of her thumb, bleeding like crazy, but direct pressure slowed it. She pulled off her shirt and wrapped her hand tight, then closed her fist around it. She one-handed her phone out of her back pocket and gave voice commands until it called Brandon.

Ninety minutes later, after a nurse had numbed up Charlotte's hand with three separate shots, a doctor entered the urgent care room. "Oh, that looks nasty." While he opened a suturing kit, he had her tell him again what had happened. "Antique?" he repeated. "When was your last tetanus shot?" Shortly he dispatched a nurse to get that for her too.

Brandon sat beside her, one arm over her shoulder. "The most important question right now is if she's going to sleep for a hundred years."

The doctor said, "Only if she pricked her finger on the spindle. This is a deep laceration in her palm, and you said something about flyer hooks." He had Charlotte open her fist so he could clean off the blood. "When it's gaping like this, you don't need a handsome prince, but you do need about ten stitches."

Brandon said, "Good thing, because we're flat out of handsome princes."

Charlotte swallowed hard. "You were joking about using super glue."

Brandon squeezed her. "Not a joke. I said if it were *me*, I'd have used superglue and then slapped duct tape over it. But this was you, and you get stitches. Or a prince if I can find one."

Charlotte rested her head on his shoulder. "You're a lunatic, you know that?"

The doctor paused, gloved hands over the suture kit. "Actually, that's sweet. He treats you better than he'd treat himself."

She analyzed the doctor's technique as he used forceps to push and pull the needle through the skin, plus the way he lined up the tissue to sew everything to its proper counterpart. He used tiny stitches and made sure not to overtighten. The doctor quipped, "Most people don't want to watch."

Brandon said, "She's got a professional interest."

The doctor looked up. "Oh, you've got a background in medicine?"

If she'd married Hunter, she'd be a doctor's wife. Today, in fact. Did Hunter make tiny stitches? "I do textile restoration."

The doctor tightened another stitch. "I can't compete with that. I'll sew up your hand, but I get my pants hemmed at the dry cleaner."

Twenty minutes later, they were in the parking lot, Charlotte's hand and wrist wrapped thick with a bandage to keep it immobile. It wasn't until they reached a pickup truck that she said, "Whose is this?"

"My sister's." Brandon helped her into the cab. "When you called, she threw me her keys."

In theory, she'd ridden in exactly this truck to get here. She must have been so out of it.

He gunned the engine to life, loud enough to hurt Charlotte's head.

She closed her eyes as Brandon drove, and he kept the radio off. Her heart kept fluttering whenever she thought about what had happened. Just one second, one stupid reflex. You shouldn't have to be told to keep your hand out of the flyer. It spins five times as fast as the wheel, so keep your body parts away from the dozen hooks. If she'd reached for the wheel instead, she could have broken her fingers. Why was she so dumb?

Her eyes burned, and she fought tears. Her hand had started to hurt, but feeling stupid hurt worse.

She should have been getting married. Married to Hunter. Talk about stupid.

Brandon's voice was soft. "You look like heck, so I'm not bringing you straight home. For one thing, you can't really do anything with your hand like that."

Urgent care had sent her out the door with a bag of sterile gauze pads and a roll of something to secure them, plus antibiotic ointment and a warning not to get her hand wet for at least five days. She hadn't thought about how she'd make dinner. She could subsist on yogurt and cereal for a while. Her mind wandered over the cereal aisle and her aunt's cabinets, the strangely shallow bowls that seemed of no use for anything liquid, and then she wondered how you wash dishes without wetting your hands.

When the truck's engine stopped, she opened her eyes and couldn't figure out where she was. She'd expected to pull up in front of Brandon's apartment, but instead they'd arrived at a two-story house with white siding and black shutters. The neighboring houses were close, so probably in town. Brandon opened the door, and out she slid, wobbly. The world felt distant and hazy, but Brandon had an arm around her waist, guiding her toward a wooden porch.

A woman who wasn't Brandon's sister rushed out of the house. "Get her inside! She's white as a ghost."

Charlotte went up three steps that didn't quite fit together and then through a creaky screen door. Shortly she was settled on a couch, and the woman handed her a cold glass of soda. "Drink that. You need sugar." Then to Brandon, "How much blood did she lose?"

"It looked like a lot, but she was fine at the urgent care center."

"She may be a bit shocky." Then again to Charlotte, "Drink it, sweetie."

She sipped, expecting the licorice taste of Moxie, but instead getting the bittersweet sting of cola. The fizz bothered her, but in the back of her mind she had the sense the woman was right. "Shocky." Was that a medical term?

Brandon tucked a blanket around her because the air conditioning was up so high she'd begun to shiver. Charlotte had more of the cola and set it aside because her stomach objected.

"You were right she shouldn't be alone," the woman said.

"I didn't realize how right." Brandon sat beside Charlotte. "Are you okay?"

No, she wasn't okay, but she could curl up here and let the world go on around her. She put her head on Brandon's shoulder, and he held her near while she let her brain wander around. Every so often he'd make her drink more soda, and then she'd return to her drifting thoughts.

Pepper had gotten over the gate. Smart dog.

She'd gotten blood on the fleece. That wasn't good. How do you get blood out of a fleece?

Five minutes later she realized she must have gotten blood on the carpet too, and Aunt Eleanor would be upset.

She blinked and found herself staring at brown carpet, not cream. Smelling Brandon's scent, her cheek against his T-shirt, her body sunken into a dark blue couch. Awareness returned, along with clarity. She reached for the soda again, and this time she was able to manage full swallows. Sugar. Suddenly it made sense, and she looked around, pushing off the blanket.

All the windows were open: there was no air conditioning. She'd been shivering in the heat. Yeah, that sounded healthy.

Brandon squeezed her good hand. "You're getting color back. You scared me there."

Now that she was coherent, she scared herself too. Where had he brought her?

They were in a wood-paneled living room with worn carpet and a couch that felt very sat-in. One corner featured an upright piano, and on the wall were a crowd of photographs.

The woman returned from the kitchen. "Oh, that's much better. If you still looked like death, I was going to have Brandon take you straight back to urgent care."

The woman turned out to be Brandon's mother, and the house was where he'd grown up. Mrs. Pelletier produced a pair of sweat pants for Charlotte to change into and then threw her blood-encrusted jeans into the wash. It seemed a given that Charlotte was staying tonight, and Brandon's family made everything fall into place. They set her up on the couch with a movie and told her not to get up; they'd handle everything. Mr. Pelletier drove back to the house and brought back Pepper. He spoke quietly to Mrs. Pelletier, who disappeared for a while as well.

At dinner time, they debated what to make until Brandon pointed out that if they threw steaks on the grill, he'd be cutting Charlie's meat for her. Burgers it was, and those bright red hotdogs. And sometime before dinner, Olivia and Dale arrived with Aria. Sure, why not make Charlotte's injury a family affair?

Olivia said to Brandon, "For one thing, loser, you didn't bring back my truck." Charlotte tensed, but Brandon only joked back at her.

The family absorbed Charlotte as though it were the most natural thing in the world to acquire a freeloader and her dog. For no reason, they all just stepped up. Worst of all, it turned out Mrs. Pelletier had gone to the house to clean her blood out of the carpet.

Yes, she'd been the cleaning lady. But that just wasn't fair. It didn't matter that she said, "Oh, I know how to do that." Knowing how didn't make it a requirement.

Still, Charlotte's hand ached, and it felt better not to have to do anything right now, just to collapse and watch Brandon on the floor playing primary-colored stacking cups with Aria. When Aria wandered back to her mother, Charlotte said, "Does the piano work? Could you play for me?"

For half an hour, he did. Aria helped by banging random keys while he cycled through "Für Elise" and the rest of his repertoire.

Mrs. Pelletier turned to Charlotte in between songs. "You're in pain? You look in pain." And then, when Charlotte admitted the ibuprofen wasn't cutting it, Mr. Pelletier rummaged in the medicine cabinet for the bottle of Percocet from when he'd had hernia surgery three years earlier.

I don't think you can do that, Charlotte thought, but everyone acted like it was so normal. Maybe that was just what you did...? Leftover painkillers prescribed for a different family member and quite probably expired...but no one was going to write a script for one dose of an opioid. And she was in pain. So she took it.

At Aria's bedtime, Brandon left with his sister's family. Mrs. Pelletier showed Charlotte and Pepper upstairs to Brandon's old bedroom, and Mrs. Pelletier even had a spare pair of pajamas for her.

Charlotte tucked herself in without immediately turning

off the light. There were still Brandon's posters on the wall. The Red Sox. Some wrestler known as The Baron. He also had a clock that looked like a cat with its tail for a pendulum, although it was stopped in a permanent frown at five thirty-five.

A breeze lifted the curtains, and Charlotte reached for the lamp. Hunter would never find her here, but Pepper got right next to her anyhow.

To the occasional hum of traffic, Charlotte relaxed into the creaky twin-sized bed. The family had enfolded her when she needed them, and she wanted to do something for them. Paying them felt like an insult, though. "Thanks for cleaning my blood out of the carpet and fetching the dog. Here's fifty bucks."

Oh. Her eyes flew open in the dark. Who said she had to pay them with money?

She had colleagues and connections. And tomorrow, after they brought her home, she'd have a whole day where she'd be doing nothing except sitting on the couch with her cell phone.

Chapter Thirty

Monday morning, Brandon got an email directly to the business account, not through his contact form.

"Dear Mr. Pelletier," it began, quite proper. "My name is Evelyn Aldridge, and I'm a curator at the Kist-Brannigan Museum of Fine Arts."

The letter went on with praise about the work he'd done for Charlie's manuscript, and she wanted to hire him to put the manuscript into their house style. That was easy.

Then she included two additional requests: could he format the other fellow's manuscript in the same way, and could he design covers for both? She requested an estimate of the cost and how long the work would take to complete.

Blinking, Brandon reached for his laminated rate sheet and started calculating. Why, yes. Yes, he could do those things. He'd never designed a cover before, but he'd figure it out.

While he was replying to the museum, another email came in, this one on his personal account. Lighthouse Athletics. Corporate Alex. Naturally, full of invective. What did Brandon think he was doing, disseminating lies about the club on Facebook, Instagram, and Twitter? "Everyone" was very upset that Brandon was smearing the name of the company that had been so good to him, but if he apologized in public, they might still consider contracting him for some advertising work.

Also, Brandon was a terrible person because the Brighthead branch had run out of towels, and who did he normally contact about the linens?

Brandon laughed helplessly. He opened a reply and typed, "Really?" but then deleted that. He typed, "You can't figure out how to call your own vendor?" Deleted that too. He tried again with, "I don't post anymore on Facebook, you idiots." Delete.

He closed that browser window and returned to Evelyn Aldridge, curator. He sent her a price quote along with his standard contract. If she signed, the 50% up front was...not bad.

Also in the inbox: "Charlotte Fletcher recommended you as a website designer. I was a classmate of hers at U. Penn, and I'm just getting started with my own career in preservation. (Wood, not textiles.) I was wondering how much it would cost to have a website similar to hers," followed by a few features Charlie hadn't needed to add.

Brandon went numb.

Charlie. Charlie was behind this.

He should be grateful and excited. A small business needed clients, and clients meant money. Clients meant the difference between continuing to rent his apartment versus moving back into his parents' house. It meant doing a job he loved as opposed to collecting tickets at an amusement park.

It was coming from Charlie, though. With her hand in a bandage and lots of time on her other hand, Charlie had sent a blast to her network. All the students graduating at the same time as her were beginning their own job searches, so they were ripe for references. Maybe she'd posted on an alumni board? Maybe she was just reaching out to everyone individually, but the effect was the same. She'd become his patron.

At the same time, half of Brighthead was up in arms about the gym, either on his side or the gym's side. People Brandon hadn't heard from since high school had shot him an email yesterday asking if that was really him. Yeah, because in a town of five thousand, there might be several dozen Brandon Pelletiers.

There had been two queries from people who'd seen the fracas (and the other logos Cashman had so helpfully posted) and wondered if he'd work for them. That was nice at least.

Everyone knew his family. His parents volunteered for everything, showed up to everything, helped with everything. The very reason he'd told Mom and Dad about Kelty's need was how often his mother brought meals to other families, organized funeral lunches, or showed up at school when a teacher requested volunteers. Cashman's outrage had unknowingly tapped Brighthead's river of gratitude toward his family. The positive responses on the public forum all had the tingle of justice: how could you do that to *him* when his family was so good to *us?*

None of this was about Brandon. Clients were emailing him because of Charlie. People were angry at the gym because of his parents' volunteer ethic.

Brandon carried the laptop upstairs. His sister had half an hour before work, and they needed to talk.

Saturday had frightened him more than he'd wanted to admit. Charlie's call, her panicked voice pleading for help, a drive in an unfamiliar truck with visions of blood everywhere—and then arriving to actual blood everywhere, her with her shirt wrapped around her hand and Pepper alert at her side. In retrospect, he'd walked in on her wearing jeans and a bra. He'd grabbed her a fresh shirt from the laundry basket, but it was all on autopilot. Even at the time, he couldn't have said what her bra looked like, not even the color. Much more vivid in his memory was the blood soaking the left leg of her pants. Mom had washed the jeans after Charlie had gone to bed. Charlie had thrown away the T-shirt-turned-bandage at urgent care.

"Don't scare me like that again," he'd begged after the

stitching was over.

Pale, she'd replied, "I won't show you my rotary cutters."

In the house, Olivia was dressed for work, and Aria sat in her high chair with a handful of bright orange crackers. Brandon singsonged, "Hey, babygirl!"

Olivia said, "Thanks! Oh, wait, you were talking to her."

Chuckling, he set his laptop on the table. "Here. Before I spend it, have August's rent."

She snorted at him. "Really? Last week you were doing calculus to figure out if you could survive on ramen if you drank the broth for lunch and ate the noodles for dinner." She took the check. "And your car. Am I mistaken that it spent five days dead in our driveway leaking blood-red fluid because you couldn't afford to fix it?"

"I got paid, and I have two potential clients who would cover *two* packages of ramen a day." Brandon sat at the table. "I may even buy an assortment of flavors rather than in bulk."

Olivia said, "I won't cash the check until either client pays you."

"You should cash it just in case they don't. That's just smart business."

Olivia took Aria's sippy cup from the cabinet and unscrewed the top. "I'm not going to kick you out onto the street."

"I'm not going to be the reason you fall behind on the mortgage and get the whole family kicked out onto the street. I was thinking," Brandon added, "if I can't make this work, I'll move out. You could rent out that apartment for real. And I could either couch-surf upstairs or go back home with Mom and Dad."

Olivia pivoted. "You're being ridiculous. Bust your butt and get clients. Go out there, beg for work, and do it. Forget your shame and your pride, and sell yourself. You're already planning to fail."

Brandon recoiled. "I'm not—"

"You're predicting rejection and the inevitable crash-and-burn. That's not the way to succeed." She put Aria's cup on the high chair tray and set her hands on her hips. "There are plenty of ways to fail. I don't need you in my kitchen cataloging them all. *Oh, and if Mom and Dad kick me out, there's an abandoned barn on route 186 that probably won't fall over next winter, so I can live in there among the fallen beams, burning pieces of straw for warmth one at a time.*"

Face in his hands, Brandon was laughing.

"Yeah, quit that now. You're the furthest thing from a failure. You've got a college degree and a useful skill."

"But—"

She slammed both hands on the table, and Brandon jumped. "Quit doing that!"

Wide-eyed and ramrod-straight, Brandon lost his voice. Aria laughed, but Olivia was staring right into his eyes.

He'd wanted her advice about Charlie and those references. He couldn't ask now. She'd tell him to shut up and take the clients, then ask Charlie if she knew anyone else.

"Pretend you're going to succeed for once." Olivia put the apple juice back in the fridge. "What would it look like if you assumed you'd get clients? What would you charge if you had a waiting list for new projects?"

Fear closed up in his throat. Risking a client felt...well, it felt risky. Without any kind of safety net, how could he jack up prices or make demands? Even the fifty percent up front felt pushy.

"Charge what you're worth," his business professor had directed, ignoring that no one could really know his own worth. You could raise your rates until people stopped paying, but if you didn't have people paying to begin with, you'd never figure it out.

What would change? Brandon managed, "I don't know."

Aria was holding her fish-shaped crackers up to her sippy cup so they could get a drink.

Olivia said, "You're hamstringing yourself because you're afraid."

Brandon protested, "I'm not afraid of failure."

She side-eyed him. "You're afraid of success."

After Olivia left for work, Brandon tucked Aria into the backpack and headed into town. She conked out against his shoulder before he made it even halfway.

How can you be afraid of success? That made no sense.

As opposed to the wintertime, Brighthead in the summer felt glorious. With the temperature only 85 degrees, the breeze off the ocean kept everything cool. Clouds drifted out to sea, and the trees stood stark green in contrast. Even the sky wasn't one solid blue. It grew deeper toward the zenith, whiter at the horizon. From the hills, you'd be able to see the ocean. In the center of town, you could feel everything alive all around you.

Snoring against his ear, Aria lay slack. "What does your mom know, anyhow?"

His sister had always been emphatic about everything. In a good way emphatic, but she was always right and she was always sure you wanted to hear about it so you could change your mind. Changing *her* mind, however, was not something she did. If that rent check got cashed before August 1, it would be because Dale cashed it.

Olivia had no right to talk about fear of success when she was the one actively sabotaging her own mortgage payment. Budgeting was about paying the most important things first. Hence, the rent. Brandon could figure out how to survive on eggs and toast, but mortgage companies showed less flexibility.

During midday, Brighthead's traffic evaporated into nothing. Brandon stopped at the post office to mail a past-due notice to a client, then continued to the auto mechanic. The guy looked pleased with himself. "That should keep it running for a few months," he assured Brandon. "As long as nothing else dies on you." Hah, as if. With a car this old, you expected vehicular death every couple of months.

He buckled Aria into her seat, but she awoke during the transfer. "You want to drive to the library? The library sounds good to me."

Just inside the library doors, Aria wriggled out of his arms and dashed through the foyer to the children's area. Aileen beamed from behind the circulation desk. "She knows what she wants."

Yeah, just like her mother. Brandon said. "I don't know if you heard from Charlie, but a museum in Bar Harbor called about a job."

Aileen bounced. "So cool! She's fun. I hope she sticks around." She leaned over the counter. "As you can tell, I had an ulterior motive."

"Dastardly." Brandon couldn't see Aria, but there was only one way in and out of the children's room.

"Speaking of which, if it would help you to give a talk, we've got a slot in a few weeks. Website design for beginners? Introduction to graphic design?"

Brandon blurted out, "Are you kidding?"

As if anyone would show up. Charlie drew attention because the afternoon library crowd consisted of sweet old ladies with overstuffed linen closets.

"I don't joke with library funds." Aileen ran her hands over the jacket of the hardback she was repairing. "Look at the list of professionals we've had. You're head and shoulders over some of them. Last year we had a podiatrist talking about calluses and a farmer who got so worked up about organic fertilizers that I felt filthy just listening to him." She shuddered. "But with that flame-fest going down on the Brighthead public forum, it would be great to have you talk. Think of the popcorn sales."

He shuddered to think of the nastiness Cashman had unleashed. "I need to make sure Aria hasn't pulled all the books off the shelves."

Aileen winked at him. "She's giving us something to do, and we want her to love books."

He found Aria at the train table, linking track pieces to one another so the anthropomorphic engines could go on a trip. Within half an hour the trains would be crashing face-first into one another, but during the track construction phase, they'd be safe.

On a couch where he could watch Aria, he opened his laptop.

Charlie had messaged him. "Boring day?"

He wrote back, "You got me two potential clients."

He checked his email, and after a couple of minutes, she replied, "Awesome! I hoped they'd follow up."

Then, "Which?"

"Museum curator and one of your friends who wants a website."

"Cool! Another friend wants his own logo. I told him you could design one."

Could he?

Yes. Of course he could. Get a grip. The whole problem started because he'd designed a darned good logo.

By the time Aria had finished smashing the trains into a ghastly railroad disaster, Brandon had finished replying to both potential clients.

Olivia claimed he was afraid of success, but was it success if he didn't do anything to earn it?

Chapter Thirty-One

On Monday, Charlotte learned it is not easy to change a bandage on your own hand.

Mrs. Pelletier had changed her bandage on Sunday morning, assuring Charlotte that she'd performed this kind of service many times. They'd sat at the kitchen table with a well-worn but clean dish towel spread out on the table, along with urgent care's assortment of bandages. Using tiny stainless steel scissors, Mrs. Pelletier had snipped off the old bandage, careful not to tug the stitches. "So deep," she murmured as she removed the gauze pad. "No wonder you were shocky."

Although seeing the gash hadn't upset Charlotte on Saturday when the doctor stitched it, on Sunday it left her nauseated, and even on Monday it left her uneasy-queasy. By now the swelling had gone way down. Mrs. Pelletier had slathered it with two little foil packets of antibiotic ointment, but Charlotte used only one. She tried to manipulate the sterile pad over the base of her thumb, but it kept sliding off. Pepper kept bumping into her, wanting attention and concerned by the medical smells.

"I'm scared," Charlotte said aloud, surprising herself. Scared of what? Infection? Hunter? Being on her own?

The roll of gauze didn't want to get back on her hand, so when Charlotte's cell phone rang, she didn't answer. Mrs. Pelletier knew some weird technique to wind the bandage back over itself and secure everything in place without tape. Charlotte...didn't.

"I should hand in my textile degree," she muttered to Pepper as she resorted to taping everything down. The final result looked like a mummy embalmed by an apprentice on his first day.

The call had come from Mom, so Charlotte called back.

"Why didn't you answer?" Mom said, miffed.

"I couldn't get to the phone." Charlotte gathered up the used gauze. "I did something stupid and slashed my hand open on the spinning wheel."

Mom said, "On the spindle thing?"

"Spindles are blunt. The flyer has two rows of rotating hooks that you shouldn't stop with your hand."

Mom said, "You worry me so much with all that dangerous equipment around."

"I won't do it again." Charlotte had avoided the whole room, in fact, which wasn't a good thing since she had a restoration project to complete and more on the docket. "For one thing, I don't want an impenetrable wall of brambles to grow up around the outside of Aunt Eleanor's house."

While avoiding the living room, she'd looked up the Sleeping Beauty legends. Brandon claimed there weren't any handsome princes in Brighthead, but with Hunter around, her story had a dragon.

"Well, Eleanor has a gardener. Let him take care of it." Mom went on without hearing Charlotte sigh. "Violet is having her second surgery later this week. The doctors wanted to wait longer, but they just can't, and the situation is dire."

"Do you know what this surgery is for?"

"Her heart," Mom said, as though Violet's heart hadn't been the problem from day one. "I'm just shocked that they can do cardiac surgery on a baby that tiny, but apparently they have very specialized equipment. Oh, and speaking of which, Hunter called me."

Charlotte exclaimed, "What?"

"He wanted to know where you were in Brighthead, and I told him to leave you alone or I would get him arrested!" Mom huffed. "What nerve. He never even spoke to me before all this, and now he expects me to tell him all about you! But everyone else blocked him, he finally decided I was good enough to talk to."

Mom went on about her hurt feelings, but Charlotte wanted nothing more than to pull down all the curtains and blinds, hire an electrified fence company, and phone Jake Farnsworth for firearms advice.

During a pause, Charlotte blurted, "Did you tell him where I was?"

"Absolutely not! It was the best day of my life when the two of you broke up, and I'm not about to invite him back into our lives."

Head reeling, Charlotte paced the kitchen. Her hand hurt. No, it was her stomach. Her head. The best day of her mother's life was the worst day of hers. But she had no time to process it because Mom launched into how thoroughly she'd told Hunter off when he dared to finally call her.

Hunter hadn't liked her mother. This was true. *Never* speaking to her was a gross exaggeration. He'd tolerated her mother when necessary. The same could be said for how her mother had dealt with Hunter.

Mom said, "Well, if he calls again, I'm going to tell him he has some nerve."

Hunter was all nerve. Charlotte was all nervous. She unlatched the living room gate. Pepper followed to the boundary and dropped to a sitting position, head straight up and eyes fixed on Charlotte. Whining. She wanted to herd Charlotte away from the wheel that had hurt her, but she wouldn't do it without a command.

Before the wheel, Charlotte touched the drive band, then extended her fingers to the flyer. It wasn't the flyer's fault. The flyer had been doing everything it was designed to do. It created beauty, but in its own way, beauty was the most dangerous thing in the world.

Mom had stopped talking. Charlotte murmured, "I knew he wanted to find me. He tracked me here because my name was in the paper after the library presentation."

She huffed. "He's stalking you."

He must have had a Google alert set for her name, to turn it up the next day. He hadn't found the Facebook mentions before the presentation, thank goodness. Imagine if she'd started her talk and he'd walked in the back door?

Charlotte breathed, "I don't understand why."

Mom said, "I'll tell him that if he calls back. He could have had you if he'd just been a good man, but instead he behaved like an animal."

Charlotte had been an idiot to fall in love with him. He'd been so sweet when they'd first started dating. He was so attentive, so romantic, so generous. Why had it changed? What had she done to lose all that?

Mom said, "Anyhow, I need to call a few more people about the surgery."

With the phone back in her pocket, Charlotte broke the end of the spun fleece. She slipped the flyer out of the mother-of-all, then slid the bobbin off the center post.

In the light of the kitchen, she examined the blood on the spool. No good. She unwound the yarn, wondering how far in she'd have to go before she found spotless wool, before the bleeding ended. Your heart could go like that too. You could unwind and unwind, and you'd have this tangle of yarn all around that represented a lot of ruined work, but when you checked again, there was still blood soaked three layers deeper.

Finally she broke the yarn end and reassembled the flyer. She might be able to spin with her left hand in a bandage. Maybe.

Her heart fluttered. Maybe she wasn't ready. Maybe she needed more time to heal.

Chapter Thirty-Two

At one o'clock, Charlie called. "What's going on?"

She sounded jittery. Brandon said, "Nothing. How's your hand?"

Truly, nothing was going on. He'd driven Aria to the grammar school to use the fenced playground for preschoolers. She was busy getting sandy.

"It's better. Hunter called my mother, and I'm freaked out."

Brandon muttered, "The guy needs to get a clue."

"She told him off, but still." Charlie sighed. "Brandon, he didn't want me."

"He does want you. He thinks he owns you."

"That's not true," she fired back.

The dude totally treated Charlie like she was his homestead where he'd put down five years staking a claim. It wasn't worth arguing. "He doesn't own you, and he doesn't deserve you. The sooner he figures it out, the better."

"I'm so fed up." She sighed. "I want to get out of the house. You took me on Saturday and Sunday, and nothing bad happened. I did nothing wrong, so why am I the one trapped inside?"

"I have my car back." It was good that she wanted to get out. Maybe she could stop being afraid of the guy. "Where do you want to go?"

Ten minutes later, he idled in her driveway with Aria in the car seat. She came out with Pepper, and they studied the layout.

"This isn't going to work." She frowned. "We can't put Pepper in back with her."

Brandon said, "Can you drive with your hand in a bandage? I can sit in the back with Aria, and Pepper can ride shotgun."

Charlie studied him as though he'd suggested they could tie Aria's seat to the roof and then he'd drive from the spare tire well in the trunk.

Brandon added, "Pepper would feel better with you and she in the same part of the car. Does she have a harness we can buckle in?"

Of course the dog had a car harness. "We're not going far," Charlie finally said by way of agreement, and shortly Pepper was riding shotgun, buckled up, while Brandon squeezed in next to the car seat. Aria, facing backward, giggled because she could see him. It was difficult but not impossible to drive with her palm taped up.

Eventually Charlie parked at the cove near the lighthouse. "The website said it would be low tide now, so this seemed as good a place as any. Plus, if Hunter were to come here, we'd see him from a mile away."

It took a while to get everything set up with the dog harness and the baby backpack, plus Brandon kept entertaining Aria by bending over and saying, "Up!" to make Pepper jump on his shoulders. Aria had embarked on a quest to have him do it a thousand times ("Again! Again!") but finally he strapped Aria into the backpack and ended the shoulder jumps. After a kiss for good luck, he and Charlie stopped at Myth Brightman's statue.

Brandon said, "We salute you for building your lighthouse in the storm."

Charlie added, "Thank you for being true to yourself. Even

if nothing about you is true."

The water lapped near the edges of the causeway, and Pepper kept looking longingly out to sea. "No swimming," Charlie said.

It took twenty minutes to walk to the island, and then they climbed. Charlie looked over her shoulder several times. Scanning for Hunter? It would be obvious if Hunter tried to follow them, but here was the fun part: if he started walking out on the causeway, they couldn't exactly escape him. There was one way onto the island and one way off. Charlie hadn't thought this through.

At a clearing in front of the lighthouse, Brandon set down Aria's backpack. She'd fallen asleep, but the frame stood just fine on its own, so he left her upright in the shade. Charlie turned Pepper loose, and she opened her own backpack to reveal it was actually a picnic basket. "Isn't this thing wild?" It had compartments for flatware, cloth napkins, plastic dishes, and a massive water bottle. She pulled out a pair of plastic stemware glasses which she set on a rock. They toasted one another, and then Charlie set out an assortment of mini sandwiches and snacks.

"You did this in ten minutes?"

She flushed. "I kind of started before you said you'd come over."

Sensing food, Pepper dropped to a seat, head up and waiting. Charlie opened a bag of dog biscuits. Aria slept the whole time they were eating, but Charlie had provided her an assortment of snacks too.

Brandon had to talk to Charlie about the referrals. Everything felt prickly whenever he tried to come up with the words, so instead they talked about nothing they ought to. She didn't mention Hunter, and he didn't talk about PacerStudios.

She said, "The day isn't as pretty as the last time we were here, but I love how quiet it is."

He paused to listen. Ocean swishes. Trees moving against

one another. A small animal crinkled over a leaf in the woods.

She leaned back on her palms. "I wish I could feel more at ease. Brighthead is beautiful."

She was beautiful. He reached for her hand, and she leaned toward him for a kiss he was glad to give. He tugged her over him, and they kissed longer, slower. Oh, to just pull her all the way onto him, the weight of her, the warmth, the breath, the need.

No, this was not the time. Not when she was hurting and scared. He sat up and sidled away, trying to get his head together. But she was so beautiful, so beautiful. Right here. Right now.

She tucked up her knees. "Evelyn Aldridge emailed me right before we left. She's pleased. You have no idea. Your work is so much better than what her administrative assistant cobbled together for the last ones. I'm trying to convince her to have you redo all of those too."

Sure, way to ruin the mood. "About that..." He'd never come up with the right wording for this. "You don't have to do that."

The breeze lifted strands of her hair. "Yeah, I didn't think you had a gun to the back of my skull. But you're a designer, and everyone needs design work."

He swallowed. "I just mean you don't need to network for me. You're sticking your neck out. What if they don't like my work?"

"They've seen your work because I showed it to them. I posted on the alumni board, and it's even been shared a couple of times." She looked up at the sky. "I'm just glad I could help."

Brandon said, "I appreciate it, but..."

She pivoted. "But what?"

"It feels awkward."

Aria picked up her head, and that was both a welcome and unwelcome interruption. Brandon freed her from the carrier, and she sat in his lap while she finished waking up.

Charlie said, "What about it feels awkward? I'm not telling you how to do your job."

"It's just—" No, it wasn't just. He couldn't put words to it, except he felt awkward.

Charlie put her bandaged hand in her lap and fingered the bandage edge with the other. "You need clients. I know potential clients. What's awkward about that? Do you not want to work with the restoration-preservation community? Or is it just that they came from me?"

Brandon swallowed hard. "I shouldn't have to rely on you."

"Don't be like this." Charlie tucked up her knees and stared out at the ocean. "You got upset when I paid for your work, and now you're getting upset that I told a few people how good your work was. Is this some kind of macho thing, where you have to do it all on your own or it doesn't count?"

Brandon actually laughed. "Macho? No one has ever used that word in relation to me."

"Or is it the misguided romantic notion that you have to suffer for your art?"

"It's not misguided that I need to figure out how to market myself," Brandon said. "You're not going to hold my hand forever while I try to figure out how to pay the next month's rent."

"Because that's just exactly how it works." Her eyes narrowed. "Two people email you for an estimate and suddenly I'm the Doge of Venice."

"I don't want you to be the Doge of Venice. I want you for you." Aria was drifting to sleep again. "You'll start resenting that you have to haul me along and turn me into a productive human being."

"Oh, please." She blinked hard. "I'm so sorry I tried to be nice."

"It's not about being nice. You're naturally nice. But if I can't make it on my own, do I deserve to make it?"

"Two clients isn't a career!"

He said, "I can't make as much money as you're used to."

She recoiled. "That's what this is about?"

Abruptly he felt shabby. He was wearing a T-shirt he'd gotten in high school, beat up sneakers, and jeans with frayed hems. She was classy and stylish, even when she'd dressed for hiking.

She got to her feet. "You think referring you to my friends is me criticising the house you'll buy after we're married? Because I expect to just get swept up into a six-million-dollar estate and cruise around in a Lexus?"

He said, "You're used to so much better."

"This isn't about my standard of living! Do you know who makes a whole heck of a lot of money? A surgeon." She was trembling. "I could have put up with a womanizer for a few years and then cleaned up in a nice divorce settlement. How about I do that? Marry the cheater, move to a fault divorce state, and let him use me for a few years before I sashay out the door with a generous nest egg. Then I can use my payout to support you." Charlie's eyes were blazing with tears. "I deliberately didn't bring up the subject of money."

"You *deliberately* didn't bring it up," Brandon shot back, "because you were thinking about it."

"Listen to yourself for once, okay?" She whistled for Pepper and walked to the other side of the lighthouse.

Aria wriggled out of his lap to pick up pinecones.

Right, Charlie had never noticed the money thing. Not the day she bought him a pizza so they'd have something to eat. Not when his car died and he couldn't fix it. Certainly not when she visited his apartment. Not when she mentioned stopping by Tempo Run to pick up real running shoes while he always ran in his regular sneakers. Not when she went to his parents' house—surely she never noticed even once in all that time that maybe there was a hint of an economic difference.

Or the fact that both his parents had been employed by her aunt. Now Brandon could be employed by her too.

Brandon got Aria's snack box from the picnic backpack (how much did something this unnecessary cost?) and Aria ate while playing.

Charlie returned. "I want to go back." She whistled for Pepper, but Pepper didn't come, so she walked off again, calling the dog.

"We need to get going, babycakes." Brandon put everything away, but Aria wanted to finish. Whatever. She could hold onto the box and spread crumbs down his back.

It took a while for Charlie to return, but maybe she'd gone to the head of the causeway to wait there. Brandon headed down in case she had, but when he got to the bottom, he found two things. First, Charlie was not there. Second, the tide had come in.

He hadn't checked the tides. Charlie had checked them, and she'd said they were at low tide.

Brandon fumbled with his phone, as if checking the causeway access would convince the ocean that oops, there had been a terrible oversight. Then like Moses at the Red Sea, the ocean would part before his phone screen and they could walk back to shore.

The lighthouse website had numbers, and yes, they were quite definitely in "causeway flooded" territory. The next low tide would be in twelve hours.

They had food, but seriously, that was not happening.

Brandon went back to the top so he'd have better cell phone reception. Who could he call that had a boat and wouldn't mind popping over to get them?

Popping over in about an hour to get them, rather. Because the tide had to get deep enough for a boat not to run aground.

He started texting. Trey didn't have a boat, but Trey knew everyone in Brighthead. Dad would know people. Olivia needed a text so she'd know Aria was safe.

Charlie reappeared with Pepper. "Let's go."

"We can't. The causeway is underwater." Brandon didn't look up. "I'm trying to find us a ride home."

"What are you talking about? High tide isn't for another five hours."

"While you're technically correct, the causeway is only open for the two hours around lowest tide. We can't walk back."

She looked startled. "Really?"

No, he was making it up because he so desperately wanted to stay trapped on an island with a princess who kept rendering judgments on his life. "You can look for yourself if you don't believe me. But we need a boat, and I'm trying to find somebody who has one."

Aileen said once that Trey didn't answer his phone during work hours, so he texted Aileen too.

Olivia texted back, "Brilliant move, Einstein."

He replied to her, "Aria has food, don't worry."

She wrote back, "You can starve to death for all I care."

He grinned. "Acknowledged."

Charlie wrapped her arms around Pepper. "I'm sorry. I screwed that up."

"It could happen to anyone. For next time, the lighthouse has its own website with the causeway hours. That's the best place to check."

"I didn't know! I'm just a rich flatlander who's used to having her butler check the tides."

Brandon lowered his phone. "You had a butler?"

"I didn't have a butler. That's called sarcasm. Just find us a ride."

Olivia would text Dale, and Dale would laugh and laugh... That was fine. This deserved to be laughed at. Brandon would be laughing himself if they weren't furious at each other.

An optimist would think, "Now we have time to work it out," but Brandon had never put much stock in optimism.

The lighthouse website had a contact form, so Brandon tried that as well. He called the number and got a voicemail. It was probably ringing in the lighthouse building behind him.

That was something. They didn't have to wait until midnight for the causeway to clear. At some point, the lighthouse operator would arrive and could ferry them back.

Charlie walked away while Aria played. They both needed time to cool down. Time walking the causeway would have been enough: physical activity, motion, and the shush of the waves all around. There would have been peace in the salt water, and at the far shore, he could have talked to her again. Instead, her misreading the tides had put another barrier between them because she felt like even more of an outsider.

A text came from Trey. "I'm asking around if anyone has a boat."

Brandon went to Charlie's LinkedIn page and followed her connections to a man who seemed to be her father. Managing director of investment banking at a multi-national bank. That probably cleared two million a year, but sure, money was no issue.

Aria started finding stones and making trails with them, and Brandon reminded her rocks don't go in the mouth. Instead of eating the pebbles, they built a little wall connecting a pair of tree roots to one another. There were lots of rocks on the path, so it wasn't hard coming up with enough masonry to keep them both occupied. Aria built a wall, and he built a tower, then set out what would be the foundations of houses. He set sticks in the ground as corner posts.

Pepper trotted over, but Brandon didn't look up until he'd finished another square foundation.

"Any news?" Charlie said.

"Trey's asking around."

She sat on the grass, watching. After a while he realized she was picking individual blades and weaving them into a square. Aria put out her hand, and Charlie gave it to her.

Brandon said, "Is that how humans figured out the whole clothing thing?"

"Reed mats? Probably. They're good for dirt floors." She stretched back. "See, I'm a source of useless information."

At least she was talking. "When did people start making clothing?"

"They're theorizing now that Neanderthals could sew clothing, based on the climate where they lived." Charlie pulled up new pieces of grass. "They used bone needles. So maybe a hundred fifty thousand years? Yarn likely predated the wheel. Drop a spindle and as it rolls away, suddenly you get a good idea."

Brandon said, "Could you restore a Neanderthal's winter coat?"

She didn't look away from the new grass mat. "No one's brought me one so far, but I'd give it a shot."

Was this how wars started? Brandon sensed it immediately: she didn't want to resume the argument, but she also hadn't let it go. He knew because he felt exactly the same.

Sometimes he heard Dale and Olivia arguing through the grate. They had a good marriage, but precisely because it was good, they talked whenever an issue came up. They disagreed about childcare for Aria, for one thing. If Olivia earned fifteen dollars an hour but paid ten for childcare, she was only earning five dollars an hour. Dale thought that was an insult; Olivia thought it was necessary.

At least with Brandon providing full-time childcare, it made more sense for Olivia to keep working. But if they had a second child, childcare would cost more than she earned, so they'd lose her income at a time when they needed it more. Enter the second disagreement: Dale wanted another baby, and Olivia was scared to make the leap.

Would Charlie understand that kind of pressure? Could she, when her parents brought in two million a year and had only one child?

He said, "Do you ever want to have children?"

"I do." She sounded subdued. "You're good with Aria, so if you're auditioning, you'll get a callback."

He said, "Where do you want to live?"

She didn't answer.

Of course. She wanted to live back in Philadelphia. Or at least in a city big enough to provide excitement. Here the biggest excitement was getting the septic tank pumped.

But then she said, "No one ever asked me that before."

He turned to her. "No one?"

She looked as mystified as he felt. "Hunter had his internship in Philly, and my parents lived there, and his parents. It was assumed we were staying put."

Brandon said, "It was assumed...by whom?"

"Everyone. You're the first person who thinks I can just uproot." Her brow furrowed. "But I could, couldn't I? I could stay here if I found a job. My aunt and uncle would like having me around for a little while. My mother would have a fit."

Her mother "would have a fit" about a lot of things. That sounded to Brandon like a personality problem, but given the interpersonal problems they were already having, he opted against mentioning it.

His phone vibrated. "Oh, we've got a ride. A guy on Trey's construction crew has a grandmother who has a motorboat."

Charlie got to her feet. "Well, then. We should head down."

"We'll see her coming." Brandon crouched down. "Pepper, up!"

Pepper jumped onto his shoulders, and Aria laughed a big belly laugh.

With their things gathered, he and Charlie descended the island, this time following the path to the east side where a pier jutted into the ocean. Eventually a boat idled up to the lower pier.

"Thank you so much." Charlie handed Pepper to the woman in the boat. "This was entirely my fault. I misread the tide charts."

"Not a problem, dear." The woman reached up for Aria, but Brandon only climbed into the boat with her in the backpack. "You're such a sweet family. I'm glad to help."

The boat's motor was loud enough to drown out Brandon's thoughts, but he could read Charlie's: such a sweet family. When he wasn't married to her, Aria wasn't their baby, and Pepper wasn't even her dog.

The woman dropped them off at a public pier half a mile from where Charlie had parked his car. Brandon texted Olivia. "Aria's back on the mainland."

Olivia replied, "I knew you'd figure it out."

Charlie had Pepper's leash in her good hand, but she was rubbing her bandage.

"Is your hand hurting?"

She forced a smile. "Yeah, I missed my ibuprofen. It's okay. It means I'm still alive."

"Surely you have other indicators."

She said, "This is the most constant."

Aria slackened against him, her head on his shoulder. It felt good. You have to trust someone to fall asleep on him. Was he auditioning for future children? He'd figured he was saving Olivia ten dollars an hour.

His car came into sight, exactly where they'd left it. Charlie said, "Are you going to be an idiot about this, or can I keep upselling your greatness to people I know?"

"You make both options sound so attractive." Brandon wouldn't look at her. "I can't stop you, but I told you how I feel."

"When the next person fills in your contact form," she said in a soft voice, "you won't know what they're responding to. You'll never trust that it's from the first post I made. At no point in time will you ever believe that they're residuals from the Sunday contact spree when I was lying on the couch grateful to you and your family."

Brandon could hear the pain in her voice. Trust. She, who'd had her trust broken.

She added, "Even if they send you screen captures of the initial post, you'll have no reason to believe I've stopped doing the thing you hate."

"Except that you're a believable person." Brandon reached for her good hand, which was currently occupied with a leash. "You've never lied to me."

"Not that you know of."

Chills shot through his gut. "What have you lied to me about?"

"I never thought Hunter lied to me either. But Hunter accused me of lying to him. He accused me of flirting with the guys in my program, the one whose publication you're formatting. I mentioned something he'd said at lunch, and Hunter told me I was leading the guy on."

Brandon huffed. "Hunter perhaps has a slight problem with reality."

"It's monogamy he had a problem with."

"Was it? Or was it that he wanted to be smarter than everyone around him, and keeping you off-balance was a way of neutralizing the threat you posed to his intelligence?"

She sniffed. "I'm not that smart."

"I beg to differ. He fooled you because you're a good person, not because you're stupid."

Charlie's hand tugged away from his, but he didn't release it.

"My mother said it should have been obvious he had wandering eyes. I was dumb to trust him."

Brandon said, "Then I'll be dumb, and I'll trust you. Because if the only way to love someone is never to fully believe them, then there's no reason to love them at all. I would rather love you and be deceived by you than anxious suspecting you."

She stopped. "Do you love me?"

Brandon felt abruptly exposed on the shoreline, the lighthouse island standing sentinel far out in the cove and the most wonderful woman at his side, hurting inside and out.

"I did say that out loud, didn't I?" He laughed nervously. "You wanted to go slow. I'm sorry."

She turned to him and stood taller to kiss him. He bent to her, and her kiss swept through him like the rising tide.

None of this was as it should be. She had the leash wrapped around one hand and he had his niece strapped to his back, and they were both exhausted. Plus she was still mad at him. And she didn't love him. It wasn't exactly the pinnacle of romance.

Charlie stepped away, sighing. "Then under protest, I give you my word that I think you're being short-sighted, but I won't reach out to more people."

"Thank you."

"If they ask who did my website, though, I'm telling them. Your info and logo are on the bottom of every page anyhow."

They reached his car. "That's only fair."

When Charlie pulled into her driveway, she was still subdued. "I'm sorry about the causeway."

"Not a big deal." Brandon smiled. "We got back."

She handed over the keys. "You've got to bring Aria home. I'll see you tomorrow, I guess."

She looked grey and distant. Brandon said, "Do you want to take Pepper running tomorrow morning?"

"My hand's hurting." She turned away. "I'll text you if I feel like it. I might just wait for the running club."

She went inside without kissing him goodbye. Aria stirred, so Brandon didn't go after her.

Chapter Thirty-Three

Charlotte knew before she knew it. Her animal brain detected a shift in the wind, a scent, a sound. Because as the door to Sparrows opened, she glanced at the entrance and saw Hunter.

She slammed herself into the corner of the booth, breathing fast, scanning for exits she knew didn't exist.

Julie looked right at her. "What's wrong?"

The first runners had returned, but Brandon and the slower group hadn't arrived yet.

Go away, go away, go away.

Julie scanned the room with her face a rigid darkness.

Cashman had his eyes riveted to the entrance. Shelly was ramrod straight. "What's going on?"

Everything in Charlotte wanted to hide under the table, but at least in the corner Hunter couldn't see her. Was it stupid luck? He was in town, and he had to eat. It was dumb to have stepped outside, but she'd been going out and nothing had been happening. Maybe he'd just order and go. She'd stay very, very still until he left.

"Who is he?" Julie said in a voice so low even Charlotte could barely hear it.

Shelly changed chairs. It was a strategic move: she'd positioned herself between Charlotte and the rest of the room. Cashman shut his laptop.

Julie stood, and then Hunter was right there before Charlotte.

Her lips went numb, and her vision spotted. Her good hand was clenched around her purse strap.

Hunter exclaimed, "Charlotte! At last!"

Julie stepped toward him. "Whoever you are, get back from her."

Cashman was on his feet as well, eyes drilling holes in Hunter's skull.

Hunter looked stunned and sad. "I've been looking for her. I don't know what she's told you, but I just need to talk to her for a few minutes."

Julie stepped into his path. "Does she look like someone who wants to talk to you? Get out before I call the police."

Shelly had her phone in her hands, but what would the police do? Hunter hadn't done anything illegal. "I don't want to talk to you," Charlotte choked out. "Go away."

"You heard her." Cashman's voice was louder, deeper. "Back up."

"Can't I explain? I love you, Charlotte." Hunter looked so hurt, so sweet. Her heart broke.

He'd been her everything for so long. They'd made plans. She'd poured her heart out to him and into him. She'd given him years of her life and had been prepared to give the rest of it too.

Cashman intoned, "I said back up. Or get thrown out."

He squared his shoulders at Cashman, who was marginally shorter than him. "Who are you?"

Cashman didn't flinch. "The second most dangerous person in the building. And you are not the first. She said go away. Back up and do not lay a hand on anyone."

Hunter turned to Charlotte. "Tell them you don't mean it. I've missed you so much. You disappeared and left me to explain everything to everyone even though I didn't understand."

Charlotte's voice broke. "I'm sorry!"

Cashman sidled in between them, which put three people between her and Hunter. Charlotte's ears whined. Don't pass out. Don't pass out. Where was Brandon?

Hunter said to Cashman, "Why are you being a pest? You don't even know what's going on."

"I don't have to know what's going on. There are professionals in this town who are paid to figure out what's going on, and I believe the club secretary is phoning them right now."

Shelly took that as her cue to call. As if the cops would come for this. For what? For a guy who wanted to talk to her?

Hunter stepped sideways so he could see past Cashman. "Sweetie, we can work this out. I'll do whatever I have to so you'll feel secure again."

Then Brandon was in the group too, and he had both hands in fists. "Don't you ever get a clue? Leave her alone!"

Charlotte blurted out, "He's not hurting me."

Hunter glared at Brandon. "You knew how to get in contact with her right from the start. You were lying to me the whole time. Did you think I wouldn't find her pictures on the club's Facebook page?"

Brandon said, "She fled five hundred miles to avoid you. She blocked you."

Cashman said dryly, "See, most people of average intelligence would call that a hint. You must be especially dense."

"This isn't about you." Hunter whirled back to Charlotte. "They've been poisoning you against me. Your mother did too, and that's not fair. We have a chance to work this out and make it right. I'd do anything to make you happy. Don't blow this chance. I came all the way out here to find you."

Charlotte teared up. "I'm sorry."

"You never trusted me. You were all set to marry me, and now you won't even talk to me?"

Julie slipped into the booth at her side and spoke quietly. "Charlie, he's manipulating you. Blameshifting. Badgering. Minimization. Gaslighting. These are abuser tactics, like he read the instruction manual."

Hunter said, "Don't try to brainwash her. I never hit her."

Cashman said, "Maybe you never listened to her either. You're outgunned, and you're too pathetic to realize it. Leave the woman alone so she can do what she should have months ago and obtain an emergency restraining order."

Doreen approached. "Sir, on behalf of management, I invite you to leave the building and not return."

Hunter spun at her. "This is a public location."

Cashman said, "And you're making a public idiot of yourself. It's hilarious, and I think someone's getting video."

Red and blue lights started reflecting on the wall, and Charlotte realized she hadn't heard sirens. No, you wouldn't hear them in Brighthead. It was still daylight, but the streets were passable. The cops would just cruise down the center of Main, leave their cars, walk inside, and appear threatening.

What if Hunter got arrested? What would that do to his career?

Hunter said to her, "Sweetheart, please. Are you the kind of woman who never forgives?"

Julie took Charlotte's hand beneath the table. "Blameshifting."

Shelly ran to the door. Cashman still had himself planted between Hunter and the corner table, and Brandon was right alongside.

Hunter said to Charlotte, "Unblock me from your phone. If you don't want to meet in person, unblock me and call. I'm not mad at you anymore. We both messed up, but we owe each other to work this out."

He spoke faster, and that must mean the police were approaching.

Charlotte choked out, "What about Vanessa? Is she

working it out too?"

"I broke up with her for you. Are you going to hold one mistake over my head forever?"

There were so many people around her, plus cops arriving in the function room. For the first time, Charlotte felt stronger. "Two people getting together multiple times per week to unbutton their jeans is not a mistake!"

Cashman laughed. "Charlie got it in one!"

Hunter shouted, "Shut up!" (which made Cashman laugh more) and then back at Charlotte, "She never meant anything to me. But if you'll forgive me for Vanessa, I'll forgive you for your fling with Brandon, and we can get back to where we were."

Brandon called, "Hey, Dylan! This guy," and stepped aside so the police could take over. Cashman smirked in triumph, and Hunter glared at him with violence in his eyes. Charlotte's stomach lurched.

Hunter turned back to Charlotte, all heart. "We deserve another chance, sweetie. It will be fine. You'll see."

The officer said, "Excuse me, sir, but we're going to step outside."

Hunter looked to Charlotte. "Her too. She needs to talk to me."

Julie said, "Just you, buddy. She's not banned from Sparrows."

A second officer appeared in the function room, shoulders squared, hands near his belt.

Hunter turned away. "They're brainwashing her. I am not a danger."

"Of course not." Dylan walked him out the front door. "It just becomes so much clearer that you're not a danger when you're in a different building."

As they left, Charlotte collapsed onto the tabletop, face in her hands. Julie hugged her, and only then did Charlotte realize how bad she was shaking.

Julie murmured, "That man is a menace, and his brain is a labyrinth. Don't ever talk to him again."

They didn't understand. None of them did. They all thought he was dangerous, but they only saw her overreacting. Hunter wouldn't hurt her. He'd broken her heart, but... But...

Brandon sat across from her and reached for her good hand. She let him take it, but she had no strength to squeeze back. With his other hand, he stroked her hair.

While Shelly was talking to the officer, Julie said to Cashman, "You put our names on the Facebook photos?"

"I tag everyone every week because it's a public page and we're a public group." When Charlotte picked up her head, Cashman wore a rare mortified expression. He said to her, "I'm so sorry. If I'd realized you were in the witness protection program, I would never have led that man to you. Your name was all over the paper and the library Facebook page, so I never considered there might be a problem."

Charlotte bit her lip. "I was scared he would hit you."

Cashman shrugged. "I wanted him to. I get why you wouldn't want a restraining order, but I'd have no qualm pressing assault charges."

Julie said, "Speaking of which, who's the first most dangerous person in the building?" and Cashman arched his eyebrows at her.

Brandon leaned across the table to Charlotte. "You sent him away. You did good."

Did good? She hadn't done anything. She'd collapsed like a house of cards in an earthquake.

Julie grimaced as Shelly approached with the officer. "Did you see the look on that man's face when he left? He considered this a flat-out victory. He's just figured out how far he can go without getting arrested."

Late that night, very late, too late, Charlotte pulled into 17 Sky Ridge Drive, relieved to see Hunter hadn't figured out where she lived.

Nice to be in a small town. Sometimes you'd look in the rear view mirror and all was darkness. No other headlights or taillights, no street lights. The only illumination was whatever your headlights revealed, and that kept changing as your car rolled along.

Not tonight. Tonight she had a police car escorting her home. Brandon had asked if Dylan could do a drive-by on Sky Ridge to make sure Hunter wasn't staking out the place, and Dylan had offered to follow her the whole way. If Hunter was on her property, Hunter would spend the night in the taxpayer-funded hotel otherwise known as the basement of the police station.

Charlotte put the car in the garage, then waved to the officer before shutting the garage door.

In the kitchen, Pepper was very excited to see her, more excited when she opened a can of food, and at peak excitement when Charlotte set the dish on the tile. The patrol car had pulled away. Now she was alone.

Hunter. Hunter. Hunter.

Brandon. Brandon had looked like a combination of distraught and furious. But the whole club had clustered up around her. If she'd been alone— What if she'd been alone?

The one thing she'd been most scared of in the world, and it had happened.

Charlotte grabbed the shopping list, but instead of writing "milk" and "more of Farnsworth's wild eggs," she listed the things Hunter had said.

Unblock me from your phone.
We owe it to each other to work this out.
I broke up with Vanessa for you.
Vanessa never meant anything to me.
You won't even talk to me.

255

They're brainwashing her.

Charlotte paused. You know what was missing here? "I'm sorry." "I was wrong." "I'll make it up to you."

The closest he'd come to it was "We both made mistakes," but really? She'd stood him up for a dinner date during which he'd have done the equivalent of hanging a framed picture over a hole in the wall. He'd conducted at least one affair for four months and quite probably longer. How were those equivalent? How was her slightest imperfection the justification for his most outrageous behavior?

Why could she not think of these things in the moment?

And his generosity in forgiving her fling with Brandon? As if *she* had cheated on *him?* Really? They were broken up! At no point had she two-timed Hunter. Why did he think she would cheat? Why was she never good enough? Nothing she'd ever done for him was enough.

The bell rang, and Charlotte went cold.

Pepper had her eyes riveted to the front door, and Charlotte didn't dare see who it was.

The lights were on, but her uncle's car wasn't visible from the outside. She could pretend no one was home. She could call the cops, who seemed eager for something to do.

Her phone buzzed. Mom. She didn't answer.

Then a text came through. "Honey, are you home?"

Charlotte's eyes widened.

"Where are you? Open the door."

"We were in the car for ten hours!" Mom said while Charlotte poured boiling water into the tea pot. "I was so worried. I knew if I called, you wouldn't tell us the truth. I made your father come right home from work and drive over here because I can't bear to see you make such a terrible mistake."

Charlotte glared at her father, who offered an apologetic smile. Of course. The only things he'd actually said to her so far were, "You look good," and, "Can you open the garage so I can park inside?"

Turning back to her mother, Charlotte said, "You talked to me yesterday morning. You didn't seem to think I was in any danger then."

"You're always arguing with me!" Mom huffed. "Is that peach honey tea? It's got to be herbal tea."

As if Charlotte would give her mother anything with caffeine in this state of mind. She showed her the box.

Mom said, "Hunter sent me pictures of you with that terrible boy. The gardener's son? And you're spending the night with him?"

Charlotte said, "Hunter lies about everything! Haven't you figured that out?"

Mom said, "Edgar, tell her not to be rude to her mother." She pivoted back to Charlotte. "There are literally pictures of it happening! Hunter said you were having a mental breakdown. I didn't believe it, but here you are telling me lies!"

"Then he's better at photomanipulation than I suspected, because I didn't spend the night at Brandon's."

Mom pulled out her phone. "Sweetheart, you're too trusting. The gardener's son is gold-digging and sees you as his ticket out of a lifetime of shoveling ditches. Here." She showed the first incriminating photo: the Pelletier Landscaping truck parked in Aunt Eleanor's driveway. "And here." The house, dark. Only guilty people turned out the lights.

The third photo was the one that made Charlotte angry: Hunter had caught a photo when Brandon had kissed her after their disastrous trip to the lighthouse.

Brandon had his eyes closed, even for a peck on the lips. He'd just told her he loved her, and she'd kissed him even though he was breaking her heart about the networking. Aria was in the carrier, and Charlotte had the picnic backpack.

Pepper was looking right at the camera. Too bad Uncle Gregory had never trained her to kill. Jake Farnsworth would have helped, too. "We didn't actually murder this man," Charlotte would have explained as Mrs. Farnsworth tossed another armload of firewood onto the heap. "Pepper just lunged, tearing the leash from my hand, and I don't want her to get in trouble with the animal control officer." And all the while Jake Farnsworth would have assured her that this was no trouble, that he held large bonfires every summer.

Charlotte took the phone from her mother's hands, and she messaged the photo back to herself, then swiped again.

The fourth photo was baby Violet, actually. She had Charlotte's crocheted bunny at her side. So sweet. So small.

Mom said, "Hunter told me everything, so you don't need to lie. We'll get you a therapist and maybe some kind of medication, and you'll see how much better everything is."

"I haven't lied to you, not even once. The only night I haven't been in this house was Saturday night, when I did sleep over at *the gardener's* house. Brandon wasn't there. He slept at his own apartment. I stayed with the gardener and his wife because of my hand."

Mom looked confused. Charlotte raised her bandaged hand. "This? Remember, I told you on the phone."

"You didn't say anything about that." She furrowed her brow as she took Charlotte's injured hand and stared at it. "Did the gardener boy do that to you?"

Charlotte pitched her voice low. "He's not a gardener. His father owns a landscaping business that caters to the most expensive properties in the area." Now she was lying: she had no idea who Mr. Pelletier serviced, but he seemed to do a few on Sky Ridge. "Secondly, Brandon is the president of a graphic design business. He orchestrates marketing campaigns for Maine businesses and manages their online presence." Another twinge of her conscience: she'd told Brandon she wouldn't upsell his business for him, and here she was, upselling to her own mother.

Mom said, "But honey, he's not up to your standards. How are you going to be happy out here when you have to live like an animal and drive ten hours to come home?"

Charlotte opened the silverware drawer. "Do you think a photo of me kissing a man means I have to marry him and live in a doghouse?"

Mom looked earnest. "Hunter is willing to take you back."

Charlotte dropped the sugar spoon. Thank goodness she hadn't been getting down the teacups. "Mom, you hate Hunter. You hired a private investigator to break off my marriage to Hunter."

Mom sounded delighted. "He explained everything to me. He's said he'll take you back even after everything you've done. He even sent me flowers."

With her legs pure jelly, Charlotte leaned against the counter.

She wasn't hearing this. A better explanation was that her hand had gotten infected, and she'd gone into septic shock. Hunter hadn't tracked her down to the runner's club, and her mother hadn't walked in the front door of Aunt Eleanor's house. Charlotte must actually be collapsed on the driveway, hallucinating vividly due to a brain-melting fever while her bodily systems shut down. That was the only way any of this made sense.

Mom said, "You shouldn't steep herbal tea for more than three minutes. It gets bitter."

Not trusting herself to take the ceramic lid off the expensive teapot, Charlotte reached for the napkins. She wondered where she'd left the cookies and when her hallucination would end. Her mother had just told her to go back to a man who'd carried on an affair during their engagement. She'd driven ten hours to encourage her daughter to live the rest of her life policing a man she couldn't trust.

Mom got up and removed the tea infuser from the teapot. "Honestly, Charlotte, pay attention. Don't steep the tea so long."

Pepper stared at Charlotte in her "herding" pose: body flat to the floor, head up, eyes never wavering.

Charlotte would have to do the same to Hunter for the rest of his life. Could she? She'd need all his passwords. She'd need location services turned on at all times, even though that wouldn't help if he hooked up with someone at his job. STI testing every six months and credit checks every three. Weekly searches to turn up any ho-phones stashed in his winter boots.

Mom said, "He even apologized to me for not paying me enough attention all those times. He said you get so jealous that he didn't want to take the focus off you. I can see that now, honey, and he told me he doesn't blame me at all for anything you did. I wish you wouldn't be so insecure, but maybe that's part of the stress you're under because of the wedding. You can see he's really a good man after all."

Charlotte blinked hard as she returned to the table.

Her hand throbbed in her lap. Mom got down the teacups and poured for them both, adding more sugar than Charlotte had ever wanted. Dad had pulled out his phone and was pecking an email on the tiny keyboard.

Mom moved Charlotte's crochet project off the table. "What are you making? You need to make me a scarf. I saw the most gorgeous scarf in Lord and Taylor, but you can make it instead."

Charlotte couldn't focus. "I'd need a pattern."

"I'm sure you could make something up." Mom sighed. "Hunter's right that you've always carried grudges. When you were ten, you were mad for months that you didn't get the Christmas gift you wanted. But it's time to stop overreacting. You can work this out. He said if you find a good marriage counselor, he'll even go with you."

"I broke up with him." That was reality. Even if Charlotte was hallucinating the rest of this, that was reality. The overly sweet tea was reality. The dog's eyes: reality. She tried to concentrate on the things she knew for sure.

Mom reached for Charlotte's injured hand and squeezed, sending a jolt of pain right up her arm. Pain was reality. "But you don't have to stay broken up."

Chapter Thirty-Four

Brandon woke up to a text from Charlie, sent at midnight. "This is a disaster. My parents drove up here. Don't come over."

A mass migration of rich socialites from Philadelphia sounded like just the thing Brighthead needed, didn't it?

Brandon lay staring at the ceiling for five minutes.

He had work to do. But he had no work to *go* to, and that was the strangest part of working for himself. If nothing else, he needed to establish a schedule so every day didn't start out seeming like a vast sea of nothing. Taking Pepper for a run every morning had gotten him out of bed, and right now he found himself limp with his phone in his hand.

What had she told her parents about that awful trip to the lighthouse? They couldn't have come because of Hunter appearing at the running club, could they? Not by midnight. Even if everything worked out perfectly, it should still be three hours door-to-door flying from Philadelphia to Bangor. But, no she said they drove. That would be what, nine hours? The timing didn't work. It had to be the lighthouse. If it had been about getting stitches, her parents would have been here Sunday night to take over where his parents left off.

It made sense she'd want to keep Brandon away from them: he was nowhere near good enough, whereas Hunter had checked all the boxes. It still stung that she'd held up Hunter's salary over his head. She could land a high-class, highly funded guy. Trying to turn Brandon into one of them was a nonstarter.

Standing in front of Hunter last night, it couldn't have been more obvious. Hunter with his expensive shirt, tailored pants, freshly cut hair, and total poise. And Brandon: sweaty and threadbare. Who would any sane woman choose?

Brandon finally got out of bed and poured cereal into a bowl. He needed a schedule. At ten o'clock he'd take over with Aria, but four hours was too long to wallow in self-pity. He jotted a schedule on the back of a junk mail envelope while eating cornflakes.

- 10 minutes: wallow in self pity
- 5 minutes: check social media for business leads
- 5 minutes: check business email
- 30 minutes: answer business correspondence (adding 15-minute blocks as required)
- 30 minutes: read up on techniques to land new clients
- 10 minutes: list possible techniques and come up with a plan for implementing the most likely

The to-do list grew as more ideas came, and Brandon eventually separated self-pity into two separate five-minute blocks rather than one ten-minute block, as smaller doses seemed more useful. After checking off prosaic details like washing his cereal bowl and showering, he got started.

There was another restoration client in his inbox, asking if he had a starter package for a beginning business and what kind of payment plans he accepted.

A business starter package... That actually... That sounded like a great idea.

PacerStudios could bundle a basic website with a contact form, logo design, color palette, business card layout, and one type of "swag" like a postcard or bookmark. Yes, sir, I have a payment plan: half up front, half on completion. (Brandon had learned a new trick too: offer a discount for paying within thirty days of the invoice rather than a surcharge for paying late. Incentivize the behavior you want to see. Apparently you needed psychology to run a business.)

Speaking of psychology, Charlie had said he'd never trust that she wasn't still pushing his business. That hurt. She'd never done anything to make him not trust her. Or did that mean *she* had no trust in *him*?

He reached over to his list and checked off the first self-pity box. He was burning right through that to-do list.

By the time he had to take over Aria's care, Brandon had everything knocked off, plus items he'd done and then added to the list. He'd accidentally wandered into the second self-pity task, but he'd avoided adding a third. His website now had a page for a small business starter package with its own special payment schedule (to accommodate for low cash flow), and he directed his new contact there. He also included a quick mock-up of a sample logo and how it would look on a sample banner and a sample business card. "Capture their imagination!" the marketing article had urged.

He'd left the gym because they wanted free work, but apparently free samples would always play a role. Go figure. Brandon's middle name must be Karma.

Upstairs, his check had vanished from Olivia's fridge, meaning Dale had seen it. Aria dragged him by the hand to the couch to read, and that ended his first four hours of work. She'd picked a book about a dog who kept behaving badly. Finally she said, "Pep."

"We won't be seeing Pepper today, kiddo."

"Pep," she repeated, a frown gouged into her brow.

Gathering up her purse and phone, Olivia laughed out loud. "Well, she told you."

"I can't just kidnap Charlie's dog." He squeezed Aria to his side. "Maybe tomorrow."

Maybe by tomorrow Charlie's family would have shoved her in the back of their car and driven her away from

Brighthead to protect her from Hunter's claws.

Maybe by tomorrow, Hunter would have gotten back to Charlie again and convinced her to give his wandering heart another try.

Too many maybes. Brandon had run out of self-pity boxes on his to-do list though, so he reached for another picture book.

Aria had a seldom-used stroller, and Brighthead had a few seldom-maintained sidewalks. In town you could push a kid around without risking her life, but the further you got into the willie-wacks, the more the roads turned into narrow cowpaths with dirt right up to the edge of the blacktop. There was little visibility and lots of speeding. He'd taken Aria for a jog in the stroller once. Once.

Today he packed her and the stroller into his car and drove to the Audubon Society preserve. They didn't have great paths, but Olivia's stroller had big wheels with treads. Aria laughed harder when it was bumpier. He dropped a dollar in the donation box and took her for a jog.

There had been a woman pushing a pair of year-old twins at Kelty's 5K. She had to have been rolling fifty pounds between the kids and the stroller, and Brandon hadn't appreciated that act of superhumanity. He'd been manning the refreshment station, so he'd just offered the kids bananas.

At the far end of the trail was a pond where Brandon removed Aria to look at the beavers. She'd destroyed a graham cracker in the seat, and he picked out the pieces. Declaring, "Let the shameless begging commence!" he tossed them onto the water. Fish darted to the surface, snapping at all the crumbs. Dozens more gathered, watching for any other crumbs...and more fish...and more fish. Aria laughed loud enough to scare the birds.

When they ran out of crumbs and the fish ran out of enlightened self-interest, Brandon jogged them back to the parking lot. By then Aria had fallen asleep.

Rule One of caring for his niece was not to wake a sleeping baby, so Brandon grabbed another water bottle and stuck it in the cup holder, then took the stroller onto the road. There wasn't much to do outside of town, but there was one place.

Half a mile up from the nature preserve was a cemetery. Brandon stuck to the shoulder and turned in at the cemetery's first entrance. He'd been here often enough that he knew exactly which paths to navigate, starting from the 1800s graves near the front and working his way toward the back. In three minutes he stood in the newest part of the cemetery before a fresh stone. Kelty Duncan.

"Hey, there." He parked the stroller's brakes. "It's been a while."

A row of tulips grew in front of the headstone. Five of the six were yellow, but one had inexplicably bloomed red. Kelty would have found that funny. If Aileen had been here recently, she'd wonder if that was a sign.

It wasn't. Just a dumb mistake. Brandon sat on the grass over the grave and craned back his neck, feeling the breeze against his skin.

In March, he'd asked Mrs. Duncan for permission to plant flowers. She'd agreed, and Brandon had spent an afternoon researching bulbs from the Lighthouse front desk. He knew from his father that you could plant bulbs on top of one another, and if you planned it well, you could have a cascade of flowers coming up one after the next all summer. Snow drops on top, shallow. Crocuses beneath. Daffodils below those. Tulips on the bottom. He'd come out with a spade and a map showing all the best depths, plus flower food and enriched soil. "You'll like what I come up with," he'd promised Kelty's mother.

It was the last thing he could do for Kelty, who'd never wanted him to do anything for her in the first place.

"You were so stubborn," he said to Kelty. "I don't understand why you balked at everything. We'd be in the same position right now, but I could have been a part of your life. You were making something of yourself. I knew you could do it. But at least your mother let me give you flowers at the end. I'm sorry one of them turned out to be the wrong color."

There's no way of knowing, of course. If you're at the garden center pulling bulbs from the bins, you're trusting everything was properly sorted from the start. A red bulb and a yellow bulb look the same in your hand, look the same when they sprout, and only show their colors when they open.

"Remember Charlie? I'm kind of with her now. Although I don't know. We had a fight and now we might not be together. She dumped the last guy without saying anything either."

A car passed on the state route but didn't pull in. The place was so quiet, but not eerie. In the early days, he'd visited some mornings with a blanket and a thermal mug of coffee, just letting the silent winter rip through him. But after a twenty-four-inch snowfall, he couldn't get in, at least not until someone died and the caretakers plowed again to do the burial.

"I'm sorry about the red flower. I hope you don't mind. If I remember next year which one it is, I can pull it up and replace it. Although with everything planted on top, that might be a disaster."

How much of life was like that? The stuff you put in first wasn't something you understood, at least not for a while. Everything came in above it, growing and spreading out, and then if you needed to change it, there was too much of a tangle. Right now there would be crocus roots and new bulbs snarled in with them, and everything could get disturbed and maybe not bloom again. All to correct one mistake.

"Was it all a mistake?" Brandon modulated his voice to

blend with the rustle of the trees in the sea breeze. "I think you made a mistake, but you'd never have believed it. We should have been together, even if only for a handful of years. You just couldn't admit you were wrong. Your family needed help. There wasn't anything shameful in accepting what we freely offered."

Dad said that to him one night in the truck after plowing. Brandon's hands and feet were frozen solid, and his cheeks stung. The lashing snow, the wind, the chill—he was miserable, and he would have to split his tips with Kelty.

Dad said, "We're all in this together. You sacrificed a little for her, but what she got back was more."

A petulant fifteen-year-old, Brandon had snarled, "I know that. I did it for her."

Dad said, "You're not doing it for her. You're doing it because it's the right thing to do. Tomorrow morning, you get to look in the mirror and know you helped someone."

Brandon still burned with shame when he remembered what he said next. "And what does she give me?"

Dad's answer was gentle, not shaming. "She gives you the chance to be the kind of person you ought to be."

A lot of people called his father "Dad." Dale had done it when he first started showing up. And in response, Dad had treated a lot of his and Olivia's friends like kids of his own. That meant sharing meals around their table. That meant showing up to their honors ceremonies or their ball games.

Not Kelty, though. Kelty had said, "I have a father, and he's a jerk."

"You wouldn't accept anything," Brandon told Kelty.

Charlie...? Was Charlie networking because she loved him, or was she doing it because she thought it the right thing? When she looked in the mirror, did she say, "I helped someone"?

Was Brandon Charlie's chance to be the kind of person she ought to be?

Brandon's hands tightened into fists. "Is this your revenge? Because Karma is my new middle name. I didn't realize when we were growing up that my family was poor, but because of you I figured out the difference between dirt poor and piss poor. Am I doing the same thing to Charlie that you did to me?"

Brandon closed his eyes. He shouldn't think it. But he had to think about it because if that was true, he was being unfair to Charlie.

We're all in it together.

Charlie wasn't ashamed of him. She just wanted to help. She wasn't saying he couldn't do it. By her actions, she was saying he could.

"I hate this," Brandon told Kelty. "I hate what you did to me, and I hate that you died after doing it."

Chapter Thirty-Five

On Wednesday morning, Mom complained that she hadn't slept at all last night. It was too quiet here, too isolated, too dark. The guest bedroom was too uncomfortable and didn't even have a private bathroom attached. The sun rose too early. Then she demanded Charlotte give them a tour of Brighthead.

Charlotte delayed by taking Pepper for a run, but she ran scared the whole time and cut it short.

Hunter had found her even here. He'd gotten photos of the house with Mr. Pelletier's truck in the driveway, and he'd watched long enough to know she hadn't come home Saturday night. If he wasn't watching her now, it was only that he'd planned something worse.

She'd missed Hunter so much in the early days. Mom had sat beside Charlotte while she blocked his number and deleted all his text messages, but in those messages had been so much of herself. Sure, there'd been things like, "Hey, want to meet for lunch?" but there were also conversations after a hard day, the funny photos, the I-love-yous.

He'd sent gifts and cards to her apartment after she found out about Vanessa. There'd been a note from the apartment office about a bouquet of two dozen red roses. She told the apartment office to keep them. Roses had arrived at her mother's as well.

Hunter had loved her once. He'd showered her with attention until she'd lost his attention by being less interesting and less pretty and less of a conversationalist. Hunter used to surprise her with tickets to shows they could see together. He'd randomly pull a jewelry box from his pocket to wait for her delighted thanks. He'd written the sweetest letters in the early weeks, romantic and perfect and thoughtful, always leaving her breathless with wonder that she could deserve someone as perfect as he was.

There wasn't a day it had stopped. Or was there? On an early date she'd made a disparaging remark about a restaurant, and he'd gotten offended. She'd learned to keep her criticisms to herself, but surely he could figure out when she didn't approve of something. Over time, her judgments might have extinguished the fire.

Vanessa doubtless agreed with everything.

Back at the house, Charlotte walked in to find a bouquet on the kitchen table, abounding with roses and lilies. Mom said, "Look what he sent! I told you he loved you!"

Mom boomeranged right back to demanding a tour of Brighthead, so Charlotte showered, changed into shorts and a T-shirt, and got into their car with Dad driving and Mom in the front. Charlotte directed them to the lighthouse, right to the statue of Myth Brightman.

With Brandon, the statue had been funnier the longer they'd looked at it. She'd taken selfies and laughed until she'd cried, but with her parents, it was just a statue.

Her father said, "This sounds like an amazing woman."

Charlotte didn't bother sharing the best part of the story. She limited her reply to, "I was certainly amazed when I learned about her."

Mom didn't want to walk on rocks and sand. After their obligatory photos with the statue of fakery, Charlotte navigated back to the center of town.

She couldn't think of where else to take them. Not to

Bright Stitches. The library? The town square? What would her mother think of the almost-but-not-quite antiques? There were two overpriced gift shops. Charlotte directed her parents to the fancier one, the one that reeked of patchouli and sold glittery things that chimed in the wind.

Shopping with her mother...was not fun. Last night Mom had accused her of holding grudges over a Christmas gift. Her tenth Christmas, to be exact. In September, Charlotte had begged for a bicycle, and Mom had finally agreed she could have it for Christmas. Armed with Mom's agreement, Charlotte had staked out the local bicycle shop and selected the one she wanted. Mom had said Charlotte needed to prove she was responsible enough to take care of such a nice bike, and had laid out conditions. A list of chores, minimum grades, check-ins after school. Charlotte had done that for October, November, and December. She'd talked about her bike all December and kept asking when they'd go get it, but Mom deferred. It would be for Christmas, after all. You don't buy your own Christmas gift.

On Christmas morning, Charlotte had gotten clothes, a pretty necklace, headphones, and an MP3 player...but no bicycle.

Yes, she'd held a grudge for months. Yes, she'd complained to anyone who'd listen that she'd been promised a specific bike, even a specific color. Yes, she'd cried. Mom had said Charlotte was being selfish. She shouldn't even want a bike.

That summer was the first time Aunt Eleanor invited her to stay with them. When they'd pulled up to the house, there on the driveway, topped with a ribbon, was the exact bike Charlotte had begged for.

At first Charlotte didn't want to ride it. She hadn't done anything proving to Aunt Eleanor that she deserved such a wonderful bike. Aunt Eleanor only said, "When you're ready, it's here for you." Charlotte had no strength of will; within two days she was cruising all over the roads with Anna, and by the end of the week, Brandon was biking with them too.

Throwing that in Charlotte's face last night had been mean. Just mean.

When they left the gift shop with a bag of nonsense, Mom checked the time and then asked about some restaurant Charlotte had never heard of. "They say it's the best place around here," Mom added, which might even be true. Charlotte hadn't explored the restaurant scene other than Sparrows and pizza, and she'd chosen that pizzeria because they had delivery and gave you a two-liter bottle of soda if you spent ten bucks.

Mom consulted the GPS for how long it would take to drive, and then she decided they should dither around more before going there for lunch. "They have live music at night," she said, as though they were going to camp out at a table consuming chips for ten consecutive hours to hear a guitarist tuning up.

The restaurant itself was an old Victorian building, three stories tall with turrets everywhere and a wraparound porch. Dad's car was the third one in the lot. Charlotte hoped the other two were the chef and one member of the waitstaff.

Mom bustled in ahead of them, but Dad looked exhausted.

"We could have stayed home for lunch," Charlotte said. "I make a decent turkey sandwich."

Dad muttered, "This was your mother's idea. I'm sorry."

"You don't need to be sorry. You're the one who's tired."

Inside, Charlotte found herself confronted with a house chopped up into multiple dining rooms. *I feel you, buddy.*

An amazing chandelier hung over the foyer, and Charlotte noted the oil paintings as they passed through a maze of rooms. Mom said, "Oh, there we are," and Charlotte turned a corner to find Hunter.

She backed up and crashed into her father.

I'm sorry, Dad had said. Mom had set her up for an

ambush.

Hunter took her good hand in his. "Oh, sweetheart. It's so good to see you without those awful people around."

He kissed her. Charlotte was too stunned to recoil.

He smelled like he always had. His hand felt familiar. His kiss was warm. Her mother had sabotaged her.

He kept her hand in his as he led her toward the table, and he seated her at his side. Numb, Charlotte couldn't look at the menu, couldn't figure out what she should be drinking. Sure, water would be fine. No wine. Keep her head clear. This couldn't be happening.

Hunter slid his chair nearer hers and put an arm over her shoulder. All the hair stood up on her neck.

Salads arrived, and Charlotte couldn't remember having ordered. Hunter finally let go of her so he could eat. With her stomach in knots, Charlotte wasn't sure she could. Her mother and Hunter carried the whole conversation, and Charlotte finally got the strength to glare at her father. He was texting.

Brandon had reacted with surprise when he heard her father was still around. Wow, wonder why?

After the waitress cleared the salads, Hunter said, sadly, "You promised you'd unblock me from your phone. But you didn't. I tried all night to call you."

Mom said, "Do it now, honey."

Charlotte pulled her phone from her purse and unlocked it with trembling hands. Hunter took the phone. "You deleted our messages? Oh, sweetheart. You could have scanned back through them and seen how happy we were. You would have remembered."

"I'll do it," Charlotte said, but Hunter kept the phone as he navigated into her contacts.

"Let him," Mom said. "You don't look very well. Was it that run with the dog? I thought it was too hot for you to run."

Hunter took forever with the phone, but finally he gave it back. Charlotte shoved it into her purse, relieved.

"I love you too much to let you walk out of my life after one mistake." Hunter turned to her mother. "Do you have it?"

Mom handed him a black velvet box, and Hunter opened it to reveal a diamond solitaire, round and glittering on its gold band. He got down on one knee as if proposing, then took her injured hand gently. He slid the ring onto its place on her finger. "You have all my promises. We'll be happy together. You'll trust me again after Vanessa, and I'll trust you again after Brandon. We have the rest of our lives to be together now that we've gotten past these wild urges. It's out of our systems, and we'll stay the course."

Mom took a photo of him holding her bandaged hand with the ring on it. "You left him too quickly, honey. This really is for the best."

The next course arrived, and Charlotte stared at the diamond. She and Hunter had the same meal, and overhead the sound system played recorded jazz music. Not live. Not real.

Sitting on the back deck, Charlotte scrolled through her photos. In May, she'd deleted Hunter's text messages, but she hadn't weeded out the pictures.

So much time invested in each other. Promises, dreams, plans. She'd thought them all gone.

Mom and Dad wouldn't be back for a few hours. Charlotte should be working on that quilt since she'd used that as her excuse to stay home instead of going out to dinner—that she couldn't leave Brighthead if the quilt wasn't finished. They, of course, were eating with Hunter. Fine. Let them enjoy each other. The quilt deserved better than this, however. As distracted as she was, she didn't want to mess up and damage it worse.

Instead she looked at Anna's most recent photos of baby Violet. She hit the contact info, then pushed the button to call.

Anna sounded exhausted. "Hey, Charlotte. How's it going?"

"I need to talk to you. Mom said Violet is having a second surgery?"

"Yeah. Later this week, or maybe early next week. Three separate teams are consulting, and it's overwhelming. Hey, can you hear the machine?" When Charlotte said she could, Anna said, "It's a breast pump. They're milking me like a cow."

"Ugh. I'm so sorry."

"They say it's helping her to have my milk, but she's so weak that sometimes she can't get it directly from me. I hate this thing." Anna sighed. "I'm glad they're keeping my milk supply up, but seriously. Distract me. Tell me about Brighthead."

Charlotte said, "I called so I wouldn't have to think about Brighthead."

Anna said, "What's wrong?"

"You mean other than everything?" Charlotte sighed. "Okay, so let's see. I visited the statue out by the lighthouse, the Myth Brightman?"

Anna howled. "Isn't that awesome? They couldn't have gotten it more wrong if they'd tried!"

Charlotte protested, "Weren't they trying? That had to be intentional."

"Totally unintentional. One of the Maine magazines did a story on it, and it was just a series of little mistakes and misconceptions, each one really small but you can see where one mistake led to the next to the next. A dated document got copied wrong. Her sister was born the other year and they matched the photo to the wrong birth date. They didn't count an adopted child. All these quiet mistakes, and all of it adding up to one hilarious disaster."

"Speaking of hilarious disasters, last week I slashed my

hand open on an antique spinning wheel. That was my medical drama."

"Ouch! How'd you do that?"

"Stupidity and bad reflexes. Pepper jumped the gate to save me."

"She's a good girl. I'm so mad they got her after I moved out." Anna chuckled. "Your hand: still attached?"

"Yes, although after I got stitched up, I nearly passed out. Brandon brought me to his parents' house, and they fed me hamburgers and soda and tucked me in on the couch like I was a little kid."

Anna giggled. "That's so cunning! Did they ask you to call them Mom and Dad? Half of Brighthead calls them Mom and Dad. My classmates were like, 'Whoa, Dad mows your lawn? You're so lucky.'"

"*Mom* got the blood out of Aunt Eleanor's cream-colored carpet, so yeah, I'm really lucky." Charlotte paused. "Okay, what's up with 'cunning'? One of us isn't using that word correctly. It means smart."

"It means adorable...?" Anna paused significantly, and Charlotte didn't bother looking it up. Of course cunning didn't mean adorable. Anna said, "And Brandon...? You called him because...?"

Charlotte sighed. "See, that's one of the things I didn't want to be talking about."

"He's *cunning*..." Anna prompted.

Charlotte exclaimed, "You think so?"

"Well, don't you?" Anna sounded dreamy. "If you want cunning, Brandon's wicked cunning. You know that. You used to hang out with him when you visited. He was always off in his own head, but when you could get him to stop daydreaming, he was a lot of fun."

Charlotte said, "Did you ever...you know, date him?"

"Of course not. Do you remember Kelty? He was totally fixated on her." Anna paused. "It's awful how she died. Mom says it was out of the blue, and I bet it was worst thing for Brandon. He was waiting for her."

"Yeah, what's that all about?"

"Have you asked him?" When Charlotte didn't respond, Anna huffed. "She wanted to be secure, and she said when she had a house and a career, then maybe she'd feel okay about getting together with him. She was humiliated that after her dad abandoned them, his family was helping her family. I mean, *our* family was helping her too, but I wasn't in love with her. She was ticked off at me too."

Charlotte decided to process all that later. "What do you mean Brandon was waiting for her?"

"Like she told him that until she was more successful than he was, she wasn't going to even consider going out with him. And then he stayed friends with her afterward. You'd think he'd get mad about that? But he didn't."

Charlotte walked back into the house, over to the spinning wheel. "His business... He didn't throw everything into it. Because of her?"

"You know, I bet that's it. By having a boring day job and not taking a risk with the business, he made sure it didn't succeed. That way he wouldn't scare her off."

Charlotte sat on the chair alongside the wheel. It smelled of lanolin and Murphy's Oil Soap, and she rested a finger on the drive band. "That's..."

"That's wicked loyal." Anna paused sharply. "Wait a minute. Are you going out with him?"

Was she? Would he hate her now after all this? Didn't he think of her help as the ultimate humiliation?

Did it matter? Because Hunter was poised to sweep her right out of Brighthead and back to the altar. Maybe Brandon would forgive her for helping him but wouldn't forgive her for doubling back to the guy who'd left her. Nor should he.

She wouldn't forgive herself either.

Anna said, "Brandon's a good guy. If you want him, go for

it."

"I don't know. He's…"

"He's totally the opposite of Hunter." Anna had taken a no-nonsense tone. "If you want loyal, Brandon would swim across the Atlantic before he'd ever consider cheating. Think of how long he was loyal to Kelty."

"Yeah." Charlotte pushed the pedal, and the wheel gave a lazy turn. The drive band spun the bobbin, and the wheel creaked. Without any fiber, nothing would spin. A metaphor for her existence.

Anna laughed. "His life is loaded with women. There was you and me back on those summers, and Kelty, and he's living with his sister, and there's his mom, and there's my mom…"

Charlotte said, "He doesn't have enough room for another woman."

"Oh, and his niece! Talk about cunning. She's going to have him wrapped around her finger once she learns to talk. You're going to have competition."

Charlotte closed her eyes. "I thought I could trust Hunter too."

"Hunter was a tool."

"Hunter's here. Hunting me down."

"Oh for pity's sake. You'd think he could get a clue."

"My mother's here too."

"Oh my goodness, like you need that." Anna's voice pitched up. "Get out of there! Call Uber and have them drive you to Freeport. Call *Brandon* and have him drive you to Freeport."

"Only if my spinning wheel fits in the back seat."

"The spinning wheel that slashed open your hand? I endorse. That's a much better companion than Hunter."

Charlotte pressed her forehead against the wheel. "What am I going to do?"

"I just told you what to do." Anna sighed. "First, you don't want to go back to Hunter."

Did she? Was dumping Hunter all her mother's idea from the start? Had she been unfair to him in not giving him a chance to explain?

He'd been good to her. He'd treated her well. He'd promised so much. He had a career ahead of him. He came from the same world she did.

Anna said, "Wait, you're not considering going back to Hunter, are you?"

Charlotte said, "My mother says I didn't give him a chance."

"Charlie, listen to me, and listen carefully: Hunter had every chance to be faithful. You had every chance to be unfaithful, but did you take it? No. He couldn't even give you his loyalty. Do you want a lifetime of being married to a man you can't trust?"

Charlotte closed her eyes.

"It's easier to play stupid and let Hunter take control." Anna sounded stern. "It's also easy to play stupid and let your mother take control. It would have been easier for me to be stupid and let the doctors do whatever they wanted with Violet, but I've had to gird up and fight for her. So help me, fight for yourself."

"Jake Farnsworth offered the use of his wood chipper." Even though she was alone in the dark room, Charlotte fought a little smile.

"Girl, take him up on it." Anna paused. "And get your mother out of there. She's railroaded you over and over again."

Anna had reason to say that. Anna was the one who'd gotten the brunt of Mom's frustration about her pregnancy.

Anna said, "I swear, I'll put *my* mother on the phone and she'll yell at you. Your mother is a megalomaniac who has never once thought about anyone other than herself."

Charlotte bristled. "That's not true!"

"If it's not true, it's because I'm *understating* the point. Violet could die, and during every single phone call, your mother makes it all about yourself. When Hunter dumped you, your mother spent the entire weekend telling people how upset *she* was over it, how devastated *she* was, what a pity that *she* wouldn't wear her gold mother-of-the-bride dress, but how wonderful that *she* had unearthed the cheating. She never mentioned you."

Was that true? When her mother had made one call after the next after the next, Charlotte had never wondered what her mother was saying.

"If your mother is pushing Hunter on you now, it's because she benefits. Trust me." Anna huffed. "Why do you think you came to us every summer? You were beaten down to the point of disappearing, and my mother said, 'We have to do something about that girl.' So we did. But then after all those summers, you started becoming independent, and then your mother leashed you up again. It wasn't us who refused to have you come up here."

Charlotte covered her face in her hands. *That's not true. That's not true. That's not true.* "Leave my mother out of this. Please."

"You're completely free right now." Anna sounded plaintive. "You get to make all these choices. You can live anywhere, associate with anyone, do anything. With your degree, you'll be able to get a job wherever you want. You could go to Europe or China or the Near East. Detach yourself from everyone and just run."

Running sounded good right now. She'd begun running for Violet. When did she start running for herself?

Hunter wasn't attached to anyone. He'd dumped Vanessa (or so he said). He'd come here looking for Charlotte, but was that attachment? Or was it possession?

By contrast, Brandon had too many attachments, and he nurtured them for so long. Kelty. His sister. Even his dead-end job was something he'd stayed loyal to when he should have bolted.

Hunter was addicted to risk. Brandon liked playing it safe.

But Anna was right. Charlotte wasn't choosing between them. She needed to choose for herself. It wasn't a question of "Brandon versus Hunter" as much as it was a question of "Charlotte versus No Charlotte".

Decide. Take on all the risks. Bear all the consequences.

Anna said, "I'm sorry. Did I hurt your feelings?"

"No." Charlotte dried her tears on her arm. "They were already hurting. You're just saying the things I should have thought a long time ago."

Chapter Thirty-Six

On Thursday, Brandon headed upstairs expecting to find Olivia, but Dale was in the kitchen. "Forgot my coffee," Dale said, holding up his thermal mug. "You look like heck."

"Yeah." He didn't bother explaining, just glanced at Aria. "Not sure yet where I'll take her today."

"You've already covered the whole state." Dale dumped sugar into his coffee as if he intended to move an entire household on nothing but carbs. "What's wrong?"

Brandon said, "You have to get to work."

"The boss isn't going to fire me." No, Dale owned the company. That's why he could run home and get his coffee while everyone else hefted sofas. "Dude, you've got my kid with you. I need you okay."

"I'm not going to drive into the ocean." Brandon sighed. "Remember Charlie, the one with her hand slashed open? She's getting back together with her ex, and I think she blocked me on her phone. He's a lying, cheating, slime-sucking manipulator, and he's got her completely snowed."

Dale got out the milk. "Don't oversell his good qualities."

"He's an emotional abuser who thinks money is a substitute for behaving like a human being."

Dale nodded. "Now you're getting started. What are you doing to do about it?"

"Exactly what do you think I can do about it?" Brandon

exclaimed. "If she's choosing a life of abuse and manipulation over respect and concern, there's not a whole heck of a lot I can."

"You sound just like my father when my mother acted like a monster. *Like what am I doing to do about her?*" Dale poured milk into his coffee. "You know what you do? You walk in there with your head up and you say, no, that's not right. How can you tell she blocked you?"

"Because her texts don't say 'delivered,' and her phone rolls me straight to voicemail, which she doesn't return." Brandon's throat closed momentarily. "She's choosing him."

"She hasn't *chosen* him yet, has she?" said Dale. "You fold like an empty moving box. Livvy said you're afraid of success, and I said no. But now you're making me wonder."

Brandon glared at him.

Dale screwed the top on his thermos. "You can hate me, but you're holding back. I own a business too, so I know how things work. You get out there and put yourself on the line. You get rejected. You screw up. People leave nasty reviews. People choose your competitors. People try not to pay you. That's business. But *you* get rejected and you stall out. You ask for work and you're afraid of people saying no. Forget that, man. That's the job. It's like being a boxer and not wanting to get hit. Get out there and do the job. Get the clients. Get rejected."

Brandon's stomach tightened. "This isn't about the business."

"It's about making the same mistake in five different parts of your life." He put the milk back in the fridge. "Go over to Charlie's house and do the job. Go to war and win her back. At the very least, tell her that guy's a user. When Charlie's hand was cut open, you dropped everything to get over there. Why are you at my kitchen table when it's her heart getting cut open?"

Brandon's fists tightened. "Are you serious?"

"Dead serious. My dad was a coward. My mother was a

witch, and he let her do things because it *kept the peace*. No, she wasn't keeping the peace. It just made the blow fall on me." Dale picked up the thermos. "If you let this happen, you're having the blow fall on Charlie."

Behind him, Olivia said, "And what about Kelty?"

Brandon pivoted, not having realized his sister was even there. "What? What blow fell on Kelty?"

"You never moved on her, and you lost her." Olivia picked up her purse. "Don't lose Charlie too. She's a good person. I like her." She kissed Dale, then grabbed her keys off the hook. "Don't keep making the same mistake forever."

"Jerk," Brandon muttered.

"Loser," she shot back over her shoulder.

Dale grinned. "You guys have the best relationship."

"I'm moving out tonight." Brandon ran a hand through his hair. "Aria and I, we'll go live under an overpass." He looked up. "But you never actually said: what do you think I can do?"

"Do what your dad did." Dale swiveled a chair away from the table and straddled it backward. "He opened his house to me. He said, anytime you want, you come here. He said if my parents weren't doing the job, he and Mom would do it, and they did. Your dad? Right there. Every time. Championship game? Awards night? Do you know who took me to take my driver's license test? It wasn't my father."

Brandon said, "What does that have to do with me?"

"I was a massive jerk to your dad. He kept welcoming me. It stuck." He frowned. "Then I see you not even trying, and I don't get it. You've got a good life, but you could have so much better. You could be on my team hauling furniture because it's good money, sure, but I don't want you because you've got all that art in your head. Put it out there."

Brandon turned away.

Dale said, "When you get bad reviews or they laugh, that's like a badge of honor. No one else is doing your art, right?" He checked his watch. "Network like a tornado today. I want you to have two clients by the time I get home."

Brandon said, "Or what, *Dad*?"

Dale said, "Or tomorrow I send my kid to daycare so you have no excuses."

Brandon's eyes widened. "What?"

Dale looked him straight on. "Yeah. If you won't do it for Charlie, do it for Aria."

Excuses.

Brandon opened his laptop while Aria played with her cars.

How on earth do you land two clients in one day? No one had written him back, which would have made it easier.

No, that was inbound marketing. What Dale intended was outbound marketing.

Brandon stared at his inbox. "And what about Kelty?" his sister had said, and his brows contracted.

This had nothing to do with Kelty. Kelty had wanted to succeed.

Succeed more than him, that was. He could have dived into PacerStudios right out of college, except what would that have done to her? If he'd one-upped her yet again, she'd have pushed the goalposts that much further back. When would she ever have succeeded "enough" to feel like he wasn't paving her way forward?

I need to land a job.

I need a better job.

When I have a house.

In the back of his mind, had he sensed his success was a threat to her? That every client was one more month he pushed back the moment she felt like his superior?

PacerStudios. You need a pacer to make sure you don't run

faster than you intend. *Brilliant, Brandon.* When he'd named his business, his unconscious mind had been telling him the same thing Dale had said this morning.

Brandon fidgeted in the kitchen. It was just him and Aria, and Aria was quiet. He could do this. Dale said he was afraid of being rejected, but Olivia said he was afraid of succeeding. Maybe he was afraid of both. He'd stayed in that dead-end job for so long, safe and predictable.

Well, time to crash and burn. Challenge accepted. Let's land a client by noon.

At eleven o'clock, Brandon packed his laptop and his niece into the car and headed to the burger shop where he'd met Hunter. "I need to speak to the owner," he said, and yes, he'd upgraded his clothes before making this trip. The owner shook his hand, and while Aria sat in a high chair making a mess of fries and ketchup, Brandon opened the laptop and showed the owner the front page he'd mocked up for his new website.

"Nice clean layout. Your phone number is here, easy to find. I've put a thumbnail map right here on the front page. One click and it expands. Your menu is immediately visible and accessible. This kind of site is easily optimized for online ordering if you ever want to expand into that, which I do recommend."

The owner leaned forward. "Click on the menu."

Brandon smiled. "I only did the first page. If you're interested in having a whole new website, then we can get to work."

The owner said, "We'll need new photos."

"I would take those." Brandon tried to remember Hunter and his charm, the way he assumed you'd do what he wanted just because he was the one saying it. "I will also rewrite the content on your interior pages to target your intended customers. We'll link to your online reviews, plus add a regular contact form and links to all your social media."

The owner chuckled. "We only have one very neglected

Facebook page."

Brandon gave him a smile. "As it turns out, I can manage my clients' social media as well."

The owner looked startled. "Let me see that web page again."

Half an hour later, Brandon stopped at the library and mocked up a front page for a different prospect while Aria played at the train table, and he spent the next thirty minutes hitting the websites for every business in town, making note of which looked to have been designed more than ten years ago.

By one o'clock he was back at the house, Aria sleeping in her crib while he ate a sandwich with one hand and worked on a prospective client's mockup page with the other.

By three o'clock, he'd gotten a phone call from the burger place, and they started hashing out details, rates, and timeframes. When the owner asked for a quote, Brandon steeled himself and said twice his normal rate, then offered a twenty percent discount on the bundled services if the guy also wanted him to provide content for the Facebook page.

"That sounds good," said the owner, and Brandon clenched the phone tighter so he wouldn't drop it.

Instead of "Holy guacamole," Brandon said, "I'll get you the contract this afternoon."

Three fifteen. Too late to land a second client for the day. Dale would have to do his worst.

While compiling the document, Brandon got another call. Lighthouse Athletic Club.

Sure, why not? A serving of awfulness would balance out the good. He answered with, "PacerStudios."

"Brandon, this is Alex, from the fitness center. You need to send me the real files for that Lighthouse Run logo."

Bristling at Alex's tone, Brandon said, "You have the real file. I saw it on the registration website."

"I'm not stupid," Alex said. "We're printing the T-shirts for the race, but the printer says the file is too small."

Brandon hit speakerphone and searched his computer. "The file I sent is the full-sized file, not watermarked. I don't know what you've done to it since then, but you can redownload it from my email."

"Don't patronize me. If I can't get the shirts printed because of you, there will be consequences."

What kind of consequences? Alex would fire him? "I'm looking at the file I sent you, and it's 300dpi, 1600 by 2400 pixels."

"And I'm looking at the email from the printer saying the file I sent is 72 dpi and 333 by 500 pixels."

Realization dawned. "That's on your end. You need to go into your email and change the settings on how it's sending the photo. Your email program is reducing the image size, but you can override that by clicking—"

"Don't blame me for your deception. I want the real file."

Brandon drummed his fingers on the table. "Look at the file in your directory. The file size is about two meg, right? That's the correct size, but your email client is sending it at a smaller size to save bandwidth. On the right-hand side of the screen you'll see the option for sending it full size. That's all you need to do."

Alex said, "You're holding our logo hostage."

"Then I'm the stupidest terrorist ever because you already have what you want. I'll talk you through the settings, step by step."

"I'm not having this!" Alex said. "You're the one who caused the problem. I expect you to solve it."

Brandon was the one who'd caused the problem? By what, by standing up for himself? Okay. If standing up for himself was the problem, he'd own it. He'd treated himself with respect. Anyone who thought that was a problem wasn't someone he wanted to be dealing with anyhow.

Brandon's voice got very low. "Here's a thought. You need that logo sent. When you're ready to work with me, call back.

Otherwise, get someone else to do it."

"You listen to me—"

Brandon hung up.

If Alex bothered to rant about the conversation to anyone, including to the guy at the print shop, even that mangled bit of conversation should be enough for the other person to say, "Oh!" and then solve the problem. Brandon himself had officially spent enough time on the issue.

Their last day to get the T-shirt order in before the race? Not his problem.

Alex having a fit because he didn't want Brandon to tell him what to do? Also not Brandon's problem.

This contract that needed to be sent across town? That was quite definitely Brandon's problem, and he returned to it.

At 4:15, his phone rang again. Again it was Lighthouse. Brandon answered with a smooth, "PacerStudios."

"Fine," Alex said. "I've got your contract in front of me, and in the contract you offered the logo design for free if we also hired you to create five ads."

Brandon rolled his eyes.

Alex said, "If I sign this, will you release the file?"

The file Alex had on his hard drive. Exactly the same one.

Brandon said, "The minute your deposit hits the bank, I will send the full-size logo directly to the printer."

Silence on the other end. Then, "Done."

Brandon logged in to his bank account and read the routing number to Alex, then took down the contact information for the print shop.

The transaction appeared. He called the print shop and asked for Ted. A minute later, Ted confirmed receipt of the file and that it was the correct size. "Shoot Alex an email saying as much," Brandon asked.

Then he texted Cashman. "Call off your internet mob. I just got paid."

Dale walked in the door while Brandon was wrapping that

up. "So?" Dale said. "Two clients today?"

Brandon started to say no when he realized he was wrong. He'd done it. And he started to laugh.

Dale grinned at him. "Good. Now, go get Charlie as well."

Text:

Aileen, to 26 members of the running club: "So many people asked what they could bring that I started a Google spreadsheet to sign up. {link}"

Aileen, 5:25 p.m. "No one has to bring anything, by the way."

Eleanor, 5:45 p.m. "Since you listed firewood, take some of ours. We have five cords."

Charlotte, 5:50 p.m. "Where would it be, Aunt Eleanor? And I'm not hauling it in Uncle Gregory's car."

Eleanor, 5:51 p.m. "Brandon, can you pick it up?"

Brandon, 5:51 p.m. "No problem. Aileen, how much?"

Aileen, 5:52 p.m. "Less than five cords."

Brandon, 5:52 p.m. "Thanks for clarifying. I won't hire a dump truck."

Eleanor, 5:53 p.m. "You may need to split some of it. Jake has a wood splitter."

Brandon, 5:53 p.m. "I have an axe. I can handle it."

Charlotte, 5:54 p.m. "Is Brandon even still coming?"

Eleanor, 5:55 p.m. "He sounds like he is."

Charlotte, 5:55 p.m. "What? Are you talking to him?"

Brandon, 5:57 p.m. "Is Charlie on this chat? Tell her to unblock me."

Eleanor, 5:57 p.m. "Well, that got interesting. I wouldn't have volunteered you if I thought you'd blocked each other."

Charlotte, 5:58 p.m. "What am I missing? Did he block me?"

Eleanor, 5:59 p.m. "Brandon wants you to unblock him."

Charlotte, 5:59 p.m. "I didn't block him."

Charlotte, 6:01 p.m. "Oh for crying out loud. I'm going to kill someone."

Brandon, 6:01 p.m. "Hey, you're back! Not killing me, I hope?"

Charlotte, 6:02 p.m. "If anyone needs me, I'm out borrowing Jake Farnsworth's wood chipper."

Cashman, 6:03 p.m. "I require live updating and video."

Chapter Thirty-Seven

Pepper charged Brandon's car as he pulled into the driveway half an hour later, and Charlotte followed more slowly.

Wary, Brandon got out. "I figured I'd come over and split some wood since Eleanor invited me."

Charlotte kept her left hand in the pocket of her shorts. "Before you go any further, I'm not angry at you, and I didn't block you. That was either my mother or Hunter, and I'm very unhappy right now with every single person who's trying to control my life."

Brandon raised both hands. "Duly noted. I'm here to chop wood. I will have nothing whatsoever to say about your life choices unless you specifically request my opinion."

Stepping back, she gestured to the side of the house.

Brandon took a pair of work gloves and a heavy axe from the back, where they'd kept uncomfortable company with the infant seat. Around the side of the house they found a disassembled tree.

Brandon dropped the axe-thing. "Really? This is what I'm supposed to split?" He pulled out his phone and took a picture. "I'm asking Eleanor if it's the right pile because this isn't firewood. It's a fallen tree that got chainsawed up."

"She said she was just going to have to pay someone to take it away."

"And I get to uphold my reputation for serving as everyone's free labor. You do realize that if I walk away, splitting nothing, the person she'll pay to take it away is my father?" Brandon examined the pile. "Well, I should maybe get started. The sun's only going to be up another two hours."

Charlotte said, "It'll take that long?"

"It's been a long day." He looked up. "I landed two clients today."

She raised her eyebrows.

"Neither one came from you. Don't worry."

Pepper sat on the driveway watching Charlotte watching Brandon. He set a flat stump on the ground, then balanced a log on end atop it. He picked up his sledgehammer-axe thing with both hands at opposite sides of the handle, then did this swing up and around his body until his hands came together and the axe-head crashed down to split the log in pieces. He picked up the larger piece and repeated the process, again with that big arc with his arms, hands sliding together, the axe moving in a circle, his whole body moving smoothly.

Pepper wasn't the only one staring. Charlotte tried to laugh at herself but it wasn't working. "That's a huge axe."

"It's just for firewood. They call it a maul." Brandon struck a second time with that amazing fluid motion. "Wood warms you three times." He struck it again. "Once when you split it. Once when you stack it." He got another log. "Once when you burn it."

In other words, he was going to work up a sweat. And she shouldn't be sitting out here thinking he was hot. "You've done this a lot."

"Oh yeah. Tree services don't usually take the trees away. Dad would do it. He'd chainsaw it apart like this." He gestured to the big pieces. "Then he'd have me break it up. Free heat."

"Free labor for him too," Charlotte said.

"I'm noticing a pattern." Then Brandon looked a bit more serious. "I owe you a huge apology. I'm sorry I hurt your feelings."

Before Charlotte could reply, Pepper got to her feet and stared at the road. Brandon followed the dog's gaze, and his face went rigid.

Charlotte didn't look. "Black Camry? Rental?"

Brandon replied, in a corresponding low voice, "Hunter."

Charlotte shouldn't be trembling.

She would be trembling with love if she were in love with Hunter, but this wasn't love. Last night, Anna had hit her heart harder than Brandon hit that wood with the maul, and everything had flown apart the same way the logs split when the blade crashed down. After a long night and an equally long day putting together all the pieces, Charlotte wondered if she'd ever been loved at all.

Wondered if what her mother said was love...wasn't. Wondered if what she'd felt for Hunter wasn't love, just her response to his attention.

Then what should love be? She'd Googled it, feeling like an idiot, and found a neat little checklist. She'd run down every point for Hunter. For her mother. For her father, who did tick some of the boxes.

Weirdly enough, the list said nothing about emotions. It talked only about behaviors. It said that love should be patient and kind, not sneering when things went wrong, approving when things went right, not easily angered, not looking after its own interests. Love should wait through anything and be supportive.

If Hunter loved her, would she be this distraught as he stepped onto the driveway? Wouldn't his apology fill her with hope? Fill her with trust that everything would be all right?

Or had something happened in the intervening weeks,

something that showed her how a man could click through every one of those boxes? Had something proved to her how real love felt from the receiving end?

Fingering her engagement ring, Charlotte stood from the rock wall.

Behind her, Brandon brought down the maul on the log, sending a chunk of wood flying.

Hunter looked irritated. "You're still around? Really?"

Charlotte's voice was cold. "He's working for my aunt, and I have loose ends to tie up."

Hunter smirked over her shoulder at Brandon.

Her parents had come out of the kitchen, and her mother didn't even notice Brandon. "Oh, how lovely. I was just going to put out dessert."

In Charlotte's peripheral vision, Brandon held that axe at waist level, one hand near the head and the other on the handle. Charlotte didn't need a wood chipper though. A low rumble went through the dog.

"I thought about everything you said, Hunter." Charlotte walked to the driveway, and Pepper stuck to her side. "You're right that I didn't give you a chance to explain anything before I ran. We both made mistakes." She looked at the ring glittering on her hand. "But I know how we can make it right. Wait here."

On the porch were two envelopes. She handed the first to Hunter.

"What is this?"

She smiled as his eyes hit the page. "That's a prenup. Yesterday you said you don't trust me after my time with Brandon, and I thought, how about we put it in writing? We both sign this, and if the marriage ends due to infidelity, the unfaithful partner keeps only ten percent of the marital assets. The other partner gets ninety percent." She twisted the ring around her finger. "The injured party also gets all the retirement funds, that way nothing has to be cashed out."

Hunter's brows furrowed. "Did you really come up with something so stupid?"

First move: head off her mother. Charlotte said, "My mother taught me about legal authority, and this seems like a wonderful way to heed her advice." She turned to her mother, wide-eyed. Please, let this work. "You're never wrong about these things."

Mom brightened. "This is a great idea. You'll both feel more secure."

Dad would never disagree now. Good. Charlotte pivoted back to Hunter. "You can thank Cashman Law Offices. Mr. Cashman said if we're making promises, we should be willing to put them in a document. Since you said you'd never cheat again, this can only protect you."

Hunter crumpled the paper. "I will not sign anything of the sort. Are you that petty and unforgiving?"

That, right there, was any answer Charlotte would ever have needed. About his honesty. About his concern for her well-being. About whatever passed for love in his heart. About whether he'd ever been the man she'd loved.

Charlotte feigned shock. "You're accusing my mother of being unforgiving?"

He exclaimed, "You, Charlotte!"

But that brought Mom to Charlotte's side, shouting at Hunter, "How dare you?"

Brandon had his phone in his hand, eyebrows raised. Charlotte nodded.

Pepper put herself between Charlotte and Hunter, growling.

"Wait, Hunter," Charlotte said. "Last night, I wrote another letter with all my feelings in it. It's everything I should have said to you right from the start." She clasped her hands and looked at him with wide eyes. "Please? Then you don't have to sign."

He snatched the second envelope from her as if striking a

match.

Last night, Charlotte had looked up templates for two types of letters. The first was the prenup. And the second...

Dear Doctor Hunter Mattingly:

This letter is formal notice that you are forbidden from entering or remaining on the property located at 17 Sky Ridge Drive, Brighthead, Maine. If you attempt to enter or remain on the property, you will be subject to legal action, including arrest and criminal trespassing charges.

This notice is effective immediately and will remain in effect unless and until you receive written notice inviting you onto the property. A copy of this letter is being provided to law enforcement.

Sincerely,

Charlotte Fletcher

CC: Brighthead, Maine Police Department

The second? Notification of Criminal Trespassing.

She picked up her phone and hit the record button. "Consider yourself notified that if you remain on the property, I will press charges. There are three witnesses."

Hunter said, "After everything I've done for you, you're treating me like a criminal? When you're the one who destroyed everything in the first place?"

Brandon stepped up beside Charlotte, still bearing that axe.

Anna's words in her heart served as a catalog of Hunter's every manipulation tactic, seconded by Julie's mini-catalog. Blameshifting: check. Accusing her of nastiness so she'd try to prove him wrong: check. Insulting Brandon: that too.

But how about that other checklist? Patience? Kindness? Support? Respect?

She hadn't gotten any of that from her parents, who'd primed her to be snapped up by a predator. But when she was eleven, Aunt Eleanor had stepped into the gap. Anna had shown her too. In twenty-four hours at the Pelletier household, she'd been protected—safe in a family where half of Brighthead called the parents Mom and Dad.

Hunter's face softened. "Sweetie, you've been brainwashed. They don't care like I do. We've been together for years. Brandon's just using you for your money."

New tactic: charm. Charlotte countered with, "Why are you saying my mother doesn't care?"

Her mother said, "You're a monster, Hunter. I always knew it."

He took a step toward her, but Pepper growled, long and low. Eyes on Hunter, she leaned forward with her tail straight up and stiff.

"You'd better leave." Charlotte kept her voice low. "You've been told to get off this property, and you can't charm the dog."

"This isn't like you!" Hunter looked devastated. "You're having a mental breakdown. It can't end this way. We need closure."

A shift in strategy: neediness. The constant changes meant Charlotte was winning because he was pushing buttons at random in the hopes of getting traction.

A police car approached. As the cop pulled into the driveway, Charlotte said, "Closure's overrated."

Hunter glared at the police car in disgust. "You called the cops? Really? Can't fight your own battles?"

Charlotte shrugged. "Why would I stay with someone who makes everything a battle?"

The officer stepped out, and Brandon called, "Darren! Good to see you."

The officer planted himself in what Charlotte had always thought of as "the police stance," legs apart and arms folded. "What's going on?"

Her mother flew over to the officer, shouting invective about Hunter. Brandon set the axe head on the ground, but he kept one hand on the shaft.

The officer said to Hunter, "Sounds like you've been asked to leave."

Hunter said, "She's not the property owner. None of them are."

Staring hard at him, Pepper had her lips pulled back. Charlotte crouched down and put an arm over her. "It's okay, girl. He's going to leave."

"I'm not leaving without you."

The officer said, "Sir, my interpretation of the state statutes says that you are leaving without her."

A second police car pulled up on Sky Ridge Drive. Twice in forty-eight hours? Brandon had been right about the cops hungering for something to do.

Hunter lowered his voice. "I gave up everything for you."

Charlotte said, "Then give up one more thing. Give up the idea of having me in your life."

He balled up her letter and threw it on the ground. "I want that ring. I spent a lot of money trying to make you happy."

Legally, that ring should be hers. She should sell it and spend the cash on a weaving loom the size of Uncle Gregory's Audi. Instead she pulled it off her hand and tossed it to him. It landed on the driveway.

As Hunter bent over to get it, Brandon said, "Up."

Pepper leaped onto Hunter's back, and Charlotte shrieked. Hunter pivoted toward the dog, and Pepper sprang down in a crouch, eyes welded to him.

The officer shouted, "Do not harm that dog!"

With teeth in front of him and two armed officers behind, Hunter stalked to his car. At the last moment he glared at Charlotte. "You're no one."

The officer stayed on the driveway until Hunter drove off. "If he returns, that's an arrest. If you want to look into a restraining order, come down to the station tomorrow and we'll get it started."

After the cops left, Charlotte's mother flung her arms around Charlotte, sobbing. "I was so worried about you. My heart's pounding. I think I need an ambulance. How could he do that? He lied to me."

Yes, all about her. Always all about her. Charlotte patted her mother's shoulder. "Well, now you know. See, you came here and it's all sorted out." She glanced at her dad. "You can go home tomorrow."

Her mother looked over at Brandon. "And you are...?"

Brandon pointed to the maul. "I'm the gardener's son. Mrs. Boucher asked me to split wood for her."

Charlotte said, "You can ask her. It's for a bonfire next week."

"Disgusting, smoky stuff." Her mother sighed. "I can't see how my sister lives out here in the sticks."

The officer went back in his car to radio in, and Charlotte took her mother's hand in her good one. "Thank you so much for everything. You've been a great help, but I know what a sacrifice you made coming all the way up here."

"I know, dear. But I did it for you. I'm so glad we could get everything straightened out with him." She huffed. "I never liked that man in the first place."

As the police cars pulled out, Charlotte's father said, "Well, if we leave tomorrow right after breakfast, we'll be home for dinner."

Mom said, "Let's have dessert first and then pack. We'll get a nice bright start."

She didn't invite Brandon to join them. Why should she? He was just the help.

As her parents disappeared into the house, Charlotte murmured, "Pack and leave. Just go. Decide you'd rather drive in the dark than endure another silent night out in the sticks."

Brandon said in an equally low tone, "Just so you know, Cashman's not his last name."

She stiffened. "That's a first name?"

"And he's not a lawyer. More like a pot-stirrer."

"That I did know. And you?" She looked at him. "What are you really?"

"I'm the gardener's son and a really lucky guy." Brandon turned to her. "Someone who wants a second chance."

She grabbed him and pressed her face into his shoulder. "Don't say that. You never used up the first chance. I swear I didn't block your phone. I got ambushed, and they manipulated me." She swallowed hard. "Can we just keep going?"

"We'd better." Brandon squeezed her. "Closure's overrated."

She chuckled. "I didn't need that wood chipper after all."

"Just a wood-splitter. And I'll take care of that for as long as you like." Brandon's hands went to her waist, and she pressed her cheek against his neck. "You did fine. You were brilliant." He angled his face towards hers. "May I?"

Her mouth was inches from his. "That depends. You said you loved me. Do you still? After everything?"

He answered by kissing her, and she hooked her fingers into his belt loops.

She giggled. "Well, then, you may. Sometimes."

He grinned at her. "We'll work out the schedule later."

"Details, details. So what was that you were saying about apologizing?"

"I've been an idiot." He brushed his lips against hers. "You seem to have forgiven me."

"A bit." He smelled good up close, a mixture of Old Spice and fresh wood. "It's going to be okay?"

He nodded. "I think so."

Chapter Thirty-Eight

While most races began in the morning, the Lighthouse Run had to start when the tide ebbed. This year's Lighthouse Run would begin at 11:36.

Brandon picked up numbers for him and for Charlie, along with eight safety pins. He returned to find Cashman chatting with her. "Safety pins," Cashman gushed. "How quaint." Then showed off four button-like contraptions that didn't leave holes in his tech shirt.

"I only aspire to be as cool as you." Brandon handed Charlie her number and her pins.

"Everyone does. Charlie told me about her contract trick. Nice work." Then he pivoted. "Would you be Alexander Smith from Lighthouse Athletics, about whom I've heard so much?"

Tense, Brandon turned. Corporate Alex was standing next to a man Brandon had met exactly once: the owner of the Lighthouse Athletic Club franchise. The owner gave Brandon a firm handshake. "Good to meet you, Brandon. I'm looking forward to working with PacerStudios in the coming weeks."

Alex looked as if he'd bitten into a lemon. Cashman shook Alex's hand. "It's nice to see you in person after all the social media. No hard feelings. Behold, I delivered you a whole running club."

Alex looked as if he did, in fact, harbor hard feelings. "Much appreciated."

With Brandon paid under contract, twenty members of the Brighthead Running Club had signed up for the race. They were too late to get T-shirts, but if Brandon's closet was typical, most of them had too many race shirts anyhow. "I'll see if we can secure one for you at least," Brandon told Charlie.

Julie approached in shorts and a tank top, wearing sunglasses, and with her ponytail stuck through the back of a baseball cap. "Why are you here?" she asked Cashman. "You swore never to run another race with me ever again, so I figured I was safe."

He said, "I don't like it either, but I have a loophole. This isn't a race. It's a trail run, and the club told Lighthouse we'd back down if they paid up. They did, and I'm a man of my word."

Julie folded her arms. "Well, don't get all gushy on me because they're still a bunch of weasels. The DJ thinks this is a charity event."

Cashman sighed. "I can't save the whole world, you know."

"Trust me, I never thought for even a second that you would." Julie turned to Charlie. "Any news about Violet?"

"The second surgery went well. Aunt Eleanor says this will be the last for a while, although when she's three or four they'll have to do something else."

Julie said, "And that jerk? He's staying away?"

Charlie nodded. "He got in one last nasty message before I blocked him again, and then my father's lawyer-friend sent him a nicely worded letter."

Julie nodded. "Let me know if you need any resources up here."

Cashman said, "She's got *connections.*"

Julie rolled her eyes. "I have *connections*, and not the cement-shoes kind of connections either."

When it came time to start, Brandon and Charlie positioned themselves near the back. "Cashman and Julie start up front," he said, "but they're going to take it at speed. We're just going to finish."

"Unless the tide comes in." Charlie made a face. "You do remember when we needed a boat, right?"

The DJ counted them down to start, and the runners began. Unlike a normal race, no one could fan out because they were limited by the width of the causeway. Within a quarter mile, Charlie said, "This is harder to run in. It's soft."

"Take it slow," Brandon said. "When the tide is lowest, it'll be easier."

The seventy runners spread into a thin ribbon as they moved, but Brandon and Charlie remained side by side. Charlie said, "I keep replaying yesterday's presentation to the museum. All the things I did wrong."

"You didn't look like you did anything wrong."

"You're not critical enough. I keep finding new mistakes." She shuddered. "They were having their meeting this morning, and they said they'd let me know. I'm worried."

Brandon said, "If you get the job, where do you live?"

"It depends on the salary and the benefits and all that." Charlie shook her head. "It's weird running without a dog."

Brandon said, "So we'll have to get a dog?"

Her nose wrinkled as she grinned at him. "You're getting ahead of yourself."

"Just making plans."

"You've got time to plan all you like. Aunt Eleanor needs me to stay in the house at least another month, unless Uncle Gregory comes home early. Besides," she added, "you can't move. Aria needs you."

"I want a stable income before doing anything that requires supporting a household," Brandon said, "and I want to give you time after Hunter. But not too much time."

Charlie's voice blended into the rhythm of water. "Thank you."

After a minute, she said, "I'll need a workroom in our apartment. It'll need lots of light."

"We'll get a two-bedroom. I can work anywhere."

"At some point you're going to upgrade from a laptop to one of those setups with two monitors and a tower. You'll need a desk too."

"So the dog can sleep under it," Brandon said.

"No dogs in the workroom," Charlie countered.

"Plus we'll need space for the spinning wheel collection," Brandon added.

Charlie shook her head. "We're up to three bedrooms now, and that's even before we've had kids."

Brandon said, "Is now a bad time to disclose my lifelong dream of owning goats?"

Charlie laughed out loud. "How many bedrooms does a goat need? Oh, wait, you meant the kids thing. Human children. Babies. If we ever have them."

Brandon felt warm. Not just from the run, but from having Charlie near. Near and talking about a lifetime together.

"I meant actual goats."

She looked horrified. "No goats."

Brandon said, "We'll negotiate about the goats."

"We won't negotiate about the goats."

He said, "I can't afford a six-thousand-dollar engagement ring, so—"

"Thank goodness. Buy yourself a six-thousand-dollar reliable car. And zero goats." She winked at him. "Maybe a sheep."

Brandon said, "Cashmere comes from goats. We should get at least one goat."

Her eyes lit up. "Angora bunnies. Dozens of them."

They reached the island and began the trail run around the perimeter. They passed several walkers and then stopped at the water station. Brandon's ex-manager Michael was handing out water. "I hear you won this round. Good for you."

Brandon said, "Did corporate ever figure out how to order towels?"

Michael said, "I've been refusing to go out of my way to solve their problems. It's actually a good feeling. They'll need to hire an extra person to replace you."

"I hope not. They need to pay the rest of my contract before they go bankrupt."

Michael snickered. "I wouldn't worry about that."

The way back was, in fact, drier than the way in. "That's good because I was getting tired too," Brandon said.

Charlie looked winded, and Brandon promised himself he wouldn't fold before she did.

He said, "Would it help if I turned on my location services and gave you the passwords to my social media?"

Charlie looked at him. "Are you seriously trying to close the deal?"

Brandon laughed out loud.

"You are! You're upselling me!" She laughed out loud. "Brandon!"

"Well, I had to learn about pitching for the business—"

"You don't get it. I do trust you. I'm not with Hunter because I wanted to trust my husband."

Again Brandon felt warm. *Husband.* Could he even do that? Could he be reliable like his father or Dale? Could he be one of those rock-solid men who formed the cornerstone of a family?

He'd have to be. Charlie was counting on him.

Charlie said, "I'm not going to be your overseer."

Brandon said, "But by the same token, I'm not going to be a toad. If you ever want access to my phone or location, say the word. I want you to feel secure."

She looked at him with soft eyes. "I do. I've learned the difference between love-bombing and love."

They ran side by side, keeping the pace even, sometimes going single file to pass someone who was walking. With the wind in their faces, it was harder than on the way in. "Nature's resistance training," Brandon suggested.

It all felt so vast out here. A world in motion around them, but the two of them moving through it together. Struggling, but together.

When they finally reached the finish line, Brandon embraced her. "For Violet," he whispered. "Look what you did for Violet."

She wrapped her arms around him. "You too. Look what you did for me."

Afterward, Brandon and Charlie drove a Ford Focus full of split firewood to Aileen's party. He and Trey carried armloads of the stuff into the backyard, and then Brandon went into the house to find Cashman hassling Aileen. "You're quite the stereotype of a librarian. No beer?"

"No beer." Aileen opened her hands. "No wine. We'll just have to spend time with each other."

Cashman shook his head. "I don't think you've thought this through. That means people will have to spend time with me too. Your guests will leave."

Julie came up behind Aileen and fixed a look on Cashman. "*You* could leave."

Cashman shook his head. "That just makes me want to compound your pain by staying right to the end," at which Julie shuddered.

They had it under control. Brandon went into the kitchen to grab a can of something that wasn't beer.

Trey's younger brother Zack was dumping potato chips into a serving bowl. Brandon flashed him a victory sign. "What is it now? Three months sober?"

Zack averted his eyes and looked down. "Yeah, no. More like three weeks."

"Oh." Brandon leaned against the counter. "Bummer."

Zack frowned. "Sometimes if you're arrogant and think

you can handle it, you put yourself into a situation where you can't." He glanced toward the living room where Cashman was smirking at Julie. "I hate that Aileen made the party alcohol-free because of me."

"Not a big deal," Brandon said. "She's just helping."

"I hate that even more." Zack's brown eyes flashed. "Like I can't make it without everyone's assistance."

"Don't think like that." Brandon steadied himself. "People help out because they know you *can* make it. They're just giving you a leg up. You wouldn't help someone up to a place where they're going to fail, right?"

Zack raised his can of Moxie. "Given my track record, failure is a given."

"You've just got to succeed more times than you failed," Brandon said. "It only takes one."

Charlie approached, looking stunned. Brandon introduced her to Zack, who then wandered off to find Trey. Brandon opened his arms, and she snuggled up to him.

"I got a call." She pressed against him. "The museum offered me the job."

"Whoa! Congratulations." He kissed her forehead. "That's savage!"

"I haven't finished processing it yet." She put her head against his chest. "I'm stunned."

"Hey, I believed in you." He rested his hand on her shoulder. "Maine is keeping you after all?"

She offered a smile. "I'm kind of liking it here."

Brandon said, "The ocean?"

She nodded. "Really like the ocean."

"And running?"

Again she nodded. "Running is pretty awesome."

He prompted, "How about the people?"

"Most of the people I like a lot." She half shut her eyes. "Most of them."

Brandon made a mock-hurt expression. "What about the

others?"

"Some of them...I don't know." She tilted up her face. "And one of them I love."

He bent toward her and kissed her again, and there she stayed. They had time to figure out the future. They could figure it out together.

Thank you!

Thank you so much for reading about Brandon and Charlotte!

Once again I thank my editor, Heather Turner, and my early readers, Amy Bartelloni and Sarah Begg. Also thanks to Charlotte Volnek for the amazing cover art and Laura Maisano for the Brighthead logo.

Please leave a review over at Goodreads or wherever you buy your books. Remember that a review only has to be a star rating and a couple of sentences, so if you can spare a few minutes, I would really appreciate it.

If you're interested in the posters on Brandon's walls, NASA has made them free. You can download them and print them at https://www.jpl.nasa.gov/visions-of-the-future/

Anyone who wants to run would do well to read the works of John Bingham and Jenny Hadfield. Their books turned me into a runner, and for that I will always be in their debt.

If you'd like to return to Brighthead for more running and romance, we've got a fun pair coming up next. If my inbox is any judge, it's the one you've been waiting for.

maddie evans

Mischief and a
MARATHON

The Brighthead Running Club Romances - Book 3

Cashman's sworn never to run another race with Julie, but Julie's just lost her marathon team. Surely it won't be so bad? It's just twenty-six miles. And the training. And a whole lot of hostility about what happened the last time they raced together.

Still, something about the open road keeps opening up the secrets between them. Suddenly Cashman can't deny that there's a lot more miles ahead of them than in their past. If only he could convince Julie...